THE
ANAHEIM BEAUTIES
VALENCIA QUEEN

BY

D. J. PHINNEY

ARROYO WILLOW
PRESS

For Sharon, Nate, Kelly, Jonas, Anders, Kayla, and Sunny.

You make me happy when skies are gray.

THE ANAHEIM BEAUTIES VALENICA QUEEN

Arroyo Willow Press

Publisher's Note: This is a work of fiction. Names, characters, places, and incidents are a product of the author's imagination. Locales and public names are sometimes used for atmospheric purposes. Any resemblance to actual people, living or dead, or to businesses, companies, events, institutions, or locales is completely coincidental.

978-1-7329034-0-1 Paperback

978-1-7329034-2-5 mobi

978-1-7329034-1-8 ePub

978-1-7329034-3-2 KDP Paperback

"Make the world safe for democracy!" the sultans of sobriety

Commanded us.

Now luster fades from Woodrow Wilson's promise.

Who were we to quarrel with their bright and shining morals?

While our emperors were naked

And dishonest.

—Canticles to an Angry God ©1929

Sr. Alma Martin, O.P.

CHAPTER I

ANAHEIM: FRIDAY, FEBRUARY 8, 1918

I didn't tell Ma I had plans today to blow through my life's savings. I was certain she'd say, "No, Deanie." But I'd made up my mind. At ten years and eight months old, I grabbed Pa's hammer from the shed and busted open my Golden State National Bank souvenir piggy bank.

With joy, I dumped my nest egg onto my yellow quilted bedspread. Mounds of dimes and quarters flowed like loot from *Treasure Island*. Three years of paper routes, mowing lawns, pulling crabgrass, digging ditches, and stuffing milk bottles with umpteen-million icky green tomato worms I'd apprehended eating Mrs. Lander's victory garden—all this work had netted me the $14.71 I had saved up since we had moved out west from Brooklyn.

I counted it all twice just to make sure.

That was enough for me to buy myself a brand new *Boy Scout*

Handbook and still have $12.21 left over. I spent my afternoon downtown, peering from fresh-cured concrete sidewalks through brick storefronts with a U S flag in most of the display windows. I loved the way it felt to be a man who earned a living. Nearly $15 begged for me to spend it buying merchandise. For now, I simply wanted to enjoy this happy feeling.

After an hour I made my way into the SQR Department Store, dashed up the stairs past their Wells Fargo office, and raced past male mannequins displaying "new men's fashions for a California lifestyle," high-water slacks and tilted hats made out of straw, bound up with hat bands wide enough to hide a line of silver dollars.

I fantasized about the day when I could dress up like my pa and sell insurance. Pa was gone a lot. I rarely got to see him. Still, he'd just come back from Belgium after blowing out his back. I was thrilled to have him home to teach me how to be a gentleman.

Boys only learned so much by reading books.

Beyond beige mannequins who studied me with razor-blade-thin smiles were the uniforms, the neckerchiefs, the khaki canvas tents. I bought myself that *Boy Scout Handbook* plus an aluminum canteen. It was a real one, emblazoned with the Boy Scout *fleur-de-lis* inside a special canvas case that I could clip onto my belt just like our troops wore, fighting Jerries on the Western Front in Europe. Me and my buddies talked a lot about the war.

All we needed were some rifles and dry ammo to assist them. We'd fly Nieuports over France, fighting the German *Luftstreitkräfte* at the side of Eddie Rickenbacker and his "Hat-in-the-Ring" 94th Aero Squadron. True Americans, dogfighting German Fokker *Eindeckers*, and watching Kraut planes spiral down in flames.

To prepare, I couldn't wait to join the Boy Scouts of America in June, on my birthday, once I finally turned eleven. My best friend, Skeeter Wilson, was in the Skunk Patrol in Troop 71. He'd passed his test to be a Tenderfoot last month. Now he was studying first aid, camping out at Tin Can Beach, and building bonfires, hoping soon to earn the rank of Second Class.

It felt thrilling to be standing on the cusp of real manhood, ready to be the next Tom Mix, Black Jack Pershing, or Douglas Fairbanks. I eagerly looked forward to my first overnight campout as I walked the seven blocks back to our bungalow.

Ma seemed troubled when I walked through our front door. "Deanie, where were you?" I avoided her, despite the smell of homecooked three-bean soup teasing my nostrils. In my bedroom I unwrapped my *Boy Scout Handbook*. I found a rope and started practicing my knots, using their pictures. I tied square knots, two half-hitches, sheet bends, clove hitches and bowlines. Sadly, my bowlines wound up a disaster.

At six o'clock I heard my father make his way up our front steps.

"Esther, I'm home." He shut the door. I made my way toward our parlor. He tossed his new straw boater hat onto its rack, making a ringer. "Ma," he said. "I closed two sales." He seemed his usual chipper self.

Pa shared an office in Downtown Anaheim at Beebe and Harrison Insurance on Los Angeles Street, one block north of Center Street, upstairs. He sold life insurance policies to veterans returning from the Great War they were fighting "over there."

He'd been having a great month. Pa was whistling a barbershop tune, *Pack up Your Troubles in Your Old Kit-Bag.*

Ma looked uneasy. I saw her silhouette from down the hallway. She stirred her pot of soup. She didn't even turn to face him. There was a letter on Pa's placemat at our tiny kitchen table.

"You got some mail from the Army," Ma told Pa. "Special delivery."

Pa looked up. "What on earth do they want now?" He shook his head.

"Read their orders," Ma said quietly. There was a tremor in her voice. It chilled the room and left the air heavy like fog along a riverbank.

She handed him the letter and returned to the steel stove to stir her soup and add more spices. "They want you training their recruits back at Fort Riley and Camp Funston to wear gas masks."

"Great," said Pa. "Just when we get back on our feet."

"I bought your train tickets. You leave tomorrow. Four a.m. Union Pacific. You're on *The Los Angeles Limited*."

"To Kansas?" Pa replied.

So unfair. Just last Christmas Pa had finally come home. After less than 40 days, Uncle Sam wanted him back.

Ma nodded, nibbling her thumbnail. She stared at it, then turned to Pa and frowned. "I upgraded to a Pullman for your back." She wrung her apron and gazed toward her lace-curtained kitchen window. "Darling, I prayed they'd never call you up again."

"Yeah, so did I. But can't complain. I'm a Reserve. Plus, I'm commissioned."

They met each other's gaze for a long time.

My heart ached too.

Ma went back to cooking. Pa was a captain in the Army. Somewhere in Europe, he'd hurt his back helping the British load their trucks with ammunition. Two days later, at the Battle of Cambrai, a German mortar hit that truck he'd loaded.

All onboard were killed.

But Pa wasn't on that truck. He'd been in France in an infirmary. Pa said they'd promised him a transfer to the Lafayette Escadrille. Like me, Pa dreamed of aviation and flying Nieuports over France. But when his back refused to heal they'd shipped him home as a Reserve. Said he'd be called up when they needed him.

They needed him.

Ma and Pa were trying hard to keep their chins up.

I had a paper route delivering *The Orange County Plain Dealer* every morning, so I wasn't going to see Pa board the train. Holding my rope in my left hand, I found Pa sitting on the chesterfield. I touched his shoulder. "Pa, can you teach me one more knot before you leave?"

Pa looked up. "I thought you knew all of your knots."

"A bowline hitch. I still can't tie it. Pa, can you...?"

I hurried down the hallway to my bedroom, and he followed.

Pa glanced down. He combed his fingers through his curly dark brown hair. "Dean, let me show you a little trick my pa taught me when I was your age."

I sat down, and I watched.

Pa took my rope and made a loop. He bent the bottom rope piece up above the circle like a tree. Pa made eye contact and smiled. He threaded the rope end through the opening. "You see, Dean, this end's the rabbit." Pa looked up at me and grinned. "The rabbit jumps out of his hole that I just made, and then he runs around the tree before he dives into the same hole he popped out of. Now *you* try it."

Pa handed me the rope.

Within ten seconds I had tied a perfect bowline.

"See, it's easy."

"Yeah," I stammered. "Pa, I'm really gonna miss you."

"At least I'm not being deployed to France where Germans can shoot back at us. Just training some recruits."

"So–how long'll you be gone?"

"Nothing much. Just ninety days."

I looked up, sad. "Write me a letter?"

"I will, Dean." Pa gave me a hug. I felt good in his strong arms, like I belonged, and he was proud I was his son.

Then Ma walked by.

She peered into my bedroom, "Soup is ready." Her eyes were red-rimmed.

"Don't worry, Esther, dear," Pa whispered. "We'll get through this, just like last time."

She didn't answer.

That night I went to bed and tied the bowline in the dark seventeen times around the right leg of my bedframe. I fell asleep dreaming of rabbits running laps around their rope trees and counted the weeks until I'd finally turn eleven, old enough to take my place among the Boy Scouts of America.

I couldn't wait to go on campouts, just like Skeeter.

At four o'clock a.m. when I got up to do my paper route, Ma told me Pa had left already. She looked at me. "He doesn't like goodbyes much."

It wasn't like Pa not to write us, but he didn't. There were no letters from Camp Funston nor from Fort Riley in Kansas.

On a damp day two weeks later when I came home from fifth grade, Ma was on the porch sweeping the steps.

She wore a mouse-brown cotton housedress. She had obviously been crying.

"You okay, Ma?"

She didn't answer. She just stared toward the sky. The fading Orange County sun lit up the tears wetting her cheeks. She shook her head.

"Tell me what's wrong."

She didn't talk for several minutes.

Then she whispered, "Deanie, he's dead." Ma stared across the street, shaking her head as if I'd just said something wrong, and she was angry. Except I hadn't said a word. She held this letter in her hand the way a child holds a butterfly, afraid to let it go.

"Who, Mama?"

Her chest was shaking.

I braced myself and sucked my cheeks in, dreading I already knew.

"Oh, Deanie." She collapsed against my chest and started weeping. It was so hard to get used to being as tall as my own mother. "Your father."

"What?" I stammered.

My spine turned into ice.

"He died of–influenza." She caught her breath. She met my gaze with steel eyes that in her shock appeared as hardened as ball bearings. It's like she'd somehow found a way to appear strong despite her grief.

I'd have to find a way to do the same.

I took a breath. Held it in. Ma stood quivering in my arms. The sun was shining, but the sunset turned this awful shade of red like it was bleeding. She buried her chin into my shoulder, and I feared she wished that *I* had been the one who'd died in Kansas.

I swallowed hard. I wasn't up to it. I hadn't even signed up with the Boy Scouts yet. I wasn't old enough to be a Tenderfoot. I felt so worthless. She kept digging her chin into my flesh, shaking her head like we could make this go away.

But Ma couldn't. And there was nothing I could do.

Old Mr. Knutson, three doors down, said we were lucky, because Pa had bought a boatload of insurance. Ma forced a smile and told him, "Thank you." Now, it seemed everywhere Ma went she hummed my dead pa's trademark tune, packing her troubles in her old kit-bag and smile-smile-smiling.

Alma Martin from next door, who sat beside me in my French class, brought me a plate of macaroons covered with tiny chocolate sprinkles. Ponytails of auburn hair hung like two ropes down Alma's back. She wore a headband. Her French wire glasses made her look like a librarian. Alma looked at me with big sad Gallic eyes.

"I've heard talk about your father." She touched the backside of my wrist, "And I am desolate." Her lower lip shook like she meant it.

I picked up a macaroon. "Thank you, Alma. Would you like one?"

"*Non. Merci.*" Alma blushed, jumped to her feet and ran inside her yellow bungalow. She came from Normandy with the accent to go with it. I had this awkward intuition Alma Martin really liked me. I ate the cookies on the porch all by myself.

The March air became as chilly as an icebox.

I watched the sun making its way past rows of ripening Valencias out past West Street, where Center Street changes its name to Lincoln Avenue, and it rolls on toward Cypress before it runs into the San Gabriel River and a maze of streets that zigzag toward Los Angeles.

It was only eight o'clock when Ma decided to retire. Behind the plaster walls I heard her weeping in her bedroom. It wasn't *their* room any more, only *hers*. I shut my eyes, trying to block out the cruel truth:

I no longer had a father.

I felt more desolate than Alma Martin ever could imagine. But I had to find a way to tough it out.

I didn't cry. Knew I couldn't. Had to stay strong. Act like a man. I laced my fingers behind my sandy hair and glared up from my bed pillow toward the stain around the edges of the parrot-green glass light fixture my father had replaced on Christmas Eve.

Because my pa had died, I didn't join the Boy Scouts of America, despite how much I hungered to belong. All those other boys had fathers. I felt like an outsider. I missed Pa, and I dared not tell a soul the way I felt.

Three months later, on my birthday, Ma presented me the last thing Pa had bought for me the week before he'd shipped out to Fort Riley. It was a baseball glove, an A. C. Spalding autographed Joe Jackson special edition, like Shoeless Joe wore in left field for the White Sox. It felt huge on my left hand, but not as big as my excitement upon receiving what I knew was Pa's last gift. Having no family to play catch with, I found a standpipe in an orange orchard. I threw my ball for hours against a hollow concrete pipe, fielding grounders when they ricocheted. I perfected my technique until I learned to throw a fastball so it bounced up from a pipe joint in a line drive I could catch in my raised glove.

One day at home I dropped my baseball. I looked beneath the dresser to retrieve it. I found my bowline hitch, still tied around the bedframe. There were dust bunnies all over it. The knot hid in the dark right where I'd left it. I thought about my pa.

I held back tears.

I kicked the knotted rope beneath my dusty box spring.

I walked outside. A trio of girls were playing hopscotch on the sidewalk. One sang a song I'd never heard.

I had a little bird

Its name was Enza

I opened the window

And in-flu-Enza.

My gut felt like they'd wrenched it inside out.

Doing my best to hide my pain, I pasted on a smile. I stepped inside. Time to get ready for my paper route tomorrow.

Ma was curled up on the couch reading her *Saturday Evening Post*.

Alma Martin stopped by, bringing another plate of macaroons.

CHAPTER II

WEDNESDAY, JANUARY 2, 1924

From my driveway on the first Wednesday of 1924, the skies seemed too blue for a January morning. Turquoise hues lit up Orange County with an antiseptic sheen that felt surreal and more appropriate for linen picture postcards. Scents of lemon and Valencia flowers wafted from the orchards to the east along the clay banks of the Santa Ana River. It gave this chilly winter break-of-day a fairy-tale veneer, too cotton-candy sweet to launch another year of high school.

My next-door neighbor, Alma, was still bringing macaroons. I knew she liked me. She was pretty, but I didn't like her back except as friends. We'd both been nobodies in 1923, but I'd been growing. I'd been five-foot nine in August. Then I'd shot up like a weed to six-foot-even, adding twenty pounds of muscle. And a smile. Ma said you always had to smile to get by. Skeeter was calling me "Big Six" after those six-cylinder engines.

I caught my breath, unloading newspaper bags off my yellow Schwinn. Alma strolled toward our front porch, wearing her calico-print dress with purple flowers. She'd brought a little bag of wax-paper-wrapped cookies. "Did you hear about poor Boomer?" Alma handed me her package. Her brow creased with a cascade of concern.

"No," I said. "Don't even know Boomer. I barely know the name."

"There was an automobile accident. Poor boy lost both of his parents," Alma's voice shook. She glanced down. "*Quel dommage*. So very sad."

Her tone made me aware I was supposed to be upset.

"Yeah," I said. "I'm real sad." Except, I wasn't, so I looked down. The kid wasn't in any of my classes.

Alma fired me a look that said I wasn't sad *enough*. "Their yellow Nash crashed east of town on Center Street across the river."

"They know what caused it?"

Alma shivered. She threw a glance over her shoulder. She lowered her voice. "The police say both the two of them were drunk." Her expression left me thinking Alma hadn't been convinced. As if policemen lied to newspapers, the way they did back East.

"We're in Anaheim," I told her. "Not in Brooklyn."

She didn't seem to know the difference. "*Au revoir*." She shook her head. She made her way across our lawn toward her yellow clapboard bungalow. She wiped her feet, slipped inside, closed her front door almost silently.

I sat on my front porch and polished off one of her cookies, before I grabbed my books and hustled off toward school.

I told myself poor Alma was a wee bit too emotional. Boomer

would survive, the same way I'd survived Pa's death. Still, it didn't pay to argue. Being a girl, Alma was complicated. "Never miss a chance to shut your yap," Pa used to say.

At lunch at Anaheim Union High School, I watched Boomer eat alone next to the picnic tables. He sat on a gray bench, peeling Valencias. I assumed these had been borrowed from the orchard south of Center Street. We weren't supposed to steal fruit, but Boomer's folks weren't here to feed him.

Eating my marmalade-wheat sandwich Ma had fixed for me this morning, I felt fortunate to have one living parent. I wondered whether Boomer's pain was anything like mine, a crater in my life where long ago I'd had a father waiting to welcome me to manhood and membership within the tribe. I tossed my sandwich crusts into the trash.

The bell rang. I grabbed my three-ring binder and my Muzzey's *American History* text and made my way upstairs toward the classrooms. En-route, I bumped into Coach Merritt. He was standing in the hallway. He clapped his huge right hand against my shoulder.

"I understand your name is Reynolds."

"Yes, sir," I replied.

"Skeeter tells me you're a southpaw."

"Yes, sir. I'm late for class."

Merritt smiled. "I watched you throwing in the orchard New Year's Day."

Smiling back, I answered, "Yes, sir. Can I..."

"Would you consider trying out? You own a glove, son?" Merritt asked.

"A Shoeless Joe special edition, sir." I said.

"Be there tomorrow on the baseball field. Tryouts. Two o'clock."

"Yes, sir," I stammered.

Merritt slapped me on the back, as if to telegraph to me I had already made the team.

My heart lifted inside of me. My smile became real. To beat the tardy bell, I sprinted into Miss Elgena's class, sliding straight into my seat like I'd just stolen second base.

Perhaps Orange County's cloudless skies hadn't been too blue after all.

FRIDAY, MAY 2, 1924

By March, my fastball had some zip. I started working on a curve. By April I'd discovered I adored the game of baseball.

Ma had taken Pa's insurance and hired Bannerman Construction to build three bedrooms on a second floor she rented out to boarders. When I wasn't on the ballfields or in class I earned good voot finishing roofing jobs for Bannerman to supplement our income. But then, Todd Larsen hurt his shoulder, Coach Merritt penciled in my name as starting pitcher for the Anaheim Union Colonists, senior varsity.

I was nervous. We were playing against the Santa Ana Saints, our arch-rival. We hadn't beaten them since 1921.

During my warm up, I felt loose. My fastball had plenty of pep, and my curve ball seemed to finally be behaving. I wore my lucky Shoeless Joe glove Pa had bought before he'd died. I'd worn that glove forever, even after Shoeless Joe was banned from baseball after the "Black Sox" threw the 1919 World Series.

"Play ball," hollered the umpire. He crouched behind home plate.

I'd known the umpire since I'd been in sixth grade. Because

he only had one eye, everybody called him "Ace." Clarkson's other eye was glass. Before the war, the story went, he'd asked this redhead, Dottie Casey, out, and Dottie'd turned him down.

To cover up his disappointment, Ace popped his glass eye from its socket and played catch with it. He said, "I'll always keep my eye out for you, Dottie.'"

Screaming, Dottie had raced home. Stayed home from school for three whole days.

Rumor was no Irish girl had said a word to Clarkson since. Still a bachelor, Ace would probably remain so his whole life, notwithstanding his insistence he'd earned a Purple Heart in France.

But right now I had to think about my game.

We took our places on the new field in Anaheim Central Park in our knee socks and our baggy blue and yellow cotton uniforms.

The leadoff batter for Santa Ana was hitting well over .400.

I struck him out with three quick fastballs.

He stormed back to the dugout.

The second batter popped up, and the third grounded to short. Six pitches and three outs. I was making it look easy. Santa Ana couldn't hit me. The game was going my direction.

After five innings, we were leading Santa Ana by a run. Sid Lowry hit a single, followed by Boomer Corrigan's double. One-nothing, Anaheim. I had a scare in the sixth inning when a kid from Santa Ana lined a screamer to right field.

But Skeeter Wilson somehow came up with a diving one-hand catch, turning a sure extra-base hit into an out.

I wrung the sweat out of my cap and mopped my forehead with my shirtsleeve.

For six innings, I had pitched a perfect game.

No one on our team said a word, afraid to throw a jinx. Except for Santa Ana's coach who tried to jinx me all he could.

"This kid's a junior for crissake, and he's throwing a *no-hitter*. And if he does, you're walking home. Did you hear that? A NO HITTER."

When the seventh inning started, the next batter was their shortstop. I threw a pair of inside fastballs, both for strikes.

He stepped out of the batter's box. He glared at me and spat. He stepped back in. I threw a changeup. He was looking for a heater. He'd swung his bat before the ball got to the plate.

"Steeerike three!" Ace Clarkson yelled.

My mouth was dry and full of cotton. I wiped the sweat off of my forehead and dried the ball off on my pants. Two outs remaining.

The angry batter slammed his bat into the dirt, walked into the dugout, and threw his helmet on the floor.

The stands were silent.

The Santa Ana coach called a time-out. A kid I'd struck out twice before was told to sit down on the bench.

The pinch hitter he sent in wasn't even five feet tall.

I threw a strike on the first pitch. Then I threw a couple balls, high and outside. Two balls, one strike. I had to even up the count. I threw a fastball down the middle, but Ace Clarkson was half-blind. Called it a ball. I took a breath. Squeezed the baseball in my hand, trying to focus. I had to throw a strike on my next pitch.

As soon as I let go of my change-up, I wanted that pitch back. Low and inside. But for some reason the batter tried to hit it. And he did. A slow roller to my left, I somehow barehanded and shoveled to first base just before he touched the bag.

Two outs. Edgar Morris, who'd grounded out in the first inning was up. Everyone told me this guy hit like Rogers Hornsby. I'd been lucky the first inning, but this time I threw him garbage, hoping he'd swing.

He didn't.

"Ball One," bellowed the umpire.

He didn't swing at my next fastball. "Steerike," hollered the umpire. An even count, and it was clear this batter didn't like my fastball. I threw another one.

"Ball Two." I could have sworn it was a strike.

The batter dug his cleats into the dirt inside the batter's box.

My gut twisted in agony. My temples throbbed. My arm felt like a heavy slug of lead.

I threw a curveball for a strike, and then another for a ball. Three balls, two strikes. A full count. And then the Santa Ana coach called a time-out to make me worry.

I tried to focus on my pitch.

Santa Ana's leading hitter stepped into the batter's box.

I offered him a fastball down the middle.

He fouled it off.

I threw a curve ball and he fouled it off again into the stands.

I threw a curve that got away from me. It dropped down to his shins.

Except he swung.

"STEEEERIKE THREE!"

Cheers exploded from the stands, and I felt as if a sack of wet cement fell off my shoulders. I raised my baseball mitt in triumph. Half the people in our bleachers started chanting out my nickname. "Go, Big Six."

This was easy to get used to. I waved back. Walter Johnson had pitched for Fullerton, and he was the "Big Train." I loved it when my friends called me, "Big Six," like Christy Mathewson, the famous New York Giants starting pitcher.

I heard a whistle and looked up to see the final score they'd hung up on the board after I'd pitched my perfect game:

ANAHEIM UNION COLONISTS	1
SANTA ANA SAINTS	0

All of us sprinted off the field and jogged the long block back to school, amazed that we had just pulled off an upset. Classmates were yelling out my name, backslapping, cheering, handing me ginger ale, and calling me a local hometown hero. It felt good to finally prove to all my classmates I could do something, if it was little more than throwing a white baseball.

After our showers, I made my way out of the locker room and was surrounded by eight girls who looked at me as if I'd won the war in Europe. I blushed. It was a game. I didn't deserve their adulation. I'd just been in the right place at the right time. What could I say? Their final two batters could have taken my last pitch and walked to first. I'd made mistakes, but so had they. I'd gotten lucky.

Coach Merritt sang my praises to a cheerleader in a tight blue and gold sweater with a jaunty silk scarf tied around her neckline, sailor-style.

"Hey, Big Six." She winked.

"Um." I smiled back. "Hello."

She was a sophomore on the B-squad who was waving to her father in his brand new silver Packard Single Eight.

I blushed and finger-combed my hair.

She met my gaze. "I can't believe I'm actually talking to Dean Reynolds."

I'd seen the girl around our high school. She used to usher at the cinema. I'd never known her name. People just called her, "the pretty one."

"Helen Webber." She smiled wide. "My father's a director on the Board at Sunkist Growers. He has an office at the Anaheim Orange and Lemon Association. He'd like to meet you. He admires how you played. Says you're 'the bee's knees.' You remind him of The Big Train, Walter Johnson."

I looked at Helen, and I couldn't look away.

"Thanks," I said, and held my breath. If Helen's eyes were pools of blue, it was apparent I had landed in the deep end. She had this flawless suntanned face framed by cascades of fair-haired curls cut short above her shoulders true to the fashions of the Twenties. Helen's lips were red as rose petals. Her necklace was a string of real pearls, the sort my mother only wore to church on Christmas and on Easter.

Helen evidently wore pearls any time she wanted.

Her father honked the car horn on his Packard.

"Care to join us?" Helen asked. "We're having malts down at the fountain."

I glanced over my shoulder and caught a glimpse of Skeeter Wilson. He slapped my back. "Go on, Dean," he said. "I'll catch up with you tomorrow."

Skeeter had class. Clearly, he understood I had to seize the moment, because Cupid didn't smile on junior boys like me too often.

"Good luck, Dean."

"Thanks," I said.

I would do the same for Skeeter.

Helen leaned against her father's Packard.

She looked almost *too* familiar. Somehow her image had

been seared into my mind like she was famous even though she lived in Anaheim. I'd seen her *somewhere*, as if her face appeared on sheet music, or lobby cards, or smiled down from billboards like the one I saw right now above the citrus orchard running south of Center Street. I saw the billboard every day from Miss Elgena's civics class. I'd stare out through the second story window to stay awake:

J. T. LYON REALTY
VALENCIA, QUEEN OF THE ORANGE
LYON, KING OF THE REALTY.

There was a lion in the center of the billboard like that lion at the movie theater introducing Samuel Goldwyn Pictures.

Footsteps were headed my direction. I looked up to see Helen. "Daddy, this is Dean," The man had stepped out from his Packard. He wore a *suit*. Helen looked at us.

She beamed. "Ain't Dean the best?"

I grinned the way my mother taught me after Pa had died.

Helen's father grabbed my hand. "Herbert Webber. Guess you know I'm Helen's dad." His grip was strong enough to juice a navel orange. "Helen, I reckon this young man of yours don't need much introduction. Heckuva game out on the baseball field, Reynolds." His handshake worked my arm the way a farmer works a pump handle.

"Thanks," I said. "Got lucky."

"Probably hard work."

I glanced at Helen, then at him. The man was staring at my clothes. He shook his head. My home-sewn shirt, my tattered leather shoes with grommets that were missing. Mister Webber wore a *custom-tailored* suit, the sort you see in motion pictures that star Rudolf Valentino, or on bandleaders who play the Bon Ton Ballroom on Lick Pier.

I hopped into the back seat, sliding my hands over the cool and supple all-leather upholstery, softer than a puppy's ears. I thought I must be sitting someplace inside of a bank. I hid the holes worn through my soles and vowed a trip to Quality Shoe Store just as soon as I had cabbage enough to buy some decent shoes.

"Don't know much about your father," Mister Webber said.

"Pa died after the war. He was a captain at Fort Riley when the influenza hit."

"I'm sorry, son."

"But I work lots and lots of jobs to help my family. We may be poor but...."

"The poor boy ain't the man without a cent," said Mr. Webber. "It's the man without a dream who's really poor."

His tone of voice left me confused. I wasn't sure whether he liked me or he didn't, and he took his time while Helen pled my case.

"Daddy, that's probably how Dean got those big muscles, working weekends."

"You go to church?"

"When I can. Since Pa died, I mostly work. Ma needs somebody on Sundays to clean rooms after her boarders. She can't afford to hire anybody else."

"See, he has paint on all his fingernails," said Helen. "He works hard. And what's that black stuff?"

"Roofing tar. I carry hods for Mister Bannerman."

She made a face, but stroked my muscle.

I flexed, and felt a blush, wondering how soon, I'd be kicked out of the Packard.

Mr. Webber made a left turn onto Center Street and drove right past the Forrest Hudnall Soda Fountain all our high school went to. Three blocks east, he signaled left and parked behind the Heying's Pharmacy. The *original* Hudnall's Fountain, was on the first floor of the pharmacy. It was more upscale, where businessmen did deals over lunch. Mr. Webber scrunched the parking brake and turned off the ignition.

I jumped out from the back seat, raced around the car's rear end so I could open Helen's door.

Helen stepped out, saying, "Thank you."

Mr. Webber stood and frowned as Helen wiggled up beside me. I wondered whether Mrs. Webber had to stay at home. There was a wedding ring on Mr. Webber's hand, so he was married. He led the way, using the back door of the drug store past the bathrooms in the rear, and we emerged beside a long white onyx bar. A line of steel pedestal stools rose from a white tile-mosaic.

Next to the cash register and cigarettes, platoons of glass jars on the counter were filled with candy sticks and goodies like salt water taffy and Necco wafers. A giant mirror on the wall reflected Alma's older brother, Donnie Martin. He was working as the soda jerk tonight. He wore a clean white short-sleeve shirt, black bowtie, pleated slacks, Donnie was busy making malted milks by hand, using a spoon. I couldn't help but wonder if he'd see me here with Helen and tell his cookie-baking sister all about us.

Still this wasn't quite a date if Helen's father would be treating. The three of us sat down around a round white onyx table. Ceiling fans spun overhead, and rows of incandescent lights glared off an advertising sign promoting Hall's Cherry Expectorant.

I was pretty sure that Donnie didn't notice who I was.

"You want a sandwich?" Helen asked, grabbing a tattered paper menu. "The grilled cheese sandwiches are dreamy here." She leaned back on her soda fountain chair with its pink loops that let her shoulders slide above them, displaying curves that could make Clara Bow or Gloria Swanson jealous.

A bug-eyed-Betty waitress came and scribbled down our order. "Three grilled cheeses, two chocolate malteds and a big order of fries."

Helen smiled, batting big eyes as if she wanted the whole store to see exactly who was seated at the table with her family.

And half the parents in the drugstore were now looking our direction, scratching their chins, seeming to wonder if Helen and I might be a couple. I wished we were. I was flattered, but for now we were just friends. I was hoping Mr. Webber wouldn't notice there were holes in both my shoes. Plus, I had to watch my manners.

"So you do roofing work?" he asked. He was staring at my hands and not my shoes.

"Yes, I work for Mister Bannerman," I said.

"Would you work for someone else? I have this good friend, Stubby Carson, with a roof job out at Sunkist. He could use another hod carrier."

"Tomorrow?"

Webber nodded. He lit up a cigar.

I hesitated, wondering if I needed to act humble or act confident without appearing cocky. "What's he pay, sir?"

"Buck an hour. Stubby will work you to the bone. He's on a

deadline. It's a temporary gig, you understand, but could turn permanent."

"I never earned that in my life. You bet, I'll take the job," I answered, nodding, as my heart lit up like fireworks inside me.

"You need a ride?"

"I have a bicycle I use to run my paper route."

"Stubby's men show up at six. They start at dawn to beat the heat. Stubby won't be all too happy if you're late on your first day."

"You bet. Thanks," I said. I'd need to start my paper route at four a.m. to finish up in time and start another job at six.

I glanced at Helen. She'd been staring at my hands, but now she looked at me and smiled in a way that seemed to mask what she was thinking. Donnie Martin came by, dropping off our trio of grilled cheese sandwiches.

Mister Webber bowed his head and offered grace for thirty seconds, his skull nodding like a German bisque-based bobble-head.

I shut my eyes and did my best to look religious. It was the first time since my father died that I thought God might care about me, giving me a job so I could buy a pair of shoes.

When my eyes opened I looked at Helen Webber.

She was smiling.

I wore that smile-smile-smile Ma had taught me, extra wide.

CHAPTER III

SATURDAY, MAY 3, 1924

B y five o'clock Saturday morning, I had finished up my paper route, and Mr. Webber's Packard Single Eight was at our curbside. He revved the engine. He had evidently been there for a while. I parked my Schwinn by the garage, raced inside to change my shoes and jump into a pair of fresh-washed overalls.

Mr. Webber wore a suit just like the one he'd worn last night. "Ready for breakfast?"

"You bet," I said.

"I stopped by a little early."

"Yes, sir, I noticed." I caught my breath, thinking I knew the man's agenda. For me to have a chance with Helen I would need to pass his muster.

"I kind of like to get to know a boy before he dates my daughter. Helen likes you."

"Thank you, sir," I said. My heart began to race.

"Can't have boys breaking her heart." I saw his right hand

slightly shaking as if he needed a cigar right now but had to break his habit.

"I like her too. She's very pretty, but I need to get to know Helen a bit more than I do right now before I ask her out."

"She's not shy. Time will take care of that, if *we* two get along. You won't find a sweeter girl than Helen Webber in all Orange County.

"Yes, sir," I said with mixed emotions. Clearly, he cared about his daughter. I had to think the reason he was here was Helen liked me. I wished my own father could be here, and I felt a pang of grief, wondering how it actually felt to have a father looking out for you.

"How 'bout we go to Warren Glover's? Best durned omelets in town. And fresh Orange County bacon straight from Schneiders by the Odd Fellows."

"Sounds delicious."

I slid into the supple leather front seat of the Packard and rolled the window down while Mister Webber started the ignition.

He glanced down at the dashboard. "Guess I need to buy some gas."

"Not a problem."

The morning's warm May air blew through my hair.

He drove straight past the Union Oil Station, turned north onto Los Angeles Street, drove past Warren Glover's and continued past La Palma north of town. Where Los Angeles Street angled toward where Palm Street became Spadra there was a Standard Oil Station I'd never noticed.

An easel by their driveway entrance said:

BUD'S CHEVRON
REGULAR $0.08
ETHEL $0.10
ayak

Mr. Webber drove his car up to the pump and honked the horn.

A slim man ambled out in overalls that looked like they'd been pulled straight off the clothes line. He seemed to squint, although there wasn't any glare. One of his eyes seemed to be lower than the other. He crossed his arms.

"Filler up," said Mr. Webber. "Have you seen Mister Akia?"

"You want ethel?"

Webber nodded.

Bud smirked and turned the pump on.

I couldn't help but wonder what the letters meant.

Bud had one of those old pumps that had that fish bowl on the top. Gasoline percolated into the dispenser bowl like coffee. "Izzat enough there, Bert?"

"Should do." Bud stuffed the nozzle into the gas tank. "Ten gallons are gonna set you back three quarters of an ace."

Webber handed Bud a dollar. I did the math and figured out these two men must have some arrangement that let Webber get a discount. Bud handed two bits back in change, and Mr. Webber dropped the coins into an ashtray he had evidently emptied out this morning.

Then he started the ignition. The Packard roared onto Los Angeles Street, signaling a left into the lot by Warren Glover's. Mister Webber scrunched the parking brake. He glanced outside and savored the attention of some local boys who whistled at his Packard. Wearing an ask-the-man-who-owns-one smile he sauntered through the backdoor of the restaurant.

I jumped out of the car and walked behind him, reminding myself Ma had said a boy should never frown. I smiled wide enough to feel phony.

I followed Mr. Webber past the bathroom and the kitchen

through its aromatic *potpourri* of scrambled eggs and bacon. Webber waltzed between glass tables like he owned the joint himself, and found a seat next to the window with real china and cloth napkins.

"Need a menu, son?" he asked as we sat down.

"I'll try those omelets and bacon you suggested."

"Good choice, Dean."

"What'll *you* have?"

"Same thing."

"I'm encouraged."

"You drink Hills Brothers?"

"I play baseball. They say coffee stunts your growth."

Webber looked up. "Mind if I...?"

"Help yourself," I said. "You're treating."

He placed his coffee cup in front of him and tapped it with his pinkie.

A waiter filled it full, and Mr. Webber took a sip of steaming java.

I took a breath and studied my surroundings.

A man behind us read the back page of the *Orange County Plain Dealer*. His wife went on about how bootleggers were ruining Orange County. On Los Angeles Street, outside, the city flagpole threw a shadow that ran several times its height before it angled up a wall. The shadow ended at a billboard ad for Murad Cigarettes, saying they "Never disappoint—never fail—never change." There were no clouds in the sky. I'd been told clouds were illegal at this hour, as if anything unpleasant could be outlawed, and all one needed were a few good laws to legislate perfection.

On the sidewalk, a stranger in a straw hat waved hello. He turned and made his way inside of Warren Glover's. I sensed

Mr. Webber knew him. He wore a brown suit with a matching vest, an orange bow-tie, and round wire-rim glasses like Teddy Roosevelt's. He took his hat off, and his head looked like an oversized potato with eyes to match, tiny brown eyes. They say the eyes of a potato can be poisonous. On his lapel, he wore a small American flag pin like that flag up on the pole or in the restaurant's front window.

"Bertie boy," he bellowed. He headed in our direction.

"Mayor Metcalf? Good to see you. Elmer, have you met Big-Six Reynolds? We're having breakfast."

"Baseball player. Glad to meet you," said the mayor. He placed his hat down on our table and extended his right hand. "Good to see you boys defeated Santa Ana. What a game."

I shook the mayor's extended hand and couldn't wait to let it go. It seemed mechanical, a handshake you might get if Dale Carnegie taught Rossom's Universal Robots how to do their handshakes. Something about this mayor bothered me. I wasn't quite sure what.

Still I bravely smile-smile-smiled.

He sat right down at our table, and my heart sank. I'd hoped to eat with Mr. Webber and enjoy a pleasant breakfast, get some tips on courting Helen, find out what Stubby needed from his roofers. I read the clock out on Los Angeles Street.

Five-thirty.

"Missed you at Pastor Leon's Bible study." Mayor Metcalf grabbed my coffee cup and plopped it down in front of him. A waiter rushed to fill it. Besides the flag pin on his left lapel, a small white metal cross was on his right lapel. He seemed to wear religion on his sleeve with those lapel pins placed like linebackers to back up his convictions.

"Business called," said Mr. Webber. "Met a grower out in

Riverside. Navy chum. Served hunting U-boats on the same destroyer I did."

The mayor took a sip of coffee, and he didn't seem impressed. "You need to bring that boy to church. We can't let Hollywood corrupt young boys like him," the mayor said, eying me over like a cop. "All that bootleggin' and liquor even here in li'l old Anaheim. We need to put a stop to it. We need to have a rally."

"I hear you, Mayor." Mr. Webber said. "I'll ask him if he's interested."

"Helen coming?"

"Of course, your honor."

"We need more good and wholesome girls like Helen Webber in our midst. That girl's the choicest bit of calico to grace the streets of Anaheim."

Mr. Webber looked as bristled as a brand new Fuller brush.

Although I privately agreed, I didn't like the way he said it. Mayor or not, I got this feeling in my throat I didn't like. Plus it appeared that Mr. Webber was afraid of Mayor Metcalf, even though they both went to the same First Christian Church.

One of the waiters brought our breakfast. I gobbled down my omelet. It was the alibi I needed to not talk to Mayor Metcalf. I wanted energy for work. The omelet tasted like heaven.

The clock outside showed ten minutes to six.

Mister Webber left two dollars on the table for our breakfast, and we hurried out the back door of the restaurant together. We jumped into the Packard, and Mr. Webber revved the engine.

We made it to the packing house with two minutes to spare.

"Sorry we didn't get to talk more." Mr. Webber shook my hand before I hopped out of the Packard down at Stubby Carson's jobsite. I saw the rusted iron roofing on the Anaheim Citrus Packing House. Another one of J.T. Lyon's billboards overlooked it.

My goal today was making money. Earning a dollar every hour I stood to make a stack of cabbage I could use to buy new shoes.

"Stop by for dinner," Mr. Webber said. "My wife is a swell cook. She won a prize last year at Fairview for her orange meringue pie."

"You mean *tonight*, sir?"

"Six o'clock." He cocked his right hand like a pistol. "Don't be late. I'll tell Helen you'll be coming. She'll expect you. We're on Clementine at Sycamore, the craftsman on the corner with the swing on the front porch, next to the olive-green front door. You'll see a steam shovel out back where we'll be puttin' in a tennis court."

"You bet, sir."

"Don't be late," he said again and turned the key in the ignition.

I feared this man had an agenda. Helen was gorgeous, and I understood her father might protect her. But something else was going on here. Helen's father wore a poker face. He fired up his Packard and drove off before I had a chance to ask.

Still it intrigued me that Mr. Webber even wanted me around. When Skeeter Wilson had his first date the girl's pa met him with a shotgun.

The work went quickly, hauling sheets of 18-gauge galvanized steel up long ladders to the roof above the packing rooms. I was grateful it was mild today. The men on Stubby's crews seemed to appreciate my strength and can-do attitude.

Somehow I kept up with their riveting. But sheet metal is heavy. After hauling several tons up to the roof, I was exhausted. My sore back wailed like a blues singer, and my hands were nicked and bleeding from the edges of the corrugated steel.

By nine o'clock, my ears were ringing from the rivet guns that hammered out non-stop throughout the morning. But I'd already earned three dollars. That was enough to buy a pair of decent shoes at Quality Shoe Store. I was going to buy them just as soon as I got paid.

Stubby Carson finally gave his men a break at ten a.m. All of us stood up on the roof. Men smoked their Lucky Strikes and Chesterfields. I didn't smoke, so I took time out to enjoy the panorama. Anaheim spread out before me. I stared down toward Lincoln Avenue and Five Points with those new mysterious "KIGY" letters on the concrete. They'd been stenciled there last month on every road that entered Anaheim.

Nobody would tell me what they meant.

Beyond the high school rose the steeples and the towers of my town, Saint Boniface, Zion Lutheran, and Salem Evangelical, the cupola downtown outside the SQR Department Store, and the flagpole just behind our City Hall.

The men were putting out their cigarettes. I had to wash my hands, and so I scrambled down the ladder to the packing rooms downstairs. I found a water closet, locked the wooden door, finished my business, and made my way out through a corridor with packing crates stacked six-feet-high on both sides of the aisle.

Every single crate had the same label.

"PRIDE OF ANAHEIM VALENCIAS" the fruit labels proclaimed. "Packed by Scott-Borden, Incorporated, Anaheim, California." Every label bore the same face of a girl.

She looked familiar. A whole lot like the actress, Colleen Moore.

But not exactly.

She had blond hair cut in a bob. She wore pearls and a black dress, and she had mesmerizing eyes.

Good God, it couldn't be.

It was.

For thirty seconds I just stared at it.

A thrill ran up my spine.

I swallowed hard and took a breath, taking a moment to recover from my shock.

I knew where I'd seen Helen's face before.

I imagined they'd be shipping Helen all over the planet. Barons in Europe, sheikhs in Hejaz, Ottoman sultans, Persian shahs, Chinese moguls, Wall Street titans, would see Helen's face on every single carton full of Scott-Borden Valencias from Anaheim, Anaheim Beauties, Prides of Anaheim, and all their other brands.

Tonight I would be dining at the home of Helen Webber who had the face that launched one-hundred-thousand oranges.

After eleven grueling hours we finished up at five o'clock. We toweled off with oil of turpentine to clean away the tar beneath our fingernails. I was grateful Mister Carson honked his horn.

"Son, need a lift?"

"You bet," I told him. Stubby's ride would buy me time to take a shower and to change my clothes to look my best for Helen.

I slid into the front seat of Stubby's Dodge two-seater pickup. He tossed aside a newspaper, the *Orange County Plain Dealer*.

It plopped into the floor well where I briefly saw the headline.

NEW CITY COUNCIL HIRES 4 MORE POLICEMEN

I wondered why so many cops were needed here in Anaheim, and why I hadn't seen the headline on a paper I'd delivered.

Stubby Carson was a sturdy man with shoulders like a baby-grand piano and muscled forearms like you saw in Popeye comics. Stubby's sleeves were rolled up tight, showing off his farmer's tan. He turned to me and flashed a crooked grin.

"Tired yet, Reynolds?"

"Yes sir," I said and grinned. "And thanks a million for the lift."

"Bert says you got eyes for his daughter."

"News travels pretty fast," I said, surprised at Stubby. Anaheim was just a small Orange County town. With only 5500 people in the 1920 census, I understood how Stubby managed to know all the local gossip.

I looked at Stubby, and I shrugged. "You know I haven't asked her out yet."

"You might want to be careful," Stubby said. "'Round Helen Webber."

"Why?" I asked, wishing I hadn't.

"Helen ain't who she pretends."

I felt the hair rise on my neck. "So do you know something?" I asked.

"I know she smokes. No decent woman needs to smoke. It jus' ain't ladylike. It's—decadent." He signaled and changed lanes.

"It's just a fad. Everybody's smoking cigarettes," I said. "In every film they make in Hollywood the stars are smoking cigarettes."

Stubby shifted into second.

"It's glamourous." I shrugged. "Modern girls want to look glamorous. I'm not setting the fashions." I stared outside.

The cabin of his pickup truck turned colder than an ice house, and I wondered what had obligated *me* to defend Helen. Some sort of instinct, I supposed and one that Stubby didn't care for.

He frowned. He made a face and floored the truck down Lincoln Avenue. "I'm disappointed in you, Reynolds. Hollywood? Glamour? You *can't* be serious. I thought your parents raised you right. Hollywood today's a moral cesspool."

Before I thought to ask him why, Stubby launched into a tirade over Hollywood, bad morals, how Fatty Arbuckle had raped Virginia Rappe, the William Desmond Taylor murder, Mabel Normand and cocaine, Pola Negri, Alla Nazimova, Rudolph Valentino. "They're all homos," Stubby said. "And Wallace Reid, dying on morphine. The studios hire fixers to hide stars' habits from the public. A disgrace."

"I thought that Rudolph Valentino had a wife."

"Lavender marriage," Stubby said, making a left onto Los Angeles Street and driving to the same gas station that Webber had this morning. The easel still stood on the corner with its curious initials:

BUD'S CHEVRON
REGULAR $0.08
ETHEL $0.10
ayak

Stubby opened up the cab door. "Bud, have you seen Mister Akia?"

Bud repeated the same ritual Mr. Webber had this morning. He filled the fishbowl with ten gallons, giving Carson the same discount.

From my seat by Mister Carson I stared northward onto Spadra Street, and there I spied the same letters I'd seen on Lincoln Avenue, freshly stenciled in white paint onto the asphalt on the highway south from Fullerton where it crossed the city limit into Anaheim.

"KIGY"

Something about it made me nervous.

Nervous enough I wanted to cover those dumb letters up with roofing tar.

"What's with all the secret code?" I asked and turned to Stubby Carson. Once again I wished I hadn't.

Mr. Carson looked away but murmured gently. "Come to Pastor Myers' Bible study, Reynolds. First Christian Church on Tuesday nights. We start at six-thirty p.m. Maybe if you come, you'll start to figure these things out."

I wondered how they fit together. I didn't have the nerve to ask.

Stubby dropped me at my house five minutes later and sped off.

Outside my house I paused a moment, hearing a loud whine overhead. It came straight out of the yellow sun and hung near the horizon. A speck of red up in the sky was suddenly straight overhead. Till now, I had only seen a couple of them. Aeroplanes. I loved them.

And then it veered off toward the south, flying toward Santa Ana, loud and faster than an eagle. Engine noise faded in the distance, but I was spellbound. *Someday I would like to learn to fly*, I thought, but chocked it off to pipe dreams. More urgent matters seemed to beckon.

Alma Martin was on my porch. This time she brought no macaroons. Her eyes were red. It seemed that Alma had been crying for a spell. This wasn't like her. She was normally a lot more put-together. The mascara from her lashes flowed in streaks down both her cheeks.

"Alma, what's up? Are you okay?"

She sat and stared down at her feet and said, "*Mon oncle.*"

Alma slowly shook her head.

"What about him?"

She pulled a handkerchief from her purse and wiped her eyelids leaving a big smear of mascara on the white and lacy cotton.

"He left this morning. They succeeded. They drove my Uncle Raymond out."

"You make it sound as if your uncle's leaving Anaheim." I said.

"But yes, he is." She shut her eyes. "These people mail him a letter, but they do not sign their names. In France we call it '*anonyme.*' These people tell my Uncle Raymond if he does not shut his hotel down before eight o'clock this morning they will..."

"What?"

She looked away. "They do not say. All they tell us is—'or else.'"

"Or else what? Who wrote the letter?"

"*They* did."

"Who?"

"People in Anaheim."

"Was there handwriting? You could talk to the police."

"You're so naïve. Why do you think the City Council hires all these new policemen, and lets the old ones go, the ones we knew and trusted?"

She shrugged. Her trembling shoulders lost all pretense of composure as she tried to catch her breath and carry on a conversation. Alma stared out past the clock towers and church steeples and wept. "Why do they hate us?" Alma asked, mopping black tears from both her cheeks, "calling us bootleggers, and Frogs, and filthy Catholics, and telling us America's for Americans. They tell us *we* should all go home. This *is* my home. They blame the *war* on us. We're *French*. We didn't start it."

"People are stupid. They don't know anything about the war in Europe. People who didn't even fight parade around like our protectors."

"Why do they treat us with reproach? They claim French people are winos. If we manifest dissent they call us Communists and say we hate America. I *love* America, but it's hard when you love them, and they hate back, and claim that everyone in France is either pink or homosexual."

Church bells rang six times from steeples all across the city. I panicked. Glanced around. "Alma, right now I can't talk."

"But Dean..."

My heart stopped. "We'll talk later. I need to be somewhere. Right now." I ran inside and changed my clothes, combed my hair, and brushed my teeth, dashed back outside and felt horrific as I ran away from Alma for my date with Helen Webber at her house.

Alma was hurting, but there wasn't any way I could console her.

She called me, and I didn't answer back.

I had a date with Helen Webber, and that date was starting *now*. I sprinted north on Citron Street, heart pounding fast as a machine gun. Turned right on Sycamore. Raced past Pine Street, Palm Street, and Central Park.

Ahead of me on Clementine was Helen Webber's residence.

Helen stood on the front porch beside her father on her left.

He was looking at his wristwatch. "Son, you're sixteen minutes late."

Helen glared at me. Her cold twin-barrel stare said she was furious. Her look bore no resemblance to the girl on all the orange crates. Her lips were trembling. She glanced toward her father, and I knew I was in serious hot water.

I took a breath.

Helen's father was still staring at his wristwatch, and I wondered why the man was so obsessed with punctuality. He sent Helen inside and backed me up against the porch rail.

"Sit, down," he said.

I sat.

"You have an attitude. A bad one."

"Sir, I'm sorry."

"It's not your fault, son. You grew up without a father. You're a good kid, but it's time you had a man inside your life. Before you go out with my daughter there are things you need to learn."

"Yes, sir." I kept my lips sealed, taking care not to point out that it was *he* who'd asked *me* here. I had yet to ask out Helen. Now I wasn't sure I wanted to. She wasn't worth the hassle, and I didn't like men telling me they didn't like my attitude. Especially when my back ached after I'd slaved eleven hours so Stubby Carson could meet his deadline on some roofing job today. I'd worked my tail off to help these people meet their stupid deadlines.

I stared down at my feet and somehow managed to stay quiet.

"You go to church, son?"

"No," I said. "After my pa died, Ma stopped going."

"Stopped going where?"

"White Temple Methodist."

"You need to come to church with *us*."

"Come to church where?"

"First Christian, Anaheim. The Reverend Myers teaches Sunday School as well. Helen goes there almost every weekend."

It was pretty clear that Mr. Webber liked to call the shots. And furthermore there was some reason he had *me* picked out for Helen. I didn't know the reason why, but I decided to keep my mouth shut. I had no father, and no mentor, and my shoes were full of holes. I'd been fending for myself, doing the best job that I could, but it was hard. And Mr. Webber seemed to know a lot of people who could help me, like Stubby Carson, even Mayor Elmer Metcalf.

Mr. Webber wound his wristwatch. "Let's go inside, son," said the man. "This lecture's over, and my wife cooked a fine meal. It's getting cold."

I hopped down from the porch rail and took a giant breath of air.

Mr. Webber grinned and shook my hand.

I hadn't yet agreed to go to church with Mr. Webber, but he seemed to think I had, and it was not the time to argue. Wiping my shoes off on his doormat, feeling the bristles of the mat poke through my socks, I stepped inside. Mr. Webber stood behind me.

I slowly made my way across an oriental carpet that was woven full of images of citrus leaves and oranges. The Webbers' huge craftsman-style dining room was filled with glass-framed fruit labels.

And Helen's smiling face was in the center of each frame.

There in the middle of the dining table a pot of three-bean soup steamed on a hot pad made of custom California mission tile. It matched the tile on the staircase in the living room that wound its way upstairs to where the bedrooms were.

Helen nibbled her pearl necklace.

I hadn't tasted three-bean soup since Pa had died of influenza. Ma never cooked it after that. She said it triggered awful memories. Our family's last dinner together was a pot of three-bean soup that smelled exactly like the steaming pot in front of me.

It seemed an omen, as if God wanted me to join First Christian Church and be a member of a family the way my life had been before the war. I had been too young to appreciate such things.

"Shall we pray," said Mrs. Webber. The swinging door into the kitchen was behind her. She wore an apron cut from the same cloth as our placemats. She had a strong angular jaw and eyes the same color as Helen's, but unlike Helen, Mrs. Webber looked afraid.

I bowed my head to join the family.

Mr. Webber bowed his head and said the blessing.

"Lord, we give thanks to thee for everything we have here in America, and we ask that you protect your town from every form of evil, from the Communists, the Catholics, the foreigners, the union thugs, the bootleggers, and Hollywood, and all forms of corruption. Father, give us back our town. Make Anaheim a model city free from vice. We pray these things in Jesus' name."

We said, "Amen."

Except for Helen, whom I noticed had been staring out the window toward that hole in the backyard where they were putting in new tennis courts. I wondered why someone would dig a hole to build a tennis court.

Helen gave me a quick glance and didn't say another word, but it was obvious she had some strong opinions.

SUNDAY, MAY 4, 1924

At seven-thirty the next morning, the Webbers pulled up into our driveway. Ma was sleeping when Mr. Webber honked his silver Packard's horn. I wrote a note to tell my mother where I was and raced upstairs, combed my hair, straightened my tie, and tried to squeeze into a sport jacket that barely even fit me since my arms had grown last winter.

My sleeves were climbing up my wrists. My slacks were clearly the "high-water" type. I cut the hem, unrolling it to stretch down to my socks. I looked outlandish, like some extra out of Keystone central casting. I raced downstairs and greeted Mr. Webber on the sidewalk.

"Mornin', Dean."

"Good morning, Mister Webber," I replied. I saw the shotgun seat was empty. Mrs. Webber sat in back, talking to Helen. It was evident the men would sit up front. I felt uncomfortable but slid onto the front seat they'd assigned me.

We made it to their church ten minutes early.

Mister Webber introduced me to his pastor, Leon Myers, while Mrs. Webber and three friends stood by discussing Prohibition. One of the ladies in her circle was as big as Carrie Nation. She must have left her axe at home. The other woman didn't say much, but I judged from all her cashmere she was terribly important.

Then Mayor Metcalf took her arm, and it was quite clear whom she was.

Helen vanished until just before the service.

She slid into the pew beside me. Her perfume smelled like orange blossoms. It didn't cover up her cigarette breath.

The service wasn't like those I was used to with the Methodists. These people sang *God Bless America* instead of the Doxology. A U.S. flag big as a movie screen was thumbtacked to the wall behind the pulpit. It dwarfed a cross that made it up to the eighth stripe.

Reverend Myers preached a sermon unlike any I'd ever heard. He was clearly a fine speaker, but all he talked about was movies. I could see where Stubby Carson might have picked up his material. Reverend Myers thundered from the pulpit.

"Ever since they made *Intolerance*, Hollywood has gone downhill. Now it's been overrun by flappers, murderers, perverts, alcoholics."

I noticed half the congregation hanging on his every word. I glanced at Helen.

She rolled her eyes.

We'd need to talk about this later.

Our opportunity came thirty minutes after the last hymn. *The Battle Hymn of the Republic* was still banging in my brain.

As He died to make men holy, let us die to make men free,
While God is marching on.

Helen grabbed me by the elbow and suggested we might march around the block, "Just you and me, Dean. God can join us if he needs to."

I said, "Sure." I needed air, and we needed to discuss things.

We stepped outside to take a stroll. One block west, we turned a corner.

She lit a Fatima and looked at me. "So how did you like Leon Myers?"

"He confuses me."

"You just need to understand *The Fundamentals*. It's this book of Christian essays Myers quotes like it's his Bible. If you believe in his pet doctrines, you don't have to love your neighbor. You could lynch the Good Samaritan, and Jesus would applaud."

"Interesting."

Helen laughed. "My Daddy says you're quite the diplomat."

"W-what does that mean?"

"What do you think? Surely you've noticed something odd about this town, all those queer letters. KIGY? AYAK? What *could* they mean?"

"Nobody knows."

"I do," Helen said. "I'll even tell you if you kiss me."

"You mean right now?"

She looked at me and laughed. "You're so naïve. Dean. Although at least you make me laugh, and you're good looking."

I took her answer as a no for the time being. But of course I hadn't even asked her out yet.

Her left hand bumped against my wrist. "My father thinks that you can tame me."

"Are you an animal?" I asked.

I heard a purr.

"What sort of cat?" I asked.

"Depends upon my mood." She blew a kiss. Then Helen puffed her cigarette and blew a smoke ring. "Meet me Monday after school."

"I have baseball practice."

"Four-thirty," Helen said. I'll be waiting beneath the J.T. Lyon Billboard."

"In the orchard?"

"Absolutely. You can be Lyon, King of the Realty. I'll be Valencia, Queen of the Orange." Helen puffed her cigarette. She snuffed it out a dozen steps before we walked into the church's field of vision. She took my hand. "This time Daddy won't show up. It'll be fun."

She winked, but I was feeling apprehensive.

We turned the corner, and I walked the block to the church holding her hand. The congregation was outside. Someone pointed our direction.

I could feel half the congregation's stares.

CHAPTER IV

MONDAY, MAY 5, 1924

Miss Elgena did her best to make the Constitution interesting, but all that I could look at was that J.T. Lyon billboard. I sat in civics class and counted off the minutes until sixth period ended. Then I had baseball. Monday wasn't my best practice. My back was killing me from Saturday. Coach Merritt asked me why my mind wasn't on pitching.

I couldn't tell him I was thinking about Helen, about kissing her and finding out what KIGY stood for. "I'll try harder," I said.

"Attaboy, Reynolds," Coach said.

I showed up at the J.T. Lyon billboard ten minutes early. Helen's father would be proud of me. I shifted on my feet. I waited for Helen to appear. I was worried she'd forgotten. Maybe this whole thing was a joke of hers to play me for a fool. I remembered she had thought I was naïve. Perhaps I was. I only hoped if she was right I'd find out soon, before I gave away my heart.

"Yoo, hoo."

Somewhere behind me, Helen whistled.

She wore a peach silk flapper dress. A bed of oysters had been sacrificed to build the strings of pearls Helen had wrapped around her neck. She twirled them in her hand, pointed her index finger toward me, flipped over her palm, and motioned me to come to *her*.

I couldn't help myself. The smell of Helen's orange-blossom perfume seemed to take over, making it known she was the Queen of the Valencias. She wore no shoes. There was that face, the one I'd seen on all the orange crates, the sapphire eyes, the fetching smile, the rosy cheeks and slender figure.

I fell into her embrace. Helen wrapped her arms around me. I could taste the scent of Jujyfruits she'd snacked on after school. She pulled me close, shut her eyes.

I felt my manhood swelling.

I'd never kissed a girl before. All of her feminine allure pressed on my chest. When I looked down, she raised her chin up so my lips brushed against hers. I felt her heart beat. Her hand slid behind my neck sending sparks of electricity up and down my spine. Her fingers frolicked in my hair. I shut my eyes. Our lips collided, and it seemed as if a dynamo sent current through my soul. I tasted Helen's gentle breath.

A rush of incandescence tingled all throughout my body.

And then she whispered in my ear. "KIGY. Klansman, I greet you."

My spine became an icicle.

She let go of me.

I froze.

The lipstick on her lips was badly damaged.

I gulped. "What?"

"That's what it means."

"You can't be serious."

She laughed. "It's the Gospel truth, I swear." Helen's gaze locked onto mine. "You're such a wurp."

I heard the backfire of a truck heading toward Anaheim on Center Street. I knew little of the Klan, other than how much you might learn watching the end of D.W. Griffith's *Birth of a Nation* at the movies where they dressed in sheets and hoods and rode on horseback with their torches. They looked creepy, even though they'd saved the day in Griffith's movie.

"The Ku Klux Klan? In California?"

"They control the city council." Helen reached into her purse. She grabbed a lipstick tube and smoothed it across her lips to fix the damage. "And our police force has eleven cops. Ten are in the Klan."

"Chief Bert Moody?"

Helen nodded. "Joined the Klan in Twenty-three."

"You're full of hooey. Bert Moody was a good friend of my father's."

"Times have changed. Surely you saw *Birth of a Nation*." Helen said.

"All twelve reels." I wiped the backside of my hand across my lips. I saw a red smear on my wrist.

She dropped her lipstick into her purse and found a cigarette. She glared at me as if she were annoyed.

"If you spend time at our church, you're gonna see them a lot more. Dean, do you know who Leon Myers *really* is?"

"You mean your pastor?"

"He's a former Exalted Cyclops of the Anaheim Ku Klux Klan Klavern Twelve. Came here from Redlands back in Nineteen-twenty-two. He started a men's Bible study that turned into our Klavern."

"Your Klavern? So you support this?"

"They're supposed to be non-violent," Helen said, dodging my question. "And they *do* support the law and Prohibition."

"But we're in Southern California. There are no Negroes here. The Ku Klux Klan has nobody to pick on."

"You think?" Helen asked wryly, elevating her penciled eyebrows.

"You mean like Mexicans, or Chinamen, or Jews? They don't cause trouble."

"Or Catholics, or bootleggers, or people who drink wine. Or don't you know who really built Anaheim Colony in the Eighties. German settlers. There were fifty different wineries in Anaheim before the plague killed off the grapes and forced them all to plant Valencias. Heck, if it wasn't for that plague we'd all be sitting in Grape County." Helen paused to chuckle at her own humor.

"So how does all this make you feel, Helen?"

"You learn to navigate these things. Being a girl is advantageous. I don't have to have opinions. That's what Crazy Florence tells me."

"But you *have* opinions, don't you?"

Helen struck a match and lit her Fatima. "You'd be wise not to express them. Daddy likes you."

"But he's in the *Ku Klux Klan*."

"It's a phase, Dean."

"A phase transitioning to what?"

"Something else." Helen shrugged.

"I hope you're right, Helen."

"I am. Now would you mind walking me home?" Helen shivered. "It's getting chilly."

"Are we okay?"

"Everything's Jake. Just walk me home, Dean."

I took her hand, feeling stupid and, yes, apparently naïve, knowing nothing whatsoever about the town I had grown up in.

I dropped off Helen on her doorstep, and she kissed me on the cheek. It was a major anticlimax after our drama in the orchard. "Daddy's watching," Helen whispered. "So we can't kiss on our porch yet. Still I'm crazy for you, Dean." She pressed her thumbs into my palms. I felt a shiver, but I wasn't sure exactly what had caused it.

"Every sheik deserves a sheba," Skeeter Wilson often said, and who was I to ever argue. Not to mention she was gorgeous.

She met my gaze, batting her eyes. "So when can I expect to see you?"

I inhaled Helen's citrus perfume, felt my manhood swell again. It ached like crazy.

"When will I *see* you?" Helen urged, pressing my palm. She gave a smile.

"I got a roofing job next Saturday," I said.

"Why on earth do you like roofing, Dean?"

"The work is pretty brutal, but it pays well, and I like a job where I can see the sky."

"Like playing baseball?"

"Or if that falls through, perhaps I'll fly an aeroplane."

"Sounds dreamy."

I glanced up toward the sky, then looked at Helen. "Say, how about Sunday?"

"Be there with bells on." Helen gave a gentle hug and nuzzled close. "But that's the night of Pastor's rally."

"At your church?"

"I have to go. But, Dean, I'd be delighted if you joined us."

"Well, I guess so. Do you think...?"

"Swell," said Helen. "See ya Sunday. I can't wait to tell my daddy. Nighty-night, Dean," Helen said. She winked and opened her front door, sliding behind it like a girl *toreadora*.

The door shut gently.

She seemed prettier than any star in Hollywood. Clara Bow or Marion Davies couldn't even hold a candle. I stepped away, still entranced with her perfume, her stunning looks, and her angelic smile with just a hint of imp.

I stood alone on her front steps, wondering how I'd live without her. That girl could tie my mind in knots no Boy Scout could imagine.

My circuitous route home gave me a lot of time to think, put things together, find my bearings, and no longer be naïve. Everything was Jake, it seemed. I had a princess for a girlfriend. I had another job with Stubby, and it paid a buck an hour. Pretty soon I would not only buy new shoes, but a new suit. After six years, life had smiled on me the way it had before my father died. I was landing on my feet and making lots and lots of money. I even knew people like Helen's dad at Sunkist who looked out for me. My life almost seemed too good to be true.

The only fly inside the ointment was my Ma. She had me worried. Since Pa had died, she never seemed to have recovered from her grief. I'd try to talk to her, but nothing I could say made any difference. It was like talking to a wraith.

"How are you feeling, Ma," I'd ask.

"Okay," she'd whisper looking at me with her smile-smile-smile.

"Just okay?"

Then Ma would rise up from her chair and walk away, as if I'd just asked her a question that she didn't dare to answer. "Cleopatra," Alma called her, "Queen of Denial."

I made my way back to Bud's Chevron and his weird AYAK sign. I watched the cars pull in and out and heard the drivers talk in code. People would answer with a reference to a strange "Mister Akia" If they did so, Bud was giving them a discount. Everybody who seemed to know the code received the discount.

Then Bud turned someone away. "Klansmen only deal with Klansmen," Bud kept muttering. There was an argument that lasted for a minute. Then the truck started. The driver pulled a U-turn in the gravel. He screeched back onto Los Angeles Street and sped into the night.

I recognized the license plate: Mister Bannerman, the contractor who'd added those three rooms onto our house Ma rented out. Evidently I knew people here who didn't like the Klan. I remembered Mister Bannerman was Catholic.

Another car drove in to take his place and honked its horn. "I need to see Mister Akia."

Bud hurried out.

I sensed the K stood for the Klan. Only I didn't know the rest. Two more cars waited in line. I told myself I'd seen enough.

I walked southward on Los Angeles Street, peering into storefronts. I found five other AYAK's in the store windows up front, next to flags that were coincidentally all placed in the window in the same place as the flag at Warren Glover's.

When I watched *Birth of a Nation*, they showed the Ku Klux

Klan as heroes. But a lot of people viewed them with suspicion in the West. I had been nine years old, too young to dare to criticize a president. Woodrow Wilson made it clear that he adored *Birth of a Nation*. In a way the Klan made sense. The word was out they wanted decency, a country free from alcohol, with law-abiding citizens. Clearly Hollywood was pumping up the sex appeal of movies that starred people very different than the good people of Anaheim. People in Anaheim were down-to-earth. They wanted law and order, old-time religion, family values. They were proud to wave the flag. Their men were patriots who'd gone to fight for freedom overseas, even the Germans who had come here in the early 1860s.

But there were lots of folks who didn't like the Klan.

Miss Elgena, for example, said the Ku Klux Klan was "scary." And Alma Martin swore her uncle thought the Klan was out to hurt him when he'd moved out of her bungalow next door the other day. The thought had never crossed my mind she might be right.

By nine o'clock I made it home. All the lights in Alma's bungalow were out. I got this feeling she was home but didn't want someone to see her, even me. I recalled our conversation, how I'd left Alma in tears and run away.

Now I felt crappy.

I didn't fall asleep till after midnight.

TUESDAY, MAY 5, 1924

I was exhausted Tuesday morning, but I stumbled out of bed at five a.m. to run my paper route before I went to class. I loaded dozens of new papers into the baskets on my rusty yellow

Schwinn. A flyer fell out from the *Orange County Plain Dealer*. I squinted trying to read it in the dusk.

Extra! Extra!

CATHOLIC CHURCH AFTER REVEREND MYERS
Rome says church will now drive Rev. Myers from Anaheim, also.
Militant pastor welcomes fight and quotes:
"Damned be he who first cries, 'Hold enough'"

Rev. Myers raises following questions:
Have Roman Catholics forced Plain Dealer *to quit?*
Is Anaheim Bulletin *now operated by Roman Catholics?*
Have certain merchants joined hands with Roman Catholics to rule or ruin Anaheim?
Is Rev. J.A. Geissinger's salary now supplied by Roman Catholics?
Will a Rome-controlled administration enforce law?
Are civic clubs of Anaheim controlled by Rome?
What merchants will support with ads a Rome-controlled paper?
What patriotic citizen of Protestant faith will take a Romanized newspaper?

HEAR GREAT EXPOSURE BY
REV. LEON L. MYERS
At Christian Church 7:30 P.M.
SUNDAY NIGHT, MAY 10TH

I finished reading. I balled the paper up. My heart was in my throat. I wasn't Catholic, and J. A. Geissinger had been my parents' pastor when they'd gone to White Temple Methodist while Pa was still alive. Why would Rome pay Geissinger's salary? Why did Reverend Leon Myers think the Catholic Church was coming after *him?*

Surely Pope Pius XI had more important things to do than seeing to it Leon Myers lost his pulpit in Orange County. Something about it seemed bizarre, fueled by someone's paranoia. Suddenly everything in Anaheim seemed so out of proportion. Most of the Catholics in Anaheim I knew were decent people. Why did Myers want to start a war?

Heck, he was quoting from Macbeth. "Lay on Macduff, and damned be him who first cries, 'Hold enough." The quote came near the end of Shakespeare's play, before Macduff cuts Macbeth's head off and raises Malcolm to the throne. Why was Leon Myers quoting tragic heroes?

I shook my head, stuffing the last of my *Plain Dealers* into their baskets on my Schwinn. I pedaled off into the morning. I wondered why people would buy a paper full of paranoia.

I didn't have an answer that made sense.

But next Sunday I vowed to pay attention at Myers' rally.

CHAPTER V

SATURDAY, MAY 10, 1924

My left arm ached after the baseball game we'd played on Friday Night. I had given up an earned run in the bottom of the sixth to Wally Hennessey of Fullerton. He'd connected with my fastball, lined it straight over the centerfield fence for a home run. That ball was probably still up there, somewhere over the Pacific. If it came down, I imagined that some Chinaman might catch it. Coach Merritt sent me to the showers. Angry, I fired my Shoeless Joe special edition glove like a bullet into my locker and slammed the door shut. I had won one game and lost one. They'd scored two runs off Toby Kellerman in relief. The final score still seared my gut twelve hours later.

FULLERTON UNION INDIANS 3
ANAHEIM UNION COLONISTS 0

Today I just wanted to work. Stubby Carson had a roofing job in Brea for Union Oil, a row of storage sheds with roofs near to the ground, good for a hod carrier, no ladders and no scaffolds. We worked through lunch and finished up the job by two p.m.

I mopped my brow and made my way over to Stubby Carson's truck to get my paycheck.

But when I got there, Helen's dad sat in the front seat of his Packard at the jobsite. *Who had told him we were done?* I thought perhaps Stubby had phoned him. *But then why had he shown up?*

Mr. Webber wore a suit which left him looking out of place on a construction site. His car door opened. He stepped out with his hat. He strolled over and spoke to Stubby Carson for a minute.

Then Stubby hollered at me. "Mister Webber needs to take you home."

Still no explanation. I wondered what this was about. Mr. Webber looked upset. He jerked his thumb over his shoulder. Glared at me. "Get in the front." He checked his watch like I was late, although we'd had no plans to meet.

I slid inside the car.

Mr. Webber slammed my door shut. Threw himself behind the wheel. Cranked the engine.

The car slammed into gear. We sped down the dirt driveway, gravel banging against the wheel wells. He swerved around sharp curves, leaving a cloud of dust behind us, spreading out across a landscape littered with clusters of live oaks and narrow farm roads lined with eucalyptus windrows.

Mr. Webber made a sharp right onto Brea Canyon Road and sped past oil wells and nodding donkeys cluttering the hillsides. My hands were still dirty with roofing tar; I hadn't even washed them. I found a rag inside my pocket and rubbed the mess off from my knuckles.

Helen's dad glanced at his watch again. He stomped down on the throttle. The Packard sped north up the canyon, leaving the oil wells behind us. There was nothing I could say. I didn't know what the man wanted, but I sensed from how he drove that something troubled him.

A lot.

"You hear from Helen?" Mr. Webber asked.

"No, sir," I replied.

"You had a game last night. Was Helen there?"

I told him, "I was pitching."

"You never saw her?"

"Not at all, sir."

He looked visibly upset. "Helen told me she'd be seeing you." He swerved around a curve so fast his hat fell from his head into the foot well just in front of him.

"Sir, I don't think she was there, and if she was, she didn't talk to me. Not that I can blame her when I gave up that home run to lose the ballgame to the Indians."

Mr. Webber rubbed his chin.

I felt his Packard slow. A wigwag signal rocked and flashed ahead. I heard a train whistle, the gonging of the bell up on the wigwag. Scents of smoke filled up my nostrils, and we watched a stack of steam move our direction through the lemon orchards just east of Puente. We had to wait for the Salt Lake Route. A black Mikado locomotive hauled a string of orange refrigerated fruit cars toward Pomona. I counted fifty-seven cars from the Pacific Fruit Express, stuffed full of oranges on their way toward the Heartland of America. I imagined every car filled up with Anaheim Valencias. I imagined Helen's face on every carton.

I finally asked, "Did she come home last night?"

"Not until this morning. We think she went down to Laguna."

"Laguna Beach? You have a place there?"

"Not exactly," Mr. Webber said.

"I beg your pardon, sir?"

Helen's father checked his watch and set his jaw. "Helen likes to ride the Red Cars down to Newport Beach on Fridays. We reckon someone picks her up and drives her to Laguna. She has a friend named 'Crazy Florence' with connections up in Hollywood. Crazy Florence owns a party house that overlooks the ocean."

Mr. Webber lit a cigarette. The smoke bothered my eyes.

"No call from Helen?" I asked.

"She told us she was going out with *you* somewhere in Fullerton."

"To where?" I asked and rolled down the front window. A warm chaparral breeze dried out my nostrils.

"That's just it. She doesn't tell us. Men from Hollywood have motorcars. They drive them to Laguna Beach, escaping from reporters. It's a party town. No trolleys, so reporters don't get down there. These men know Helen's down in Newport Beach and stop to pick her up. She's pretty, and she hopes someone in Hollywood will notice."

"I see," I said. "So you're concerned."

"Very much so," he replied. He reached down toward his feet and retrieved his missing hat.

The train continued on its way. We drove more slowly after that. Mr. Webber stopped in Walnut at a Gilmore Oil Station and bought gasoline. We headed north across the Southern Pacific tracks and made a right turn at the junction. We were now on Valley Boulevard, the old Santa Fe Trail across the San Gabriel Valley.

Heading east, we sped through Spadra. "Hungry?" Mr. Webber asked. A wooden sign marked the Pomona city limit up ahead. "Elevation 850, Population 13,505." Groves of walnut trees spread out in all directions.

"Sir, I could eat a herd of cattle. And I'm worried about Helen."

"So am I. Let's grab a bite." He checked his watch. "It's three o'clock, late enough for early supper at the Edgar Hotel lunchroom." We made our way into Pomona, turning onto Garey Avenue, heading south past numbered streets and stucco houses toward downtown. I saw the brick Edgar Hotel, kitty-corner from the Fox Theater tower ahead at Third Street. We found a parking place in front.

I followed Mr. Webber through the lobby to a lunch counter with several wooden booths along one wall. I found a men's room and washed my hands. When I returned, an aproned waiter poured me coffee. I didn't drink coffee, but was more worried about Helen.

Mr. Webber ordered steaks for both of us.

"Has Helen disappeared before?" I asked.

"Twice," her father said.

"How do you know she's in Laguna?"

"Got a phone call. From a friend."

"Somebody saw her. I'm surprised you folks aren't calling the police."

"In Laguna, police let Hollywood do anything they please."

"I see," I said. "Town wants their business."

"Kid, you're brighter than you look."

"But *I* can't help you."

"Sure you can."

"Excuse me, I don't understand."

"Helen likes you. I do too," said Mr. Webber.

"But sir, I can't compete with Hollywood. I'm *poor*. My family doesn't even own a car."

"You can drive *my* car."

"Who are you kidding, sir? The *Packard?*"

Mr. Webber paused to grind his cigarette out in an ash tray. "Helen needs somebody wholesome. I'm afraid you fit the bill. That's if you're willing."

"You want me...."

"To be her boyfriend, and her escort."

"Sir, I'm...."

"...Grateful is the word I think you want. And yes, you're welcome."

"But sir."

"Dean, I don't want to be pushy, but I hope you see the upside. Helen's brother died a year ago. My son was just a sophomore at Stanford. He got drunk one night and fell off of a balcony. It's not something we talk about, but someday, Mister Reynolds, there's a spot for you at Sunkist."

I inhaled a deep breath.

"That's if you want it. It's serendipitous. I need a son. And I believe you need a father."

His mouth expanded into an incandescent smile.

He lit another cigarette and blew a smoke ring.

The aproned waiter came out with our steaks.

I'd never tasted meat so tender. I'd fallen into a swell spot, I told myself and pushed away all of the doubts I had been having. It felt too good to be true, but now I dared not pop the bubble.

And I still couldn't believe this man would let me drive his Packard.

Mr. Webber tipped the waiter, paid the bill, and we stepped onto Garey Avenue. The lights of the Fox Theater came on. Mr. Webber checked his wristwatch. It was ten minutes to five. The Packard was still parked beside the curb.

He handed me the car keys. "Let's find out if you can drive."

"I have no license, sir."

"We'll take the back roads. High time you should learn." He opened the right door and found his way into the passenger seat. "Come on, Dean," he said, checking his watch. "Don't have all night."

I climbed in behind the wheel.

"Check your mirrors," Mr. Webber said.

I took time to adjust them. I gripped the steering wheel with hands planted at ten o'clock and two.

Mr. Webber handed me the keys.

"Press the gas pedal," he said. "Ease up slowly on clutch there in the middle.

I placed the key in the ignition. Turned the key. The engine purred. I stepped down on the clutch, shifted the gearshift into first and raised my foot up off the pedal.

The Packard lurched and screeched. The engine lost its power. "Nuts," I said.

Mr. Webber looked at me. He laughed out loud. "Try it again. Ease out the clutch."

This time I let the clutch out slowly. The gears feathered into place. I gave the car a little gas. I crept out onto Garey Avenue, looking over my left shoulder. I rolled the window down and signaled a left turn using my arm. Then I drove the car uphill, nearing the end of Garey Avenue.

"Good job, Dean," said Mr. Webber. "See, it isn't all that hard. Now at the end of Garey Avenue the concrete pavement ends.

The road veers left. I signaled, hearing the tires touch the gravel. Near the foot of the Puente Hills, I steered the Packard out of town onto the unpaved Pomona-Corona Road.

The barns and orchards disappeared, and I drove through chaparral. There were no cars.

"You like this, Dean?" Webber lit a Lucky Strike.

"I can see why men love cars." I laughed out loud and honked the horn, and Mr. Webber laughed beside me. The road rolled through a grove of oaks. A marker pointed left,

CHINO—3 MILES

"Keep going straight," said Mr. Webber. "Two miles ahead, let's make a right on Carbon Canyon."

The sinking sun dropped like an orange over Orange County.

A wooden signpost up ahead showed nine miles to Olinda. It pointed right.

"This is Carbon Canyon Road. You need to signal."

I did and turned.

A dusty road rolled down a hillside to the base of Carbon Canyon, lined with sycamores and groves of gnarled oaks. A bouquet of scarlet clouds ahead cast shadows from the cattle who were grazing on the south slopes of the bare Puente Hills.

I set my foot onto the clutch and shifted from second into third. My face stretched into a smile. Scents of sagebrush filled the air. I made my way along the canyon road and back down through the sunset toward the Union Oil hillsides that were forested with derricks. Eucalyptus lined the roadway through Olinda.

We made our way down dusty dirt roads through the sleepy towns of Carlton, and Richfield, and Olive. Ahead, I saw another signpost. We were six miles from Anaheim.

"Turn right," said Mr. Webber.

We passed a white cross wreathed with flowers on our right. It marked the spot where Boomer Corrigan lost his parents in that car crash. Word was his parents had gotten drunk and crashed their Nash into an oak tree.

I sped past, and Mr. Webber rolled his window down.

Ahead, the lights of Anaheim glowed brighter than the moon. "How do you like it?" Mr. Webber asked.

"Love it," I replied.

The lingering scent of lemon blossoms permeated the evening.

We barreled into Anaheim at twenty miles an hour. The road had made its way straight onto Center Street downtown.

I heard a whistle.

Flashing headlights.

A black car pulled behind me at a stop sign.

They yelled, "Move over."

I shot a glance at Mr. Webber.

He checked his watch and sat expressionless.

I pulled the Packard to the shoulder.

Two tall cops leaped out from both doors of a shiny black police car.

One had a clipboard and a whistle. His partner wagged a nightstick

I got this feeling like I'd just swallowed a shotput in one gulp.

"You have a license, son, to drive?" The clipboard cop stared through my car window. His partner slapped his nightstick against his palm and stood behind him.

"No sir," I said, feeling a jolt of terror rifle up my neck.

"Step outside."

I slowly opened up the driver's door.

"C'mon!"

I glanced around. My heart raced faster than a Barney Oldfield speedster. My stomach wrenched up into knots, and sweat cascaded down my brow. I slid outside, feeling the chilly evening air, fearing a billy club might crash down on my skull at any moment.

The two policemen boxed me in and backed me up against their car hood. The nightstick cop spun me around. He yanked my arms behind my back.

He slipped on handcuffs. Snapped them shut. Shoved my face against the car hood.

I shot a glance at Mr. Webber, but he didn't seem to notice.

The cops gestured toward the rear seat of their ugly black police car.

I heard the passenger door open on the right side of the Packard. Mr. Webber stepped outside. He put his hat on. Glanced around. He lit a Lucky Strike and stared out toward the hills on the horizon. My pulse throbbed in my temples till I felt like they were steam hammers.

A full moon made its way above the Santa Ana Mountains. A Model T drove past on Center Street. I shut my eyes and hid my face. I feared if anybody saw me they could kick me off the baseball team.

Mr. Webber coughed to clear his throat.

"I understand both of us know a Mister Ayak," Mr. Webber said. He grinned at the police like he expected a response.

The two cops' jaws dropped, and they turned to him. "He lives up on Akia Street," the clipboard cop said. "Cyknar." He finger-drummed his metal clipboard.

"Three-five-eight-nine-double-seven in the Realm of Kalifornia, Anaheim Klavern number twelve," said Mr. Webber. "I helped your people get onto City Council. I need a favor."

The two cops stared at him.

At *me*.

"You need to let this fellow go," Mr. Webber lowered his voice. "Mayor Metcalf is a friend of mine. We eat breakfast every week at Warren Glover's. I'd hate to bring up both your names in klonversation."

Startled, I shivered in the night. The pair of cops glanced at each other, then looked away like Mr. Webber had mouthed some magic incantation. "Abracadabra." "Open Sesame." "Ayak." "Akia." "Cyknar."

I had no idea what any of it meant.

Except the handcuffs were unlocked from both my wrists, and I was free as if the episode tonight had never happened.

I felt the way I did when roofing loads were lifted off my back. I breathed in deep, but kept my mouth shut. I didn't want to press my luck.

"What will you do about his license?" said the clipboard cop to Webber.

"He'll get a learner's permit Monday." Mr. Webber said and tossed away his cigarette. "I promise on the name of Leon Myers."

The nightstick cop stepped toward their car. "Y'all know we really shouldn't do this, Mister Webber. He related?"

"I plan to take him to a rally tomorrow night at Christian Church. My daughter kinda likes him, and I think he's seen the light. He's one of us."

Both cops laughed and shook his hand. "Well, let's just keep this klonversation to ourselves."

I took a breath.

"See you tomorrow, Mister Webber, at Christian Church. Midway past the doleful hour. Itsub. Klasp."

"Orion," Mr. Webber answered.

The cop put away his clipboard, and they walked toward their patrol car, climbed inside, and drove away into the orchards east of town.

I heaved a deep sigh of relief.

I mopped cold sweat from my brow and took a huge breath of night air perfumed with citrus blossoms. The Packard cast long shadows from the moon. I gave the keys to Mr. Webber. "I think you need to drive us home."

"Sure, Dean," he said. "Lucky for us you got pulled over by some Klansmen."

"So what does 'Ayak' mean?" I asked.

"Are you a Klansman?" said Mr. Webber.

"No, sir,"

He laughed out loud. "I wasn't talking about you. It's the initials. A.Y.A.K. That's how we ask—Are. You. A. Klansman."

"Oh, I get it now," I said. "So what's Akia mean?"

"Our sign of recognition. AKIA. A Klansman I am." Mr. Webber turned the key in the ignition.

"How about Cyknar?"

He shifted gears and pulled the Packard onto Center Street. A bicycle raced past and swerved to miss him.

"Whoa. Slow down there. Hard to keep up with your questions, Dean," he said. "Cyknar stands for 'Call Your Klan Number and Realm.'" He signaled left.

The Packard made a left and headed south onto Los Angeles Street past Warren Glover's Restaurant. I remembered our first breakfast when Mayor Metcalf had walked in on us and sat down at our table. It seemed our mayor was in the Klan.

So it was true. Mister Webber seemed to eat this business up. The Klan was almost like its own secret fraternity I thought, maybe even his religion.

"What does 'Itsub' mean?" I asked.

"In The Sacred Unfailing Being," Webber said. "You ask an awful lot of questions." Mr. Webber checked his watch and signaled right.

He made a turn onto my street. Mr. Webber's tone of voice told me I'd pushed things far enough. He was entitled to his secrets. If I were smart I'd keep my yap shut. Bad things happened when outsiders know too much. So far I didn't know enough to be a threat.

I changed the subject. "What time tomorrow should I come to pick up Helen?"

"The doleful hour," Mister Webber said. "And don't keep Helen waiting."

"What time again?"

"Seven p.m." Mr. Webber rechecked his watch. He pulled up to the curb and let me off outside my house.

I jumped outside.

He sped away.

The lights were on upstairs, and on our porch, and in our living room. I knew something was up.

When I walked in through our front door, Alma Martin sat on the sofa. She was reading. A noisy fan blew chilly breezes from the kitchen

I swallowed hard. "What are you doing here?"

"Dean, your mother broke her arm. We need to talk."

I swallowed harder. When women said that, it meant trouble.

CHAPTER VI

SATURDAY, MAY 10, 1924

A s if to mourn the "doleful hour," the bells of Saint Boniface Catholic Church tolled desolately seven times to mark the time of evening. My mother shuffled from her bathroom, wearing her tattered towel-cloth slippers and her bathrobe. Her broken arm was in a splint and in a sling. For once the smile she always pasted on her face had disappeared.

"Ma," I called, "Are you okay?" I felt a sudden pang of guilt for being absent on the one day she had needed me to be here.

"Dean, I'm tired. I'm going to bed."

"You need an aspirin? Some tea?"

"Good night," she said. "I took a sedative. Arm hurts. I'll be fine."

"I'm so sorry." But Ma seemed too worn out to care and walked away.

She didn't sound fine. She looked exhausted, and she clearly needed sleep. I watched her shuffle down our hallway. Her bedroom door slammed shut. I closed my eyes and said a prayer, hoping my mother might forgive me, wishing I'd picked a better day for my adventure with Mr. Webber.

Alma was still reading on our sofa.

I turned to face her. "Is Ma okay?"

I felt like Alma hadn't heard me. She turned a page and kept on reading Charles Dickens' *David Copperfield*. She took another sip of tea and set her cup onto its saucer once again without a sound. Our mantle clock rang seven chimes. My heart climbed up my throat. I swallowed hard.

Finally, Alma set her book onto her lap.

"Where *were* you?" She fired a glare at me. "I walked your mother to the doctor."

"I was working up in Brea."

"Mister Bannerman drove to find you at the job site. You weren't there. All of us were worried sick."

"I rode home with Mister Webber," I said, shrugging. "You barely missed me."

Alma frowned and shook her head. "They said you finished up at two. It took *five hours* to drive home?" She shut her book ever-so-gently. She raised her glasses above her forehead. Her blue eyes matched her cotton blouse. Her auburn hair flowed from underneath a woven scarf that left her looking like a cross between a Victor Hugo heroine and Theresa of Lisieux. I'd heard Theresa had been beatified last year from Alma's uncle, who kept a picture of the nun inside his wallet. He said they'd both grown up in Alençon in Normandy in France. I wondered why he'd left, why he had sailed to America.

I also wondered why they'd run him out of Anaheim.

Alma took another sip of tea.

I took a breath and met her gaze. "Mister Webber had to drive up to Pomona. Had some business."

"This wouldn't be about his daughter?" Alma asked, tilting her head.

"What?" I stammered.

Alma glared.

Uh-oh, she was jealous. I'd tipped my hand that I liked Helen. Alma must have picked it up at once.

"I never figured Helen Webber was your type," Alma replied. She took another sip of tea and set her cup back in its saucer.

"So what's my *type?*"

She steeled her gaze like she was trying to stay calm but glanced away. "I'm sorry. It's just...." She took a breath and held it in. She tried to smile. "I care about you as a friend." She looked beyond me toward the bay window that overlooked our lawn.

A Model T putt-puttered past our house.

"Should I apologize for caring, Dean?"

"I'm grateful for your help."

"Are you?"

She set her chin into her palm and turned her stare toward the motorcar outside. I watched her gaze follow the Model T's two taillights as if her heart had hitched a ride inside the rumble seat and gone.

After that, she went back to her reading.

I feared I'd hurt her. But I chose to let her question go unanswered. We'd been good friends, had grown up close, but distance clawed its way between us. She'd helped my mother. I was grateful for her friendship, but I still worried Alma liked me way too much. She hadn't brought me macaroons today. Thank heaven. Alma's baking came with *strings.*

I needed *wings.*

I had to find a way to change the subject. "How bad's Ma's fracture?"

"It's just broken." Alma's terseness chilled the room several degrees.

"How'd she break it?" She made it hard to hold a simple conversation.

"She fell." Alma replied. "Took a spill off of the porch steps."

"You're very kind for looking after her," I said. I smiled in a manner I hoped conveyed that I was grateful.

"You're welcome, Dean." She rose up. "It's very late." She looked upset. She faced the door as if I'd ordered her to leave our house at once.

"Good night," she whispered. She slipped outside and shut the door without a sound.

I felt cruel, hearing her footsteps pad away across our driveway. They faded. I breathed in deep and prayed that Ma would be okay. I thought of Alma and was sad to know our friendship might be over. I took a breath. My weariness descended into my gut.

I worried that our bond had been irreparably damaged.

SUNDAY, MAY 11, 1924

Watching Model Ts and Maxwells circling in the foggy streets outside First Christian Church, I saw why Mr. Webber loved punctuality. By seven o'clock we had arrived while there were still places to park. I had come to pick up Helen almost fifteen minutes early. I hoped after the lecture I might walk her home alone.

Crowds made their way up concrete steps into the narthex where a pair of wooden poster boards were set up on two battered wooden easels. A hooded man next to the boards pointed a finger my direction. There was a cross over his heart. Below the picture was the caption:

WHAT HAVE YOU DONE FOR YOUR RACE AND FAITH TODAY?

Flags and crosses were assembled on a table in a corner with a stack of printed flyers with the caption at the top.

"DON'T BE HALF A MAN, JOIN THE KLAN."

I picked one up. I noticed "P.O. Box 16" down at the bottom, and returned it to the table as if I'd seared one of my fingers. On a side-table a basket was stacked with red and white carnation buds for Mother's Day. The sign said men could take one for their wives.

I saw people there I knew, Stubby Carson, Mayor Metcalf, and Coach Merritt. The Harris twins, Colleen and Ed, came with their parents. Plus, both the cops who'd tried to pinch me had shown up, wearing their uniforms. Four other cops had joined them. The guy who'd handcuffed me last night gave a thumbs-up and then winked. I felt the blood run through my face and looked away, wondering what I had in common with that thug.

Soon Helen made her way between us, and the cops left us alone. She grinned and whispered in my ear. "How about Friday let's play hooky."

"Doing what?"

"We'll ride the Red Car to the Lick Pier Bon Ton Ballroom. See Harry Baisden and His Orchestra." She opened up her purse. "See! I have tickets."

"Where'd you get those?"

"I know people."

"In Hollywood?" I asked, remembering all the things I'd picked up from her father.

Helen grinned. "We can't confine ourselves to boring little Anaheim. Say we leave at nine a.m. It's just an hour on the trolley."

"All the way to Ocean Park?"

"We'll be there by ten o'clock. Or as my father might say...." Helen's voice descended half an octave. "We'll be there before the frightful hour." She looked so stern.

I had to laugh at her deep voice. Helen checked a phantom wristwatch the way her father always did, except Helen never wore one. She laughed. "I got our tickets. You can reciprocate by paying for our trolley fare." She licked her lips and offered me her orange-crate-label smile. I could feel myself being reeled in.

Mr. Webber and his wife had found their way into the church and motioned toward us. He was sitting in a pew, checking his watch. While other women wore carnations, I saw Mrs. Webber didn't. Again they waved for us to join them. Reverend Myers stood up front and asked for all of us to stand and pledge allegiance to the flag.

After that the room fell silent. Reverend Myers scanned the audience as if he might be looking for a Bolshevik or two. He skimmed right past me.

"Shall we pray," he said. "I sense that we're all friends, and happy Mother's Day."

"Thank you, Reverend," the women said in unison.

I bowed my head, swallowed, and braced. The congregation shut their eyes. I held my breath, and Reverend Myers cleared his throat.

"Father, our country is in peril." Myers stopped to take a breath, letting the 'country is in peril' part re-echo through the loudspeakers. "Bands of merchants in our city have joined hands with Roman Catholics to rule and ruin Anaheim by rewriting our laws. They plan to shut down our free speech and force the *Orange County Plain Dealer* out of print." It was clear the man was not praying to God but rather lecturing the Lord about the downfall of America, and his secret plan to save it from the cruel conniving Vatican. Myers' "prayer" went on forever. I was struggling not to laugh.

"AMEN," Leon Myers said at last.

Helen heaved a sigh of resignation.

I shut my eyes and thanked the Lord the man had finished.

Except he hadn't. The lights were dimmed, and Reverend Leon Myers' voice dropped to a whisper. "What I will speak about tonight might we must keep secret. I've just returned from New York City, a town within the grip of Rome, Tammany Hall, and organized crime. And puppets like Governor Al Smith, an outspoken opponent of any form of Prohibition. The Eighteenth Amendment is ignored there. Neighbors, that can happen here...."

Mrs. Webber's gaze was riveted to Myers' every word.

"You do know Anaheim was founded by a cult of Catholic *winemakers*. They built Saint Boniface Church and private schools to raise their offspring, such as Saint Catherine's Academy on Palm Street here in Anaheim." He stopped again, letting the reverb make him sound like he was God.

"They are bootleggers, and rum-runners, and winemakers." His voice dropped. "But there *is* a way to fight them if Klansmen only deal with Klansmen. In the name of the unfailing Being, let us band together, people. We are the last hope for America and we must only deal with 'right' merchants," vetted and accepted by patriotic Klansmen. I beg you folks to boycott any

Catholics, or Jews or other merchants advertising in the papist *Anaheim Bulletin.*

I noticed Mrs. Webber dab her makeup with a handkerchief.

Helen looked away as if she didn't want to be here.

I tried to pull my thoughts together. How on earth could I survive around a family who believed in things I didn't understand? Helen's parents seemed to be grieving for the son they'd lost last year. Helen seemed trapped between her parents' dreams and those she had herself. I wished I knew a way to somehow help her.

"Now Rome has turned its sights on *me.* Curse those who dare to fill our churches and our schools with their dark heresies. Curse their whiskey and their gin. Curse their disciples of debauchery who contaminate our theaters with movies fit for demons. Damned be papists who destroy us. Let us *fight* to save our city, *fight* to preserve our God and country...."

Leon Myers seemed to like to fight a lot.

Helen glanced at me and rolled her eyes.

I heard amens and hallelujahs. He wound the people in the pews up like a box of Waltham watches. More applause. I had to wince. While Leon Myers blathered on, I made a promise to myself to get my learners' permit and buy a pair of decent clothes next week. I needed shoes, needed a suit. If I showed up wearing overalls or baseball clothes the Bon Ton ballroom wouldn't let me in. I'd need to speak with Mr. Webber about getting me a discount the way he did when he bought gas up at Bud's Chevron.

Mrs. Webber put her handkerchief away while Mr. Webber smiled wider than that grinning man at Coney Island's Steeplechase.

The reverend moaned on like a carnival calliope. "Today the civic clubs of Anaheim, Rotarians, Kiwanians, and Optimists are run by Rome who peddles its depravity. There is but one organization who dares to stand between them and our children. I beg you to learn more about the Klan."

"Lord, we give thanks to thee for everything we have here in America, and we ask that you protect your town from every form of evil, from the Communists, the Catholics, Father, give us back our country. Make Anaheim a model city, free from every vice. We pray these things in Jesus' name and say, amen."

I felt Helen grab my elbow, and we shot out the front doors the way pellets leave the barrels of a lever-action shotgun. She said she had to smoke a Fatima. We walked around the block. I wanted to ask Helen about the lecture.

She stopped and looked at me. She wrapped her slender arms around my neck. She tugged me near, so close her pearls seemed to squeak against my collar. Helen smiled.

The evening fog should have felt chilly on my face.

Then Helen kissed me.

I surrendered.

We melted into an embrace.

SANTA MONICA PIER

FRIDAY, MAY 16, 1924

The cogs tugging the bobsled-style cars up on the scaffolds of the Whirlwind Dipper Roller Coaster pounded on my spine. The ocean breeze dampened my cheeks. It flapped wet hair across my forehead. Our car shivered and shook. In her raccoon coat, Helen snuggled up beside me. Her cigarette breath overpowered her perfume.

She was fully flappered out, wearing a sleeveless slinky dress. She'd tied her purse around her shoulder to make certain it stayed put. Her slender neck was wrapped in scarves. Bangs of bobbed hair were cut to frame her glowing face beneath a zig-zag-seamed cloche hat shaped like a bell, holding a single ostrich feather sewn with silk threads into felt.

We tottered. Looff's Pier was ten stories below us.

Helen screamed. Our knuckles choked down on our galvanized restraining bar.

We plummeted. My stomach did a somersault in place.

Ocean mist drenched both my eyelids as I shut them out of terror. Steel tracks rumbled beneath us. Our salt-sprayed cheeks fluttered like flags. Another coaster shot above us as we dipped beneath the scaffolds into darkness, hearing rumbling and groaning wooden timbers.

We banked into a curve. Helen was shoved against my thigh. I smelled her perfume, felt aroused, yet more amazed that Helen liked me, while we were lifted toward the sky into a spiral as the car tipped. The coaster kissed the fog then dropped back into the darkness.

I tugged her close, hearing her shriek as we careened though ocean fog, bounced up and spun through a 180-degree turn that left me dizzy. We hurtled back along the pier, feeling our stomachs rise and fall as if we were seasick, feeling the gravity of the dips and weightless crests. Helen laughed. The squeeling brakes locked underneath us. The stench of rubber-asbestos brake pads smoked around us, and we slowed.

The car screeched to a stop beside the platform.

The restraining bar popped loose. Helen stepped out of the car, grabbing my hand, laughing and asking me to light her cigarette.

I still felt dizzy. The thrill rides we had ridden on that morning lit their lights to greet the evening, leaving shimmers on the bay, the Circle Swing, the Looff's Carousel and Hippodrome, the Whip Ride, and the Aeroscope Ride's whirling steel cars, the Eli Ferris Wheel, the shooting gallery, Bennett's Seafood Grotto, such wondrous memories. I cherished every hour of the day that had raced past.

Helen squeezed my hand and whispered in my ear, "Dean, we need to catch the Red Car."

I saw the trolley by the shoreline, rolling south.

She ran beside me, and we sprinted toward the trolley stop. We dodged the record crowds. There'd been a fire on Lick Pier, so all L.A. had come to Looff's. The Looff's Pier Hippodrome calliope blew circus tunes and whistled out a waltz.

We hopped onto the Red Car just in time.

She sat beside me on the trolley with her purse and raccoon coat looking like something from a dream. Her pale complexion almost cloudlike, Helen sang with the calliope, Paul Whiteman's big hit, "*Whispering*." Her sultry voice tickled my earlobes as the trolley rumbled south:

> *Whispering while you cuddle near me,*
> *Whispering so no one can hear me,*
> *Each little whisper seems to cheer me,*
> *I know it's true, there's no one, dear, but you....*

The lights came on across the bay, spreading north and toward the burnt out barns of Inceville and the cabins of Pacific Palisades. I scanned the highway running south along the cliffs of Santa Monica, watched the sun beyond Looff's Pier, sending flames between the scaffolds where the new La Monica Ballroom was to open in July. Once more, Helen squeezed my hand. We passed the L-shaped Crystal Pier. The Rendezvous Ballroom over the ocean advertised Art Hickman's Orchestra. A brakeman checked our trolley ticket. "Next stop Ocean Park," he said. "Lick Pier. Have a nice evening. This is where you kids get off."

I buffed my shoes against my pants, straightened my jacket, checked my reflection in the plate glass of the windows of our well-lit steel Red Car. I blushed, and Helen dug into her purse to find our tickets for Harry Baisden and His Orchestra at the Lick Pier Bon Ton Ballroom.

Outside, the remnants of the Giant Dipper Roller Coaster skeleton ascended like a ghostly souvenir of what had been before a fire had burnt Lick Pier and all its structures to the waterline last January. The Bon Ton Ballroom was the sole surviving building.

The setting sun cast eerie shadows through the wayward wooden piles and steel scaffolding that rose above formations of charred pilings. I recalled my pa had brought me here in 1917 after the Fraser Million Dollar Pier had burnt down just like Lick Pier.

I got this sense this pier was cursed. I could almost hear the tunes of prior years, the wails of Dixieland, the crooning of Al Jolson, and I thought about my father and the way I had looked up to him. I wished that I could tell him I had finally found a mentor, Mr. Webber.

I wished my pa could see Helen beside me.

I don't think Helen saw me wipe a tear.

Helen squeezed hard on my hand. I felt like European royalty descending the iron steps of the Pacific Electric Red Car. The ocean breeze whipped through my hair and sent its salt spray through my nostrils. Across the tracks, the restless surf pounded the sands of Ocean Park.

I breathed in deep, preening the jacket I had just purchased on Wednesday. I hoped I looked like an adult, wearing my pressed and laundered suit. The glitz that lit the Bon Ton Ballroom drew me forward like a moth toward an incandescent glow. Its lights reflected off the waters. Bulbs undulated in the moonlight. Helen massaged my shivering hand. Two towers rose above the entrance like a pair of minarets holding a row of blazing lightbulbs in-between, reading as follows:

BON TON BALLROOM
HARRY BAISDEN & HIS ORCHESTRA

We crossed the trolley tracks and Speedway, making our way toward the marquee. An usher stood outside the door. Helen handed him our tickets.

We stepped inside. Helen looked at me. "Wait here," she told me sternly. Thousands of light bulbs lit the foyer, and I paused to take it in, picking lint and brushing crumbs off the lapel of my new jacket.

She hurried off to find a powder room, returning in five minutes, freshened up and somehow looking even prettier than ever. She took my arm. It felt like Christmas. Helen glowed in her silk dress and buttoned gloves. Her strings of pearls matched Helen's cinematic face that launched one-hundred-thousand Anaheim Valencia Queen oranges. Helen grinned and held our ticket stubs, reminding me she'd paid for our admission, and this evening was exclusively for her. After checking her raccoon coat, she clutched her purse, straightened her necklace.

A twelve-piece orchestra was warming up beneath a rainbow archway.

They played Al Jolson's newest hit. Helen smiled. Her gaze

met mine. She took my arm. I got this look that said I needed to escort her. We strolled inside, as if they'd just cued Helen up for her grand entrance into a ballroom lined with people whom I'd seen somewhere before. She sang aloud, raising her sultry voice so everyone could hear. Heads swiveled our direction. Helen crooned in her contralto:

A Sunkist miss said "Don't be late!"
That's why I can hardly wait,
Open up that Golden Gate!
California, here I come!

To applause, whistles and catcalls, we made our way into a ballroom full of high-hats smoking cigarettes and drinking Coca Cola, swells I knew I'd seen in pictures. But I didn't know their names. Next to their European suits I felt embarrassed to be seen in my new duds from Turton's Men's Wear back on Center Street in Anaheim.

There were a few faces I recognized. Bebe Daniels, Hobart Bosworth, and John Gilbert, one of the newest stars at Metro-Goldwyn Mayer. It seemed surreal, as if we'd walked into a fairy-tale world I'd seen in popcorn-scented theaters on Center Street Downtown.

A red-hot jazz number began. Helen dragged me to the dance floor, swung her arms, and I felt foolish trying to learn to dance a Charleston. I stepped back, kick-stepped, moved my elbows, feeling clumsy and ridiculous while flappers all around us danced like Hollywood professionals. Perhaps they were. After a round of *Ain't She Sweet*, and *Toot-Toot-Tootsie*, I staggered off toward the sidelines for a chance to catch my breath. Helen was still out on the floor as if her night was just beginning, and every partner Helen danced with only added to her energy.

I'd felt waaaay out of my league out there, a complete and utter heeler and a wurp. They played a waltz. A woman twice my age was asking me to dance. She was a face-stretcher with a half-sack of Gold Medal on her face. "Get a wiggle on," she said and dragged me out onto the dance floor. Banjos and trumpets echoed loudly through the ballroom.

Helen was dancing with a man in a tuxedo who wore patent leather shoes so black and shiny they looked almost like obsidian. He was a cake-eater, a ladies' man, who clearly had designs, but from the way that Helen looked at him, he also looked connected.

I glanced toward Helen, except right now she scarcely noticed I existed. Her attention was fixated on her shiny-shoed companion. I swallowed jealousy. He appeared to be an agent or a talent scout, and Helen turned the dial up on her charm.

"Whazz your name?" my partner asked. Making her way into my arms, she felt as stiff as those Egyptian girls on Tutankhamun's tomb walls. People smirked at me and stared as if I were the woman's gigolo. I smelled brown plaid on her breath, and it was clear that she was zozzled. Golden bangles on her arms announced she'd come into some money.

"Wheee, I'm Margaret," she said. "Margaret Hollingsworth. My ex-husband's a big cheese at Julian Pete. You heard of Julian Petroleum?"

"Oil outfit," I replied. "Their ads are all over the papers."

"Biggest outfit in L.A. Put the spring in Santa Fe Springs. You heard of *them?*"

I said I had.

"Now you're on the trolley, Willie."

Once again, I glanced at Helen. Some matinee idol–I knew his face but not his name–cut in on shiny-shoes and serenaded Helen. *"What'll I do,"* he sang, *"when you are far away and I am blue? What'll I do?"* Helen was smiling as he spun her in his arms.

I wanted to leave this joint right now. I had no place among this crowd. I was a humble boy from Anaheim, and these people had money. *Lots* of mazuma they could spend on things I'd never even dreamed of. I feared I'd even felt more comfortable at Leon Myers' Klan lecture.

Margaret serenaded *me. "What'll I do when I am wondering who is kissing you?"* she cackled, looking up as if I cared. I stared past Margaret, saw Helen take a long draw from a flask that *Monsieur Matinee* had handed her. No secret what was in it. She lowered the flask, opened her purse and shook a fag out of her hope chest. "Butt me, darling," Helen cooed, and *MonsieurMatinee* lit her cigarette. She laughed and waved its tip around like flappers do in movies. She was clearly showing off to lots of men who paid attention. I wanted to get out of there.

But she had bought our tickets.

The stench of Margaret's bad breath now nearly drove me off the dance floor, but she wasn't letting go of me. Our waltz number had ended. They played a tango. Margaret begged for me to dance, but I refused, saying, "I'm sorry, but I wouldn't know a tango from a mango." Time to go check up on Helen, tell *Monsieur Matinee* to beat it. Helen had come with me. I had to bring her home while she was sober.

I made my way toward Helen, but John Gilbert got there first.

He asked her, "May I have this dance," and Helen swooped into his arms.

I wanted to knock John Gilbert's block off. His wealth was far out of my league with that thin moustache like a caterpillar camping on his lip. The man was married to Leatrice Joy, and he was hitting on my date. I screwed my courage up. Strolled up to him. Put my nose into his face. "Excuse me."

Helen glared at me.

John Gilbert glanced at Helen. "Is he annoying you?"

"Everything's Jake," Helen replied.

"Want me to tell this chap to beat it?"

Helen stared beyond my face across the ballroom. The orchestra struck up another jazz tune, and the pair began to dance. Everybody watched them shimmy.

"Get hot. Get hot," people around us called, while Helen and her partner kicked their heels up. My temples throbbed in angry syncopation. I had thought she was my date, except she had other agendas. She loved Hollywood, and clearly Hollywood did not love *me*.

I wondered who had given her those tickets.

Margaret tapped me on my shoulder. "Willie, dahling, where ya been?" She grabbed my hand and tried escorting me to somewhere we could talk. Margaret took a snort of giggle water. She grabbed me by my elbow.

Helen tapped me on the shoulder. "I'm afraid I need to leave."

I calmly reached toward Helen's hand and felt her slap me on the wrist. John Gilbert made his way between us. "Sorry, chap, you're not invited. I think we have to see a man about a dog."

"You mean get drunk?" I said. "Or laid?"

Helen glared as if she wished I'd disappear. "If that's the way you choose to put it," she fired back.

"Rude," said Gilbert. "Young men no longer have a vestige of propriety."

"She was my *date*."

"I bought your *ticket*."

"Aren't you married, sir?" I said.

He threw a punch that landed squarely on my jaw and knocked me down.

I lay there numb. The ballroom swirled around me like a carousel.

Helen walked off with John Gilbert, out the door.

I rubbed my jaw, feeling an ache, tasting my angry bloody gums, grateful no teeth were loose, but furious at how I'd just been sucker-punched.

Laying sprawled out on the dance floor, I wondered what I'd tell her father, knowing tonight I would come home without his daughter.

"Willie, dahling?" I looked up. Margaret charged across the dance floor my direction. "That brute hit you. I know good lawyers if you need one."

"No, thanks, Margaret."

"That was a whale of a sockdollager. Poor baby...."

"Everything's Jake, ma'am." I rubbed my jaw and flashed a grin, making my way back to my feet as Margaret grabbed me by both wrists."

"Well, if you need someone to comfort you...."

The orchestra played excerpts out of *Rhapsody in Blue*.

"Ma'am, I could really use a drink."

She yanked a flask out of her purse and raised the opening to my mouth. I took a belt of Scotch that stung my bleeding gums and left me reeling. But it helped to numb the pain. I wiped a dribble off my chin as three security cops pinched us and escorted us outside.

The evening sky was raining pitchforks. The lights of Speedway and the lamps above the trolley tracks were glistening in puddles on the asphalt. "Wait here, Willie," Margaret said. *Why did she keep calling me Willie?* I rubbed my jaw and heard the cold surf from the ocean pound the shore as Margaret opened an umbrella and made her way toward a red Cadillac.

It seemed the Cadillac was hers, a lipstick-red V-63. They sold for several thousand dollars and had more horses beneath the hood than even Mr. Webber's Packard. Margaret opened the right door, jumped in the passenger seat and honked the horn so loud I felt embarrassed.

"What are you doing?" I yelled out.

She yelled, "Willie, drive me home."

"Where do you live," I asked.

"In Inglewood."

I opened up the door. She shoved the keys at me. "Get in."

"I think you're drunk."

"Willie, you slay me, kid. I'm posolutely spifficated. Drive me to my house, and let's make whoopee."

I swallowed back revulsion.

The last person I wanted to make whoopee with was Margaret. I was still goofy about Helen although tonight she'd acted awful. But I had little use for Margaret. Her breath repelled me, like that whiff you get when walking down an alley full of trash cans. Margaret paused. She opened up her compact, powdering her face with more munitions.

"*You* want *me* to drive you home."

"Now you're on the trolley, Willie."

It seemed I *was* on Margaret's trolley, and I wanted to get off. It's just that Helen had left the ballroom with *our* trolley tickets home, tickets John Gilbert didn't need. I was penniless and stranded.

"I live in Anaheim," I said.

"Hey, let's drive out there tomorrow."

"No. Tonight."

"I can't drive home." She grabbed her flask and downed a snort, shaking her head. "Baby, I'm drunk. No way can I drive home from Anaheim tonight."

"Don't call me baby, Mrs. Hollingsworth," I told her. "And my name is Dean, not Willie," I shot back, pulling the keys from her ignition.

"I thought you said that was your name."

"I never told you what my name was."

"Well, you remind me of a Willie. Hot dawg." She clapped her hands. ""An' you look tight the way my husband did before he chased that skirt at Julian Pete, last July before the scalawag walked out on me. You won't walk out on me, will you, Willie?"

A plan was forming in my mind as Mrs. Hollingsworth went on about her ex.

I could drive Margaret to Anaheim, to Saint Boniface Church. She could dry out there. She looked Irish, and the Catholics knew the territory.

It was a short walk to my house from there while Margaret slept it off.

But what on earth would I tell Mr. Webber?

Margaret was sleeping. The asphalt ribbon of the roadway unrolled east. We drove through Inglewood and out the other side. The song that Margaret had sung to me still echoed through my brain. But I was thinking about Helen and the end of our romance. Things had started out so swell. Tears were forming on the edges of my eyes as I reflected and sang lyrics Margaret had failed to sing while Helen's picture on an orange crate label flitted through my thoughts. My heart sang along in pain.

What'll I do with just a photograph
To tell my troubles to?
When I'm alone
With only dreams of you
That won't come true
What'll I do?

I signaled onto Slauson Avenue. A grunt arose beside me, moaning, "Willie!" I felt my arms stiffen. "Pull over, Willie," Margaret groaned. I yanked the steering wheel right, slammed on the brakes, and pulled to the shoulder.

Margaret clawed open her door handle. Her passenger door opened.

She plopped outside onto her knees, bellowing louder than a moose. "Ugggh," she said. "I need to pull a Daniel Boone." And then she upchucked.

"Well you just did, right on your skirt." I found a towel in the back seat and mopped her off.

"Uggggh," she moaned.

I jumped aside, and she sprayed all over her car door.

I mopped her car off with the towel and helped her back into her seat. I threw the towel into the bushes and got back behind the wheel.

"Where are you taking me?" she asked.

"We're going to Anaheim."

"What? I hate that place. Everybody calls it Klanaheim."

"I don't."

And then she unloaded an earful.

It seemed the Ku Klux Klan in Inglewood had dressed up in their robes and staged a raid against some Basques who had been bootleggers. There'd been a gunfight, and a cop named Medford Mosher had been killed, some said by Klansmen, but the Ku Klux Klan had never been convicted. Plus Medford Mosher was a Klansman and an Inglewood policeman. Accusations had been made Mosher was murdered by a bootlegger. "Klan makes him out to be a martyr," Margaret said, slurring her words. "Just some cop doin' his job breaking into some guy's barn, murdered in the line of duty by a lawbreaker."

"So *was* he murdered?"

Her alcoholic breath was laced with sarcasm. "Oh, yeah. Of course." She looked away. Margaret's voice dropped to a whisper. "Another cop told me a fellow Ku Klux Klansmen murdered Medford. Lousy killjoys. Breaking and entering into decent people's barns. It's not their beeswax if we drink, or Fidel Elduayen makes moonshine. Bible-bangers, far as I'm concerned. I hope they rot in hell, forcing morality down other people's throats," she said. "Pull over, Willie."

I pulled over.

Her door flew open, and she vomited again.

At two a.m. I parked the Cadillac in Saint Boniface's parking lot and hightailed down Palm Street straight to Mr. Webber's craftsman. The lights were on. Seeing his silhouette, I staggered up the steps and wiped my shoes off on the doormat. My broken heart was in my throat.

What would I say to Helen's father? What would he think that I had done, leaving his daughter, stopping by two hours after midnight to explain what had transpired. I felt ashamed, and yet afraid how Mr. Webber might react. I took a deep breath. Shut my eyes, trying to rehearse how I would tell him I'd left Helen with that womanizing actor.

I rang the doorbell.

The window curtains parted. Mr. Webber stared at me. He glowered. He still wore an ironed dress shirt, open collar. His sleeves were rolled up like a prizefighter's. He frowned. He checked his watch and shook his head.

I swallowed hard.

He flung the big front door wide open. Fire raged in both his eyes.

"Where the hell's my daughter?"

"With John Gilbert."

He stepped back. "The movie star?" He looked down at his watch again. Looked up.

I pointed to the swelling in my jaw.

"He punched you out?"

"Sucker-punched me."

Webber stared at me and didn't say a word. There was a pause. A Model-T engine backfired half a block away. His anger seemed to fade, as if he realized I'd been punched out already. No point in beating me up twice in the same night.

His face grew serious. "Dean, you need to come inside and put some ice on that."

"You sure?"

"We need to talk." He pointed inside toward the table.

Again I braced, amazed the man would let me inside of his castle.

We made our way across the mission-tile floor into his dining room and sat down at his table. He dug some ice out of his ice box, wrapped it up inside a kitchen towel. "For your jaw, Dean. Hope this helps. Looks like he smacked you pretty hard." He made a fist and gave a grin.

"He did," I said and pressed the ice against my jaw to feel its chill. It numbed the pain and took some of the edge off my embarassment. There was that photograph of Helen on that orange crate label, framed. She smiled down on us as if we both amused her. I felt like she was watching us. It made things seem surreal.

Still, I spilled out everything I knew.

"Helen skedaddled with John Gilbert. He had evidently met Helen and purchased both our tickets. I was nothing but her patsy. Helen thinks that Mister Gilbert's gonna help her be a movie star. I think she was just using me."

"She wasn't."

"What?" I said, confused. *Was this man blind?*

Mr. Webber filled a pipe with some vanilla-scent tobacco. Helen's portrait somehow seemed to change expressions, like she listened.

"I've seen her looking at your picture. Dean, she isn't using *you*. She's using Mister Gilbert, trying to navigate through Hollywood. You're a good boy," Mr. Webber said. "I want us to stay friends, Helen or no Helen. And Helen needs a boyfriend to look out for her."

I was angry, and I wanted to lash out at Mr. Webber. I didn't need this man to patronize me, call me a "good boy." I fought to swallow back emotion. I wiped my sleeve across my face, only to notice Mr. Webber's eyes were both redder than radishes.

Evidently Mr. Webber had been crying before I'd come. He inhaled on his pipe.

I said, "I need to call my mother."

"Use our telephone," he said.

I called my house.

Ma didn't answer. She was evidently sleeping.

I returned to Mr. Webber.

He dabbed his eyes with a silk handkerchief. He rolled down both his sleeves, letting them dangle with no cufflinks to secure them. It seemed he needed to unburden himself. "Missus Webber doesn't speak to me," he said.

I mentioned I had noticed.

"It's not her fault. She's been afraid of something, ever since we took the train out west to California, clear from Mason City, Iowa. In 1898, we lost our first girl, Anne, in infancy. Diphtheria," he said.

The man inhaled on his pipe.

"Your wife has seen her share of suffering."

"Then Herbert Junior died at Stanford in that accident last spring when he was drunk. Even before that, Emily'd fought for Prohibition and blames their deaths on me. Helen's all that I have left other than Sunkist and my church. You see, I'm desperate to keep my baby safe."

"She's not a baby." I looked up at Helen's picture, and I shivered. "She's a very pretty girl, but there's a curse in being pretty."

"You know she likes you."

"What Helen really likes is Hollywood," I said.

"Our girl's a dreamer who doesn't know some dreams are perilous."

"Sir, I'm not strong enough to love her. It's tough enough being her friend." I rubbed my jaw, and Mr. Webber somehow conjured up a grin.

"I'm not strong either," Mr. Webber said. "But life gives us hard choices. If you and I don't love Helen, will *Hollywood* take care of her?"

"I see your point."

"Do you?" He puffed his pipe and looked down at his watch. "Okay then promise me you'll take care of my daughter like a man."

"Okay, I promise."

He shook my hand. "And I know that as a man you'll keep your word. Thanks," he said. He grinned and dabbed a tear from his left eye.

Then he stood up. It was evident he'd cry more once I'd left. He wiped his face against his shirtsleeve, and he helped me to the door. "Get some sleep, son," Mr. Webber turned the porch light on. "I spoke with Stubby Carson. He knows you won't report to work today. Not safe to work on rooftops when you're sleepy."

"Probably true."

He shook my hand. "Listen, I need someone to lean on. So do you."

I told him, "Thank you." I had doubts, but it felt good to hear the words.

"I think you're right, sir."

"Goodnight, son."

The front door slipped shut behind me.

Sore and fatigued, I stumbled home at five a.m. to run my paper route, exhausted. Angry at Helen, I filled my bags up full of newspapers.

An engine purred behind me as I climbed onto my Schwinn. *Who drove this early in the morning?* I glanced over my shoulder.

Then I panicked.

A bright red Cadillac had tailed me to my house. I glared at Margaret.

She honked her horn. Then she sped off into the morning.

I felt uneasy, knowing Margaret had found out where I lived. I hadn't planned on seeing her again.

CHAPTER VII

SUNDAY, MAY 18, 1924

By dawn, the streets of Anaheim were slick with muddy tire-tracks and puddles from a cloudburst that had dumped an inch of rain. A butter-yellow sun peered down through cotton candy clouds east of the orchards, its light reflecting off the freshly washed brick skyline. Musty scents of moldy leaves mixed in with gasoline aromas. They rose from gutters filled with road oils and mud left by the storm. Rain provided me a respite from a week of arid Santa Ana winds. These had left everyone in Anaheim on edge.

At Mr. Webber's invitation, I joined him and Mrs. Webber at the 7:30 service at First Christian Church on Sunday. I felt awkward. Leon Myers gave a sermon on the flag and Betsy Ross, who'd lost two husbands in the war against Great Britain. We sang patriotic songs ending in glory hallelujahs, while the choir marched downstairs and filled the sanctuary with candles. I smelled the scent of burning paraffin. The smoke watered my eyes. We clapped our hands and told each other it was good to be American and good to know that God was on our side.

I was surprised when Helen showed up during a "glory hallelujah" and slid between me and her father as if last Friday'd never happened. She evidently had come home, put on a lime-green cotton dress and come to join us, knowing nobody would lecture her in church.

"How'd you get here?" I asked Helen.

"Got a lift from Crazy Florence."

Whoever *that* was. She kept referring to this invisible friend named Crazy Florence who taxied Helen around Southern Califorina. I wondered whether Florence was as good looking as Helen. Perhaps this Florence lived vicariously, riding Helen's coattails.

I fired a glance at Mr. Webber. He removed a gray silk handkerchief. He dabbed it on the corner of his eye.

Mrs. Webber didn't even turn her head to look at Helen. Her chin was set at the same angle as those cow-catchers on steam engines or fenders in front of trolley cars that scoop up rogue pedestrians. She stared at Reverend Myers as if the man were called by God to speak for Jesus, for America, for all the Ku Klux Klan. She wasn't nervous in his church the way she seemed everywhere else. She seemed entranced within his spell, much like a tsar hearing Rasputin. I didn't understand quite what she saw in him.

We finally were dismissed. Mr. Webber went for coffee.

Helen grabbed me by my wrist, saying, "Dean, we need to talk."

I looked away. I wasn't ready.

"Dean, we need to talk right now."

"You left *me* holding the bag, Helen. Like some worthless dumb palooka."

"I didn't have a choice."

"Sure you did. You *lied* to me. Fed me a crock full of baloney. You didn't tell me how John Gilbert bought our tickets to the Bon Ton."

"Well you don't have to cast a kitten. I didn't...."

"Helen, I don't even want to know."

"Okay, don't ask." She stared straight forward like a woman on a ship prow. The weird thing was that Helen didn't cry, just set her chin at that same angle as Mrs. Webber's chin this morning, as if only one thing mattered and she knew just what it was.

"John Gilbert offered me a screen test."

"How thoughtful," I replied.

"This is huge, Dean. Can't you at least show some excitement for a change?"

I smiled back to mask my anger. Helen had left me on my own in Ocean Park. Taken our trolley tickets. "You didn't even care how I got home. I had no money and had to hitchhike. That's not how girls should treat their dates."

"It was *John Gilbert*. Don't you see?" She waved her palms. "Opportunity only knocks but once."

"Well he's an eighteen-carat jerk." I rubbed my jaw. "He sucker-punched me."

"He knows his onions," Helen said. "He knows the ins and outs of Hollywood."

My ears burned full of rage. "*I'll bet* he knows the ins and outs of much, much more than Hollywood."

"You're sounding like my Daddy." She looked away. "The so-called 'war hero.'"

"Well, you should listen to him, Helen. Can't you see your dad adores you?"

"Lots of men adore me, Dean."

"Lust isn't adoration."

Helen's deer-in-headlights stare appeared as if I'd struck a nerve.

"I was afraid of this," said Helen.

"Afraid of what?"

"You and my father. Why do you think he finds you work with Stubby Carson every weekend?"

"He's a good guy."

"You need a father, and my father needs a son. You think I'm blind? Can't you see Daddy is a lecher and a liar? He wasn't even *in* the Navy. He had a heart murmur. Four-F." She looked away, smiled and sashayed out the door, then spun around. "And why do you think my mother never talks to him?" asked Helen, her voice tone punctuating something wasn't right between the Webbers. She spun around and resumed walking. Her footsteps echoed through the narthex and faded outside toward the street.

Conversations hummed around me.

My mind was spinning in a whirl. *Why did Helen hate her father? Why would Helen claim her father lied about his Navy service?* Voices closed in on all sides and made it difficult to think. Colleen Harris and her brother, Ed, were talking about baseball. Mrs. Webber spoke with Mayor Metcalf's wife about a patriotic rally in July at Central Park in downtown Anaheim. She said thousands of her friends would come from all over the Southland. Mr. Webber and Stubby Carson spoke of how the L.A. Angels had beaten the San Francisco Seals in extra innings Friday night. Stubby said he'd heard the Angels would be building a new ballpark, Wrigley Field in South L.A.

Just then, Stubby waved me over.

I joined their conversation. They liked the Cubs, Gabby

Hartnett, Charlie Hollocher, and especially Grover Cleveland Alexander. We spoke of baseball and how they loved watching the Cubs on Catalina for spring training. I hadn't known how much these men loved watching baseball.

"So how's your pitching arm?" asked Stubby. "Heard you're pitching for the Colonists this Friday."

"It feels loose."

Mr. Webber stepped outside.

Stubby Carson dropped his voice a half an octave. "Still seein' Helen?"

"On occasion."

He elbowed me. "Don't say I didn't warn you. Still, I'd stay close to Mister Webber. He's a very decent man who needs a friend. He seems to like you. Likes your work ethic like I do. Both of us'll be there at your game this coming Friday. Make us proud."

Stubby Carson slapped my back, and that felt good.

It felt better to share the company of men I had grown up with. For once I felt like I belonged, no matter how Helen had treated me. I grinned and picked my chin up. I had a great job and good mentors.

Then it dawned on me.

I needed Mr. Webber more than Helen did.

FRIDAY, MAY 23, 1924

Sitting once again in Miss Elgena's civics class, I stared out through the window toward the orchard where I'd kissed Helen. The J.T. Lyon Billboard with the lion in the center was papered over with a new message beneath a pair of eyeglasses:

I TREAT BOTH CAUSE AND EFFECT STANDPOINTS
DR. LOUIS J. ELWOOD, MODERN OPTOMETRIST
106 E. 4TH STREET, SANTA ANA, PHONE 43-R

It saddened me the lion who had chaperoned our kiss was papered over with a pair of eyes that glared back from our orchard, as if reminding me I had no need to fantasize about Helen, and I needed to bear down and pay attention to my lessons.

Miss Elgena lectured on. Something about the Tenth Amendment and how people had opinions that were manifestly different. Some thought the states should have more power. Others felt Washington knew best.

I had too many problems of my own to pay attention.

We had a baseball game today. We were playing down in Orange against the Panthers, an away game. I'd been penciled in to pitch. We were in second place. If Santa Ana somehow got past Fullerton, and *we* defeated Orange, we'd tie for first and make the playoffs. My stomach turned over and over like a giant concrete mixer, and I nibbled on my thumbnail while Miss Elgena spoke about the Bill of Rights. My head was spinning. I grew more nervous by the minute, and I longed to go outside for some fresh air.

At last the bell rang.

I set my jaw, making my way toward the locker room at double-time.

The baseball game would start in ninety minutes.

Our team bus navigated the circle on Chapman Street in Orange and made its way past Watson's Drug, then turned a sharp left onto Shafer Street. We rode past bungalows and orchards. Eastward, the Santa Ana Mountains rose like cardboard silhouettes above the arid chaparral.

My nerves constricted in my stomach. I had to focus on my pitching. I didn't want to think of Helen, but our prom night was approaching, and we had tickets. Next to the Bon Ton ballroom, proms seemed adolescent, but at least I knew John Gilbert wouldn't come and punch me out.

I was wishing I could bring someone who might enjoy my company. Alma Martin, for example used to bake me macaroons. We'd had a falling-out the night I wasn't home when Ma got hurt. But it was possible to fix that. I'd heard no one had invited her. I knew if she dressed up she would be stunning. But I'd promised Mr. Webber I'd take Helen. He said he trusted me. I hadn't earned that trust but had to keep up my appearances to get work with Stubby Carson who was paying very well. Helen was gorgeous, and she liked me, but I didn't need her drama. She was too Hollywood. I longed to have a girl with simple tastes, someone who thought of people other than herself.

Our bus parked north of the new high school, a two-story brick fortress with provisions so a third story might be added in the future. A makeshift ballfield was carved out from the Stoneman family's wheat field a block north of the new school beyond the gravel lot for parking. There were no bleachers, and the infield had grass but not the outfield. A rail fence had been constructed to mark the limits of the outfield. Two horses had been tied up to the outside of the rails. I shuddered when I saw another J.T. Lyon billboard. It reminded me of Helen. I had to focus on my pitching.

To make it worse, Skeeter told me there were two Pacific Coast League scouts. One from the Los Angeles Angels, the other from the Vernon Tigers. They were somewhere in the stands and I knew both were scouting *me*. If Helen had her shot at Hollywood, it suddenly occurred to me I had a chance to play pro ball for a Pacific Coast League team.

I shook my arm to loosen up. I threw some catch with Skeeter Wilson.

"How's that arm feel?" asked Coach Merritt.

"Feels swell," I hollered back. I hurled a fast ball. Heard it sizzle into Skeeter Wilson's glove.

He shook the leather like I'd thrown the ball so hard he'd bruised his hand.

"Hey, Big Six."

I turned my head, surprised Helen had shown up. She wore a loose dress with a dropped waist and a scarf tied like a sailor's, both cut low to show her figure. She had come with Colleen Harris and Helen's father, who'd parked his Packard in the gravel lot just south. I almost wished they'd stayed at home. I wasn't up for her shenanigans. It subtracted from my focus, which it seemed I'd left in Anaheim. To make the playoffs, I'd have to pitch the best game of my life.

The Orange baseball team sauntered out onto the diamond.

Two rows of girls in orange sweaters and black skirts lined up with pom-poms just outside of the first-base line on the edge of Orange's benches. They yelled a cheer for the Orange Panthers. Orange's coach hit several fungoes to his outfield.

"Play ball," the plate umpire yelled out.

I sat down, letting my teammates take their first-inning at-bats. Skeeter Wilson led the game off. He swung and missed on three straight pitches. Toby Baker came up next and popped the ball to second base. Then Tommy Harrington fouled out. We'd been retired on five pitches.

I made my way out to the pitcher's mound and stared toward home plate.

"Go, Big Six," Helen yelled out. She had even brought a megaphone.

I pushed her voice out of my brain and squeezed the baseball. I'd heard Sam Collins was much stronger than he looked and very dangerous. From the batter's box, he studied me.

I glared back from the mound and chewed a wad of Adams Blackjack.

"Go, Big Six," Helen yelled out.

He was as skinny as a fungo bat. He stepped up to the left side of the plate. Glaring at me, he dug his cleats into the clay. He mopped his cap against his brow.

Toby Baker held two fingers up.

I shook away the sign. Sammy leaned over the plate. Toby held one finger, a fastball. I nodded and bore down. I had to telegraph a message, send Sammy Collins my best pitch.

The baseball sizzled toward him on the inside of the strike zone near his chest.

Sammy swung. I knew that pitch was hard to hit.

There was a loud crack and the ball shot toward the center field fence rails like a mortar had been launched. The outfield turned around and watched. It sailed far beyond the fence, half the way to Yorba Linda, beyond the wheat field, landing somewhere in the middle of an orange grove.

Sammy Collins grinned. He slowly circled all the bases, clapping his hands, perhaps applauding his own heroics. Or perhaps he meant to taunt me. I hung my head, trying to focus. I couldn't show the on-deck batter how that last home run had rattled me. I wiped my palm against my rosin bag and dug my steel cleats into the pitching mound.

The plate umpire threw another ball out.

Orange's cheerleaders went crazy, shaking pom-poms while I tried to push my nerves out of my throat. That guy had hammered my best pitch. I had to swallow back my fear and appear confident. I buckled down. I waited till the next batter stepped in.

Threw him a curve ball.

He lined it to center field for a double.

"C'mon, Big Six," Helen called out, breaking my focus yet again.

Coach Merritt glared back from the bench. Toby Baker held two fingers up. A fastball. My last fastball had been crushed for a home run. I wound up tightly. It didn't feel right. Threw the ball high and outside. It got past Toby for a wild pitch.

The runner raced to third.

No outs.

Coach Merritt walked out to the mound.

His face was red. "What's going on?" He kicked the dust beneath his shoes.

"Coach, I don't know. First pitch felt good, but Sammy Collins had its number. Same with my second pitch."

"Calm down. Take a deep breath," Coach Merritt said.

I did exactly what he asked, holding the breath for several seconds. I exhaled.

"I'm counting on you." Coach Merritt turned and walked away. I took another long deep breath and blocked out everything except the batter facing me.

The batter's name was Andy Mathews.

I threw the first pitch for a strike. Low and inside. He swung and missed and fouled away the pitch behind it.

No balls. Two strikes. I threw a change-up.

Andy Mathews was in front of it.

"Strike three!" the umpire called out.

I heaved a hard sigh of relief and squeezed the baseball in my fist.

Orange's next batter popped a foul ball which our third baseman took care of. The next batter hit a slow roller to first for the third out. After one inning I had stranded a man on third to end the inning.

One-nothing, Orange.

Angry, I paced toward the bench and took a seat.

After six innings, the score remained one-nothing in Orange's favor. Archie Schmidt had hit two singles, but two double-plays had followed. Orange seemed unbeatable today. But at last their pitcher's throwing arm grew weary. He walked two batters, Larry Nelson and Boomer Corrigan. The fastball didn't have its zip. I made my way toward the plate, and hoped that somehow I could drive somebody home to tie the game. I knew I had to. If I didn't I'd be blamed for today's loss, blowing our season. I loved baseball and could not afford to choke. I couldn't let my teammates down. I had to win it for my father. I imagined he looked down on me. I couldn't disappoint him.

I took two balls, low and inside. I took the third pitch for a strike, then fouled the fourth pitch for a second strike. The count was two-and-two. The next pitch sailed right down the middle. I took a swing and watched it loop toward center field. The center fielder sprinted in to field it.

But it bounced underneath his glove. Larry hustled in to score followed by Boomer as the ball rolled all the way center field. I steamed past second toward third, except the ball bounced off the J T Lyon billboard. The center fielder threw a perfect strike to third.

I was out by twenty feet.

"Yer out!" the umpire yelled. The third baseman had yet to even tag me. He just grinned and shook his head, slapping his glove against my thigh to make it legal.

I shook my head and shuffled to our bench.

The next two batters lined to second base for two quick outs to end the inning. Two-to-one Anaheim. But our season was on the line.

I made my way out to the mound to pitch the seventh and last inning, knowing a single run would tie the score and cost our team the playoffs. I'd had a sore spot on my finger and looked down to see a blister. But I knew since there were scouts here that I had to win the game, not just for Anaheim, but a chance to play pro ball.

"C'mon, Big Six," Helen called out, breaking my focus yet again. I wished a teammate or Coach Merritt might tell Helen to pipe down. I chawed down on my Blackjack gum to focus on my pitch and bit my cheek. I winced. It somehow felt like a bad omen.

I threw the first pitch for a ball, low and inside, then threw another. I threw a curveball for ball three, feeling it rub against my blister. I spit the gum out, tasting blood along the inside of my cheek.

"C'mon, Big Six," Helen repeated, raising her megaphone again, making it sound as if she yelled from somewhere inside my right ear.

She sat down behind third base. I threw another pitch.

"Ball four," the umpire hollered. (It was a strike, but it was not the time to argue.) Mort Rifkin tossed his bat aside and sauntered to first base as Jim McCormick made his way into the batter's box, hitting lefty.

I threw another ball. Another. Then I finally threw a strike, only Mort Rifkin broke for second, and the catcher held the ball. Mort had stolen second base. I threw another ball. A strike, except the umpire called, "Ball three."

I threw my hands up, shook my head. Another pitch was way outside.

"Ball four." McCormack sprinted to first base.

Orange's cheerleaders were screaming. Mort took a lead off second base halfway to third. I threw to pick him off, but Morton scrambled back. Orange's batter laid down a bunt. I grabbed the ball. Lobbed it to first.

"Yer out!" the umpire called, but runners were now on second and third.

That meant a base hit won the game if they could score from second base. Sam Collins stepped into the batter's box. He'd singled off me twice. He'd slammed that home run in his first at-bat for Orange's only run. He took the first pitch for a strike. Coach Merritt glared out from the bench as if he wanted to replace me.

Collins fouled the next pitch off.

No balls. Two strikes, the way I liked things. I could risk throwing a junk ball. It didn't need to be a strike. Sammy Collins had to swing. I threw a curve down and outside.

Sammy Collins fouled it off.

I looked down at my finger. My blister had just popped.

"Go, Big Dean," Helen was shrieking.

Morton Rifkin led off halfway toward home plate. I lobbed to third and felt my bleeding finger sting.

Morton dove back. I was lucky Tommy Cunningham had octopus-long arms to grab my pickoff throw, two feet above his head.

I threw another strike and Collins fouled it off.

It hurt to throw now. After allowing two straight balls, my hand was throbbing, and my shoulder hurt. Red streaks covered the baseball.

"Let's go, Dean," Helen shrieked out.

Collins was glaring. I wound up. A sinking curve ball down the middle.

I heard a crack, and I looked up.

The ball launched upward like a rocket.

Mort Rifkin tagged at third, waiting to score after the catch. Jim Cunningham had tagged at second. Boomer Corrigan was circling in right field, but the wind had caught the pop fly in the air, and it was drifting toward centerfield out of Boomer's reach. He sprinted for the catch.

Mort raced for home.

Boomer threw a bullet to Toby Baker at the plate.

"Yer out," the umpire hollered as Toby tagged him with his glove.

I exhaled. It was the third out. That meant we had won the game. I stuck my finger in my mouth and started licking off the blood.

The final score was two to one, and now I noticed both my temples had been hammering like Thompson submachine guns while I pitched. I knelt down to catch my breath.

Coach Merritt raced onto the field.

Helen ran out right behind him.

I wiped my glove across my face.

I tried to mop sweat from my brow, except my shirt and glove were soaked. Merritt hugged me, Tommy Harrington and Boomer piled on. Then Eddie Harris made his entrance with a pail full of ice water he dumped over my head so ice went streaming down my jersey.

My baseball cap was full of water. Ice piled up above my belt, and I was freezing. Helen hugged me, and her hands found Eddie's ice. She rubbed the ice against my spine, laughing and kissing both my cheeks, pressing her dress against my shirt until its front was fully soaked, and I could see beneath her sailor scarf she hadn't worn a bra.

Teammates were staring at her, winking my direction in approval. I felt helpless with her father on the sidelines. My manhood swelled up like a rocket that was ready to ignite as Helen reached to grab my glove hand, since my throwing hand was bleeding. She tugged me like a horse might tug a sulky toward the Packard. There was nothing I could do to camouflage my bulging pants. Teammates were clapping for me, cheering me. I hurried off the diamond.

"Dean, wait up," said Skeeter Wilson.

I couldn't glance back. I was aching.

Her father opened up the rear door of his Packard Single-Eight. Helen yanked me in beside her. I was still catching my breath, trying not to stare at Helen.

She was screaming through her megaphone. "Guys, let's party down at Hudnall's. Follow us."

They didn't hesitate to follow.

"You were splendid, Dean," cooed Helen.

I was trying not to gloat.

Her father turned down Chapman Avenue and drove around the circle several times, honking his horn, as Helen hollered through the window, "Anaheim is number one!"

The team bus had caught up with us.

Her father shifted into gear and broke the speed limit down Chapman. He was smoking a cigar with only one hand on the wheel. We made our way across the Santa Ana River where the Mexicans drank wine outside their citrus camps.

They waved as we sped past.

Mr. Webber signaled right and sped toward Anaheim on Manchester. We crossed the Anaheim City limit with its KIGY letters. These were stenciled on the asphalt and a half a dozen stop signs. Webber drove above the speed limit, but Klan cops didn't care.

"We won," shrieked Helen, and the town cops on their motorcycles grinned.

At Palm and Center Street I noticed a big man atop a backhoe worked to excavate the concrete base that held the City's flagpole. "What's he doing?" I asked Helen.

"Moving the flagpole," Mr. Webber said.

"To where?"

"Central Park. You didn't hear about our rally?"

"What rally?"

"A Klan rally with twenty-thousand people."

My heart dropped like a sinker. I wasn't sure about the Klan. And yet it seemed they had befriended me. I needed a few friends like Mr. Webber and Stubby Carson, father figures to look up to. For some reason the Klan made them look small.

But tonight I was still riding atop their world.

Mr. Webber signaled left. He parked his car behind the drug store, and the bus parked alongside us. Mr. Webber scrunched the parking brake and turned off the ignition. Helen and I jumped from the car. Half our high school had shown up.

In we paraded through the back door past the bathrooms in the rear and down the mosaic-tiled corridor that led to Forrest Hudnall's. Helen plopped her sequined purse atop the long white onyx bar and took her place on a swivel stool above a steel pedestal.

I sat beside her near the cigarette rack. Donnie, Alma's brother, worked the register and sold a girl in glasses a roll of Necco wafers. I saw Helen in the mirror with its Coca Cola corners. I glanced at Donnie. He had sold the Necco wafers to his sister.

Donnie left to grab a spoon and mix a double-chocolate malted.

Alma was looking at me, wearing an embroidered cotton blouse trying hard to hold her chin up. I saw her sad face in the mirror. Couldn't look at her directly. Wished I could. She'd been a good friend since we'd moved out here from Brooklyn.

Alma looked away.

Helen nudged my elbow. "What do you think about the merger?"

She was talking about Hollywood and Metro-Goldwyn-Mayer, the merger engineered by Louis Mayer and Sam Goldwyn. "Now John Gilbert, Alice Terry, and King Vidor will share one studio. Think of the movies they can make. They're keeping Samuel Goldwyn's lion." She smiled at me. Her figure made her dress appear invisible but her mention of John Gilbert made me cringe.

My stare returned to Alma's image, a ship passing in the

night two feet away, yet I was seeing her reflection in the mirror. The mirror made her seem more distant, even though I smelled her perfume, while we both acted like strangers who'd been friends not long ago.

Coach Merritt slapped me on the back. "Hey, did you hear Fullerton lost? We're in first place."

"No," I said.

"Just called my brother at the *Orange County Plain Dealer*. He's a reporter. Saw the game. Nine-to-one Saints. We're in the playoffs with Santa Ana, and you're penciled in to pitch."

I rubbed my finger and hoped my blister on the tip would heal soon. I had no-hit them our first game. But lightning rarely did strike twice. They might be eager to get even, and I couldn't throw a curve ball with my finger.

Boomer Corrigan sat down and seemed to hit it off with Alma. Everyone liked Boomer, a natural-born athlete. He had an Irish face with freckles and red sloppy hair to match. He wasn't handsome, but he'd led our team in RBI's all season.

Mayor Metcalf shook my hand. "Heckuva game you pitched," he said. The man liked baseball, and he'd seen the game along with Aaron Slayback, who owned a grocery store and sat with Mayor Metcalf on City Council.

Helen raised a bubbling cherry coke.

"Here's a toast to Big-Six Reynolds. Wasn't he swell?" Helen called out. Colleen Harris sat by Helen, and she raised her glass as well. Colleen had platinum blonde hair that framed a face she covered up with too much makeup to cover chickenpox scars she'd had since seventh grade when she'd moved to Anaheim from Mississippi.

Teammates joined in, raising their glasses in a toast. "Hooray, for Dean."

I raised my soda glass.

A cheer filled Forrest Hudnall's. "Hear-hear-hear."

I sipped my soda, then looked up.

Alma was walking out the rear, not looking back. The door closed quietly the way she always closed them.

It made me sad after our victory, and all the effervescence of the evening went as flat as month-old cherry Coca Cola. People chattered on all sides of me, but I now felt upset.

Alma and I hadn't shared a word.

With Alma gone, and Helen telling me Glen Oswald's Serenaders would be playing at our prom, I did what boyfriends had to do.

I asked her out.

She seemed excited, letting everybody know she would be going as my date.

Except it didn't feel right.

"Big Six, just asked me to the prom." She held my hand up like a trophy, pressing her luscious ripe tomatoes against my chest so I could feel them. She snuggled near me like a baby vamp and flung my arm around her like a stole.

I smiled weakly.

"Way to go, Dean-o," Skeeter Wilson said and raised another glass.

"You're a very lucky boy, Dean." Colleen Harris turned to Skeeter. "Hey, what about me?"

"I guess," said Skeeter.

"He's so romantic, Helen, isn't he?" Colleen asked, letting her sadness pierce her Mississippi drawl.

"And how," said Helen, her voice chilly with a double-scoop of sarcasm.

Colleen blushed. Her face was redder than her badly applied lipstick.

Skeeter glanced at me. "So, Dean. Think maybe we could bum a ride?"

"Sure," I said. The evening buzzed into cacophony. The sun went down. The gas lamps lit up Model T's on Center Street outside. Helen was still talking about Hollywood. She had big plans after high school. Plans for Hollywood and stardom. Plans that didn't involve me. She was a star. I was a property, a gigolo, an escort.

Someday I had to talk to Alma. But I knew that would be awkward.

Donnie Martin handed me my tab and rang our bill up.

I walked home in the darkness by myself.

SATURDAY, MAY 24, 1924

The next day when I came home after I'd run my morning paper route, I parked my yellow Schwinn and noticed Rollo Earnest at my doorstep. He stuffed an envelope behind the iron scroll that ran across the screen on our front door. Then he took off. He didn't even smile or say hello.

He had penciled in my name outside a plain manila envelope, no postage stamp, no address, just my name:

MISTER DEAN REYNOLDS

I ripped it open. It was weird seeing my name as "Mister Reynolds" like my father. I rarely saw myself as being an adult. And why was Rollo writing *me*? He owned the *Orange County Plain Dealer*. He was friends with Stubby Carson and with Mayor Elmer Metcalf. They were bigshots here in Anaheim.

I'd seen them eating lunch at Warren Glover's on Los Angeles Street, talking local politics. Rollo always rolled his sleeves up, even when he wasn't working. He didn't even roll them down for church.

I unfolded the letter. It was hand-typed with no signature. My name was at the top. "Dear Mister Reynolds," it began which still felt strange. I read it slowly. Here is what it said:

"Your best friends state you are a 'Native Born' American citizen having the best interest of our community, city, state, and nation at heart and believe in The Tenets of the Christian Religion, White Supremacy, Protection of our Pure American Womanhood, Promotion of Pure Americanism. REAL MEN, whose oaths are inviolate are needed. Upon these beliefs and the recommendations of your friends, you are given an opportunity to become a member of the most powerful, secret, non-political organization in existence, one that has the Most Sublime Lineage in History. Discuss this with no one. If you wish to learn more, address PO Box 16, Anaheim, CA."

I swallowed hard. Holy crap. I was only seventeen, but evidently my celebrity had put me in the spotlight. I had no clue what this was all about or why these people flattered me. It piqued my curiosity. I needed to find out.

And so I readdressed their envelope to P.O. Box 16, scrawled off a message on the porch using a sheet of loose-leaf paper from my notebook. I wrote my name down. Said I was interested but needed to know more, given I didn't even know who I was writing to.

Heading to work, I dropped the letter in the mailbox downtown. Then I forgot about it and sprinted, late, to work for Stubby Carson.

CHAPTER VIII

TUESDAY, MAY 27, 1924

Before my Tuesday morning paper route, I read through several letters in *The Orange County Plain Dealer*. Most seemed to be about the flag. Folks asked why the city fathers had to move the giant flagpole from outside City Hall several blocks to Central Park.

It seemed like there weren't any answers. The flag belonged at City Hall, everyone said, and I agreed. The council's logic still escaped me. But it was "progress." Rollo Earnest said so in his editorial, and my job was not to argue with the paper but deliver it.

There was other news today. It seemed some man had been offended at that shrine for Boomer's parents on the east side of the river. The story was a group of Bolsheviks had uprooted the whitewashed cross, and they had smashed it into splinters with a sledge outside of town.

I felt mighty bad for Boomer. It was rough losing a parent. I knew *that* much. He'd lost both of his and set the whitewashed cross up to remember them. It's not like he was trying to evangelize. But someone had told Boomer not to put another cross up, because Anaheim could not afford the lawsuit.

Colleen Harris tracked me down outside my locker during lunch. She reminded me I'd told Skeeter they both could bum a ride to senior prom. I asked, "Where's Helen?"

"Didn't y'all hear? She stayed home sick. Told me she couldn't hold her food down. With prom so close let's pray poor Helen doesn't have the flu."

"Right," I said, feeling awkward that I felt so little sympathy. Helen could be selfish, and it bothered me a lot. What made pretty girls so selfish? Why were nice girls always plain, like Alma Martin, who *could* be gorgeous, but she didn't seem to want to?

Afternoon classes went by quickly. I felt alone in Miss Elgena's class with twenty other high school students sitting in my classroom. The eyes of Dr. Louis Elwood stared from that billboard in the orchard where J. T. Lyon's lion had chaperoned my kiss from Helen. I rubbed my elbow, swollen up larger than a navel orange since Friday. Plus my blister wasn't healing. I had a game to pitch this Friday afternoon. I was starting to get worried for our chances.

The bell rang, and I made my way downstairs to dress for practice. My arm muscles were tied in knots no sailor could untie. I threw light to loosen up, but my motion didn't feel right. I had no curve ball with the blister on my finger and no fastball with my elbow. It was clear Coach Merritt noticed I was struggling. After practice Merritt tapped me on the shoulder on the mound.

"Reynolds, see me in my office."

My stomach crawled into my throat. "Yes, sir," I said.

"But change your clothes and take a shower right before."

"Before we meet?"

Coach Merritt nodded.

"Okay, if that's the way you want it."

"Go," he said. He tapped his whistle.

I turned and sprinted toward the locker room.

I showered, and I changed into my street clothes just as quickly as I could. My nerves were firing like a box of Roman candles.

The door outside Coach Merritt's office was locked when I arrived, and Skeeter Wilson was outside. "Here for the meeting?" Skeeter asked.

"Yeah," I said. "What's this about?"

"Guess we'll find out," was all that Skeeter had to offer, but it made me feel better.

We waited outside for five minutes. Then I heard the door unlock, and we were ushered into Coach Merritt's small office, both at once. Four wooden folding chairs were crammed into an office that was big enough for two. Deflated volleyballs and brick-red Voit utility balls were stuffed into a steel drum to clear space for four chairs.

"Have a seat, sons," said a man I recognized as being the cop who had arrested me the night I'd driven Mr. Webber's Packard.

The cop gave me a look, and I remembered our first meeting. I'd deserved to get a ticket, but the cop had let me go. Perhaps he'd had a change of heart. Or perhaps someone had tried to rat him out.

I took in shallow breaths, dreading what was going to happen.

But what was Skeeter doing here if this was all about the ticket? Aaron Slayback was also in the room with Merritt and the cop. Aaron Slayback was soft-spoken, but he *was* a city councilman. He looked down at his watch like Mr. Webber always did.

Someone had lathered Coach's office with the scent of *eau de basketball* with subtle hints of body odor laced through the aroma. On Coach's desk, a can of Odorona functioned as a paperweight. Its contents, evidently, hadn't seen the light of day. Two faded photos of Coach Merritt showed he'd once played for the Nashville Volunteers, a minor league team in the Southern Association. He'd been an outfielder who'd lasted for a season and a half before they'd cut him, and he'd had to make a living coaching high school.

Coach reached into his desk drawer. He retrieved a pair of envelopes. He handed one to Skeeter and the other one to me, the same envelope I'd dropped off at the Post Office last Saturday.

"You recognize these?" Aaron Slayback asked.

"Yes, sir," we mumbled.

A wall clock tick-tick-tocked. An industrial-sized desk fan rattled loudly on the file drawers and oscillated slowly. I took a long hard look at Skeeter, and he shrugged. "You got a letter?"

"Yup," I said. "Guess you did too."

Skeeter puckered, nodding slowly.

Aaron Slayback stood and cleared his throat, proceeding with the meeting.

"We're assuming neither one of you are old enough you served on active duty during the War between the States?" Slayback deadpanned.

"No, sir. How could we?" I replied. "Skeeter and I weren't even born yet."

"Of course," Coach said. "He needs to ask though. Due diligence and all that."

"And I assume you have no sympathies with Radical Republicans, the Union League, the Loyal League?"

Skeeter laughed, "Pacific Coast League?"

"He isn't talking about baseball. He's talking politics," Coach Merritt said.

"Never heard of them," said Skeeter, "except Radical Republicans, and they ain't been in business since the Reconstruction ended."

"Same for me," I blurted out.

"And you are too young to be Freemasons. Were you both born in America?"

"Yes," I said. "In Brooklyn."

"Born in Anaheim," said Skeeter.

"And both of you are Christians."

"I was raised Methodist," I said. "And so was Skeeter."

Aaron Slayback rubbed his chin.

"Reynolds, I've seen you at our church with Goblin Webber," the policeman said. "Our pastor, Leon Myers, is a Klokard in our Klavern."

"What's a Klokard?" I inquired.

"Klokards are lecturers," Coach Merritt said. "Two thirds of our Klokards are ordained ministers," he added.

Slayback cut in. "And you don't drink?"

"It's illegal," Skeeter said. I was glad he took the question. As for me, I'd had a snort when Helen abandoned me at the Bon Ton. Except I wasn't drinking now, and we were in the present tense here.

I said, "Me neither."

That seemed good enough for everyone concerned.

Councilman Slayback locked Coach Merritt's office door.

"What I say from this point forward must be kept on the QT. Mind your potatoes, boys. I wouldn't want for us to have to hurt you." Slayback met both of our gazes.

"What are we here for?" Skeeter asked.

Slayback laid a laminated card out on the table. It said:

PERSONAL CODE
KNIGHTS OF THE KU KLUX KLAN
I PLEDGE

1. To untiringly work for the preservation, protection, and advancement of the White Race.

2. To forever be loyal to the Knights of the Ku Klux Klan—as the only true Klan.

3. To obey all orders from officers of the Empire.

4. To keep secret all fellow members and Klan rituals.

5. To never discuss any Klan affairs with any plain-clothes officer on a state, local, or national level.

6. To fulfill social, fraternal, and financial obligations to this order as long as I live.

Signature Aaron Slayback
Realm of Kalifornia

My mouth went dryer than a furnace. Skeeter looked at me. At Merritt. "You're asking us to join the *Klan?*"

"Very few men are invited."

I gasped and said, "But don't you...?"

The wall clock tick-tick-ticked, and Aaron Slayback rubbed his jaw. "Lynch people?" He glared at me as if I'd said the words. "Name one Negro who's been lynched in California. I dare you. We don't need the bad publicity. We're working hard to save our country and make the world safe for democracy."

"Save it from what?" I had to ask.

"Isn't it obvious?" said Slayback.

"I'm sure you read about that cross just east of town someone just savaged," the policemen interjected.

"The one the atheists...."

Coach Merritt met my gaze and nodded. "Yeah." He looked away.

"Why isn't Boomer in this meeting?" Skeeter asked.

"Because he's Catholic," I whispered.

Aaron Slayback winked, and his companions nodded with him.

"I still have a lot of questions." I stood up.

"And, so do I." Skeeter stood too.

"Sit down, boys, not so fast," cooed Aaron Slayback. "You just got here. There's something Coach Merritt never told you. He laid two slips of paper down before us on the desk.

My mouth went dry, and something tightened up inside my throat the first moment I discerned what I was seeing.

This certifies that _Dean Reynolds, Jr._
Has donated the sum of TEN DOLLARS to the propagating fund of the
Knights of the Ku Klux Klan (Inc.)

And same is accepted as such and as full sum of "KLEC-TIKON," entitling him to be received on the acceptance of his petition under the laws, regulations, and requirements of the Order, duly naturalized and to have and hold all the rights, titles, honors, and protection as a citizen of the Invisible Empire. He enters through the portal of a Klan.

To be initiated at Anaheim
State of California Date July 27, 1924

Received in trust for the
KNIGHTS OF THE KU KLUX KLAN, (INC.)
K.O.I.E.
E. N. "Harry" Harris
Klabee

There was another one just like it, except Skeeter's name was on it.

"That's Colleen's father!" Skeeter stammered.

"He's our treasurer. Our Klabee. He's paid the full sum of ten dollars so that *you* won't have to pay us. I've already placed his money in the bank. Don't disappoint him."

I cleared my throat. "Can I assume that Mr. Webber...?"

Slayback nodded, and he grinned. "It would be a crying shame if you turned down our proposition. I advise you not to do so. Girls like Helen and Colleen deserve real men to be their escorts. We consider the protection of pure American womanhood our duty, and our daughters need to date men we can trust."

He looked at me, and dots began connecting in my mind. I'd promised Mr. Webber I'd take Helen to the prom.

No one acted like they'd threatened me, but evidently Slayback was a genius when it came to making threats that looked like favors. We were cornered. There was no way I could turn down Mr. Webber. I had given him my word that I would take care of his daughter. Plus he'd mentored me. I needed him for jobs with Stubby Carson. And Coach Merritt. With the season on the line I had no choice. Evidently they were testing us to find out if they thought we might be man enough to stand up for the honor of their daughters.

I nodded slowly.

"We're initiating several hundred members at our rally next July the twenty-seventh." Slayback. said. "It's on a Sunday at Central Park."

"You need to mark that on your calendars," Coach said.

Slayback showed us where to sign.

He gave a fountain pen to each of us. "Keep the pens as souvenirs. You men, have made the right decision." We took a quick glance at our pens. They had the Ku Klux Klan insignia, the "blood-drop cross" on each of them. I swallowed. I had seen that cross before.

"That's not much time," said Aaron Slayback. "But I think you two can manage. It'll be just like in the Boy Scouts, except this time you'll be *men.*"

I felt a knot inside my stomach that was worse than all the tightness in my arm. I had to sign. Mr. Webber had my word that I would take care of his daughter.

We signed where we were told to.

"Swell," said Slayback. "Stubby Carson, our new Kladd, will get in touch with you."

The knot inside my stomach just got tighter.

CHAPTER IX

THURSDAY, MAY 29, 1924

Our final playoff with Santa Ana came on the Thursday before Decoration Day. Our game was at Birch Park across from Santa Ana High. Behind the plate, Ace Clarkson, glass eye and all, served as our umpire. It was our championship meet, and half of Anaheim was there.

Helen hadn't come. Said she was sick.

And I'd been struggling on the mound despite the knowledge some more scouts had come to watch me. My left arm felt sore and as awkward as an anvil. The ball was caked with bloodstains from the blister on my finger. There was more blood on my baseball glove across Shoeless Joe's name. The score was Santa Ana six, Anaheim four when I struck out. It was the bottom of the sixth. I made my way back to the dugout to ice up my swollen arm for one last inning. I hoped my teammates could do something to score runs.

The Santa Ana Saints had played like anything but saints, even spiking poor Sid Lowry in the bottom of the third. Tensions were high, except our anger hadn't translated to runs up on the scoreboard.

Eli White dribbled a slow roller to third.

The ball bounced off a rock, and Big Stan Gurtz of Santa Ana muffed the play, hurried his throw and tossed the ball wide of the reach of their first baseman. He stretched to catch it and his foot came off the bag as Eli White touched down at first. One out, and one man on at first.

Terry Anderson hit next. He looped the ball into right center between two outfielders. It rolled all of the way out to the fence. Eli steamed into third, and Terry stopped at second base. He'd hit a double. That put the tying run at second with one out.

Skeeter Wilson made his way toward the plate.

Skeeter was having a great game. He'd hit a single and a double to drive in two Anaheim runs. It was the best game of his life. He had no power, and his talent was at shortstop, not at hitting. His batting average barely topped .200.

The Santa Ana coach walked from the bench out to the mound to point to first, telling Bob Metz, their lanky pitcher, to walk Skeeter.

Bob Metz kept shaking his head. Toby Baker stood on-deck. He'd slammed a home run the first inning off a vicious Bob Metz curveball. After an argument, the Santa Ana coach pointed his finger and sent Metz back to the bench and called Lou Morgan to relieve him.

Lou Morgan could throw fastballs just below the speed of light. Lou claimed he'd hurled a couple faster, but the umpires never saw those. He tossed five warm-up pitches sizzling past the plate into the catcher's mitt. They sounded like five fire-crackers popping in the glove.

After five pitches, Morgan signaled he was ready.

He threw a fastball for strike one, hard and fast, straight down the middle.

His second fastball hit the corner. Skeeter swung at it and missed. No balls, two strikes.

"C'mon, just hit one to the outfield," yelled Coach Merritt. Sacrifice.

Skeeter stepped out of the batter's box to focus.

Eli White took a long leadoff. Skeeter knocked a lump of clay off from his cleats using his bat and then stepped back up to the plate.

Morgan lobbed the ball to third and nearly picked off Eli White, then threw a fastball Skeeter Wilson fouled away.

Skeeter fouled off two more balls.

The Santa Ana bench was taunting him.

'Eybatta, 'eybatta 'eyyyyyyy….

Here came the pitch, straight down the middle.

Skeeter looked at it.

"Ball One."

"WHAT?" The Santa Ana coach came storming from their dugout. "Can't you see that was a strike?"

"Siddown," yelled Ace. "Or you're ejected."

The coach was pointing at the umpire's glass eye, and within moments he was thrown out of the game.

But we all knew he'd been right.

After tempers had cooled down, Lou Morgan threw a couple warm-ups and then bulleted a fastball on the inside of the plate.

And Skeeter swung.

The inside fastball bounced off Skeeter's bat. It came so fast I don't think Skeeter even saw where it was going.

He looked away, as if he'd fouled away another pitch. Then he ran. Our whole team leaped up from the bench, and our jaws plummeted. The ball sailed out past center field. Amazed, we watched it soar above the grass out to the sidewalk, where it bounced and dribbled somewhere into traffic out on First Street. Cheers erupted from the stands.

Eli White and Terry Anderson both sped around the bases to the plate, and we watched Skeeter circle first and make a sprint to second base. Only then did Skeeter realize he'd hit a three-run homer.

He pumped his fist into the air and circled home.

People from Anaheim went crazy. We mobbed Skeeter at the plate to shake his hand. I never had seen Skeeter smile so wide. He'd hit a home run. Skeeter couldn't even hit a deep fly ball. But he'd just *homered*. His first ever. I was happy for my friend.

Morgan walked back to the mound, and he struck out the next two batters.

But Anaheim was leading, seven to six.

Coach Merritt asked if I could pitch another inning. I said no. I touched my elbow; it was swollen up and bigger than a softball.

"Dean the scouts are here to watch you," Merritt said.

"I know," I answered. "But my fastball isn't working any more. It's like a slowball."

He met my gaze. "Okay," he said. "I'll put Walt Riley in this inning."

We were thrilled to see Walt Riley throw three pitches for three outs to end the game. "Anaheim," we screamed. We shouted out our victory. We sprinted off the field and watched the Santa Ana players hang their heads and walk away knowing the league trophy was ours.

We'd won our season for the first time I remembered.

My arm throbbed like a steam hammer, but deep down I was thrilled. Eli White grinned wide and hoisted Skeeter Wilson onto his shoulders. Skeeter waved around his baseball bat. He doffed his sweaty cap, still half-amazed he'd hit that homer. Everyone liked Skeeter. It felt biblical, like David had just put away Goliath. Ed Harris threw a pail of ice water onto all of us.

A cloud of dust ascended from the gravel beyond left field.

A yellow Chevy pickup had jumped the curb onto the grass.

The vehicle sped across the outfield, tires tearing up the foul line. It screeched to stop next to third base. Out jumped the same cop from the Klan who had arrested me, off-duty, in plain clothes. The man looked frantic. He waved his arms, screaming at Skeeter and at me. And then the umpire yelled, "Get into the truck. There's been an accident."

We sprinted toward the pickup.

"Stubby Carson rolled his truck up Carbon Canyon. He's hurt bad." Ace Clarkson shredded all his umpire gear to join us.

Stunned, Skeeter and I jumped onto the flatbed on the truck.

My heart pumped like the ballgame wasn't over.

Five more teammates piled in with us. The euphoria of victory descended back to earth like a pop fly to centerfield. Four more jumped into Coach Merritt's car. He followed right behind us. We sped north toward Carbon Canyon Road at thirty miles per hour.

My left arm was in agony. I knew I wouldn't be able to pitch for several months. But at the moment I was worried about Stubby. Had to be serious, or maybe Stubby already had died.

My heart was in my throat again, lodged up there like a baseball.

We veered right on Carbon Canyon, the same road I had

driven with Mr. Webber, and we sped uphill for three-and-a-half miles. I heard the brakes screech. A left turn signal. We bounced against the wheel well, and the truck climbed a dirt road four-hundred feet along the canyonside.

We stopped. We all jumped out. Didn't even lower the tailgate.

A Santa Ana wind blew in our faces.

There was Stubby's truck below us, rolled upside-down against a boulder at the base of the ravine with a scattered and burst pallet of clay tile. Stubby had piled so much weight above the axle on his pickup truck it had broken while he'd driven up the road with all those pallets. Three other pallets had miraculously been spared.

The truck had rolled onto his arm. He was trapped beneath his cab. His blood streamed down the boulder and then soaked into the dirt.

I shimmied down the hillside around greasewood and white sage to get to Stubby. "He's got a pulse," I shouted, tearing off my jersey.

The cop was fifteen feet behind me. Two more police cars had arrived, bringing a total of six cops. They'd brought chains to move the pickup truck.

Skeeter helped me tie my jersey for a tourniquet on Stubby Carson's forearm. We used a stick just like the *Boy Scout Handbook* said to stop the bleeding.

Stubby was in and out of consciousness, moaning and then stopping. Cops wrapped chains around the door hinges and rolled the truck off Stubby. In spite of my sore arm I somehow helped pull him to safety. We carried him uphill to the police car.

He was unconscious now. His left hand was so mangled we all knew there were no doctors in Orange County who could save it.

We stuffed him into the back seat, and the car raced back to town, carrying Stubby, red lights blinking, sirens wailing into the evening.

I said a prayer for Stubby. A lump lodged in my throat when it occurred to me I shouldn't call him Stubby any more.

The Orange County General Hospital rose like an antebellum mansion up from beanfields and orchards in West Orange off Chapman Avenue. It boasted 27 acres of Valencias on-site, plus a herd of pure-bred Holsteins that were needed for fresh milk. Skeeter and I rode in the flatbed up its palm-lined concrete driveway. It had been more than an hour since we'd watched police cars race down Carbon Canyon Road with Stubby. Still, our hearts were in our throats. I sprinted toward the lobby to find out all that I could.

Inside, a nurse informed us Stubby was alive and still in surgery, but that was all she knew. He was in critical condition. We waited for more news, reading our pamphlets in the lobby telling us Orange County General was built in 1914. It had 125 beds. It had an almshouse for the poor, it had a psychopathic wing built just last year, and it had three surgeons, three obstetricians, a pathologist and six graduate nurses. I didn't care but read my pamphlet several times. It was the only thing I had to keep my mind off Stubby Carson.

He'd been a friend to me, a mentor. I didn't want to see him die.

His wife, Elaine, walked in, escorted by the Webbers and Coach Merritt's new wife, Caroline. I hadn't known that Mrs. Webber's name was Hope. It seemed appropriate right now.

Stubby's wife wept uncontrollably while sitting in a cushioned wicker chair off in a corner in-between a pair of sagging potted palms.

Sunrays poured in through the window. Mrs. Merritt and Mrs. Webber sat with Elaine. Coach Merritt paced across the white honeycomb tile, the way he paced when we were losing. "You heard anything?" Coach asked a nurse.

"He's in surgery."

"I know." Coach made a face.

"Doctor Burlew is quite capable."

Coach Merritt huffed and turned away.

We bit our lips, swallowing anger at the hospital's bureaucracy.

I went to speak with Mrs. Carson. Asked her how I might help out.

She told me, "Finish Irwin's roofing jobs."

I promised I'd take care of them. Skeeter and Ed and Colleen Harris said they'd work with me tomorrow, and Mr. Webber even offered me the car keys to his Packard.

Aaron Slayback strolled inside with Mayor Metcalfe right behind him.

Skeeter looked at me. "Impressive how they take care of their own."

"Yeah," I said, recalling Pa's death, when Ma and I had felt abandoned.

Skeeter looked at me again. "Good thing Stubby has his Klan friends."

I nodded, and a quiet understanding passed between us.

It was dark, and many hours had passed. The waiting room was filled with men and women. Reverend Myers was here praying with Mrs. Carson. I noticed all the men around me wearing little blood-cross pins in their lapels. They'd come for Stubby, and to show their solidarity.

It occurred to me how all of us need somebody to talk to when life hurts us, and the Ku Klux Klan was there to fill the vacuum like their family. Stubby's family, Mr. Webber's family. All of them were hurting, needing friends in a tough world.

Ten minutes later, Doctor Burlew made his way into the lobby. He had a word with Mrs. Carson. Reverend Myers went back with them. White steel doors swung back and forth as half the lobby held our breaths.

Reverend Myers walked back out and motioned all of us to join him in the corner by the potted palms where the women were all sitting.

"Is he okay?" Coach Merritt asked.

Reverend Myers dropped his gaze. "He's out of surgery."

"What's that mean?"

"They...." He took a breath.

"Don't sugar-coat it," Mrs. Merritt said.

"The doctors had to amputate. They cut off Irwin's arm leaving a stump below the elbow."

"But he's stable?" Mr. Webber asked.

"For now. We need to pray. He won't wake up until tomorrow when the morphine has worn off." We bowed our heads, and we stood silent for a minute and a half. Weeping men and women cleared their throats like they were trying to act strong. They were hurting for their friend, who'd lost an arm. And he was *my* friend and my mentor.

"Amen," said Reverend Myers.

After that there wasn't very much to say.

Mrs. Webber said she'd organize the women to bring casseroles.

Coach Merritt looked at me. At Skeeter. He said, "You both played a good game," then looked away.

Mrs. Carson and Mrs. Webber said they needed to go home, and Mr. Webber walked us all out to his Packard in the dark.

As we rode back into Anaheim in Mr. Webber's Packard with his wife and Mrs. Carson, my thoughts whirled like a toy top. There were those KIGY letters on the pavement and on stop signs. For those inside the Klan, it told them Anaheim was their home.

And people needed a safe place, a place where they could be themselves, admit to others they were scared, and help each other through their troubles. The Klan provided that for them. It was their family, their lodge. The Ku Klux Klan was there to help them when their churches let them down the way my own church had the year my father'd died.

We let out Mrs. Carson at their well-kept orange bungalow on Palm Street. Mr. Webber dropped his wife off at their house then drove us both to Warren Glover's since he knew I hadn't eaten. "Order anything you want, Dean."

"How about meatloaf?"

"Let's have steak." I saw a grin and knew that Mr. Webber needed me tonight.

We sipped our coffee. He told us Ed and Colleen's father, Harry Harris, would be replacing Irwin Carson as our Kladd the next months. He also told me there were lots of jobs that Irwin had lined up. His superintendent could handle school days, but I'd need to take the weekends.

I told him, "I'll do everything I can to help him out."

"You're a good man," Mr. Webber said. "You're going to be an asset to the Klan."

I changed the subject. "How is Helen, sir?"

He frowned. "Dean, I'm concerned."

The waiter came and brought our steaks, with baked potatoes and a teepee of asparagus stalks fresh from Slayback's market cooked in butter.

"I hope she's healthy by next weekend."

"She better be," he said. "Hope bought her prom gown last Monday night. Set me back almost thirty dollars. It's gorgeous, and I'd hate to think I wasted that much money on a prom my lovely daughter and her beau never attended." He met my gaze and touched the back of my right hand and told me, "Thanks."

I said, "You're welcome," feeling odd, as if my pa had never died, and I'd grown up, and Mr. Webber and I ended up best friends.

I cut a bite out of my steak.

I don't remember ever tasting meat so sweet in my whole life. After that we didn't speak of Helen.

SATURDAY, MAY 31, 1924

The next morning I woke up at five a.m. to the alarm clock shouting at me. I had my paper route, and then a roof to finish tiling. I dusted off a faded picture of my father on my nightstand. Today was Decoration Day, the remembrance for the war dead. Pa had been sitting there and smiling for so long he'd gotten dusty. I wiped the glass off on the leg of my pajama pants and stared back at his photograph. What would Pa think if he had not died in the war? Would he be proud? I'd grown taller than he'd stood in all his life. Would he be angry he had died, serving his country and the Army without receiving any medals in remembrance? I had no way of ever knowing. I only knew how much I missed him. As did Ma. But somehow both of us had managed to survive, pasting on smiles while our hearts had never healed.

I passed my mother in the hallway in her tattered towel-cloth slippers and her bathrobe. I noticed the doc had taken off her cast. I hardly saw her any more with all my studies, and my baseball, and my jobs. I said, "Morning, Ma."

"Good morning, Dean," she murmured, her voice showing no warmness or expression.

I hurried out the front door to the porch to fold my newspapers. I had meant to do it after supper but had spent all night at the hospital. I had a stack of them. Skeeter's photo was on the bottom of Page One below the fold, where it said Anaheim had beaten Santa Ana. It made me smile we were champions. I wrapped the papers with rubber bands, folding and wrapping.

Then I ran out of rubber bands.

There were more in the garage. I found them in their Mason jar. I brought the jar out to the porch to finish folding all my papers. Someone had parked a shiny V-63 Cadillac a block away. The car was lipstick red.

I knew exactly who it was.

Margaret.

I froze. *What was she doing here?*

I glared at her.

She waved. Margaret started up the engine and skedaddled.

A knot reformed inside my stomach.

I finished folding newspapers, so nervous both hands trembled. I loaded up my saddle bags and pedaled off to work. I was troubled about why Margaret's car was parked outside my house. It was creepy, and I had this feeling Margaret was trailing me. I was beginning to have thoughts being good-looking was a pain. I had several women chasing me. I wished that it might stop. I understood now Helen Webber had the same problem as me.

Except she liked how men adored her.

I preferred to be monogamous.

There was so much more to process. Irwin Carson had lost his arm. Helen was a wild child. I'd wounded Alma Martin. There was the matter of the Ku Klux Klan. My life had gotten complicated. It was the weekend of Decoration Day. I needed time to think. And time to grieve. And time to catch up with my ma who rarely saw me.

But I'd promised Irwin's wife I'd work to finish up their roof jobs. I was concerned who would take care of Irwin once his jobs were done. It was hard to sign new clients when he was sitting in a hospital.

I grabbed my bicycle and pedaled toward the dawn. The sun peeked over the horizon. I needed to race to finish my paper route in time to start my roofing job. Too much was on my plate, but I was glad it kept me occupied with so many hard challenges ahead.

Mr. Webber had his car running with Skeeter and Colleen in the back seat when I returned. They both wore dungarees and t-shirts. Colleen wore makeup, clearly trying to look her best to impress Skeeter, who hadn't even combed his hair to Colleen's marked disappointment.

I rolled my bike to the garage and tugged the door down, locked the padlock, ran and jumped into the front seat.

We pulled out into traffic. Mr. Webber asked if I could find the map inside the glove box.

Skeeter told him we had both been at the accident site yesterday.

Mr. Webber shook his head. "I like a map to know exactly where I'm going." He checked his watch the way he did when he was nervous. I pulled the glove box open, sorting through its contents. A coffee-stained and stapled pamphlet tumbled down into the floor well.

I glanced down at my feet and cringed. It said this:

KLORAN
Knights of the Ku Klux Klan of Kalifornia
K-Uno
Karacter—Honor—Duty
This book is the property of the
Knights of the Ku Klux Klan (incorporated) and is loaned to
358977, Realm of Kalifornia

My throat went dryer than a slag furnace. I turned the pamphlet upside-down and placed it back into the glove box.

Mr. Webber hadn't noticed.

I found his Rand McNally road map of the Los Angeles basin, folded it open to show Orange County and handed the map to Mr. Webber.

He signaled right at Carbon Canyon. Five minutes later we all stood where Irwin's truck and his clay tile pallets had rolled into the ravine. We tied a chain to the rear bumper frame on Mr. Webber's Packard, and I scrambled down the gully and wrapped more chain around the pallet.

Colleen gathered up loose roof tiles. Skeeter lugged them up the slope. Mr. Webber threw his Packard into gear and let the clutch out. The chain jerked taut. Colleen and Skeeter hacked black sage out from the pallet's path as Mr. Webber dragged it up the hillside to the roadway.

The next two pallets came up even easier than the first.

Aaron Slayback arrived in his grocery truck. He shifted into first and hauled the pallets up to the jobsite, a hacienda overlooking Carbon Canyon. The Anaheim cops who had arrested me showed up riding their motorcycles. Two more cops in cars brought us an extra roll of felt.

We got to work. I showed Colleen and Skeeter how to tack the felt down to the roof deck while the four policemen nailed down the battens. I laid down flashing. By lunchtime we were ready to set tile.

Mr. Webber and Aaron Slayback had returned to bring us sandwiches. We wolfed them down along two cold bottles of Ward's Orange Crush apiece. Then we started laying tile. With nine of us, the work went quickly.

By sunset we were finished. I set the bird stops and the cap tiles, mortaring the last pieces into place.

I'd hang the gutters and the downspouts up tomorrow.

We piled into cars and drove to Central Park in Anaheim to celebrate.

For the first time since my father died, I felt like I could have a family if I wanted one.

I just wasn't sure my parents would approve.

I missed my simple life. I'd been confused since meeting Helen.

The flagpole I had seen them digging up after the baseball game was already in place at Central Park when we arrived. But for the moment I was spellbound. This time *two* aeroplanes flew north from Santa Ana. I stood beside the flagpole and admired them.

One was fire-engine red, the other black and yellow like a wasp. They even sounded like two wasps as they approached. They separated. One of them swung north and flew toward Fullerton. The yellow one winged westward toward Long Beach.

I shut my eyes. I fantasized and wished that I could fly. It seemed impossible right now, but *they* were flying. Boys could dream. But I was full of dreams my mother said, like pitching in the Majors. Ma told me I needed to be somewhat more pragmatic.

"Hello, Dean." I looked up, surprised that Mayor Elmer Metcalf had just greeted me.

Mr. Harris said they'd both been there for hours. Warren Glover and his wife showed up with tubs of deep-fried chicken. Aaron Slayback brought two crates of Bubble-Up and two big watermelons. All of us were starved and couldn't wait to start the feast.

Mrs. Carson carved the melons, handing each of us a slice while Mr. Harris told Colleen that this was where they'd have their rally. His drawl was thicker than Colleen's.

He said, "That's why we moved the flagpole." He explained how when he'd moved here people all around Orange County drove to Anaheim to drink. "It was a wet town in them days. Most of the other towns were dry. Then Leon Myers came from Redlands, and he started his men's Bible study at our church.

It grew so fast it turned into a Ku Klux Klan Klavern. The last election four of our members were elected to City Council."

"Four of them?" said Skeeter. Colleen Harris raised a finger to her lips. "Shush," she whispered. "Such things aren't publicly known."

"Because their membership is secret," I told Skeeter. "Like the letter said."

"What letter?"

"The one we both mailed to P.O. Box 16?"

"It has to be that way. Did y'all know ten of eleven policemen on the force are in our Klavern?" Mr. Harris asked.

Skeeter asked, "What about the other guy?"

"He's half Mexican. He probably won't be with us too much longer, but we can't get rid of everyone at once. It wouldn't look right."

My jaw dropped. This had been going on in front of our own eyes, while Anaheim was unaware of the extent of Klan control.

"We've all been praying this big rally makes Anaheim a model Klan city," said Leon Myers who'd just walked up along with councilman Aaron Slayback.

A model Klan city?

A chunk of watermelon stuck inside my throat. I coughed and stammered out, "Excuse me." I rose and tried to walk it off.

"Y'all okay?" asked Colleen Harris.

I nodded, staggering toward the restrooms, feeling the watermelon painfully inch its way down my esophagus. It even hurt to breathe, but I needed a time-out.

There was so much here to process. I had no quarrel with the Klan, and they'd been nice to me. Exceptionally nice. Too nice, in fact. Now as a local home-town hero taking Helen to the prom. I had no wiggle room. I had to stay the course.

People depended on me. Helen needed her escort. Skeeter and Colleen needed a ride. Mr. Webber needed me to spy on Helen. Irwin Carson needed me to mind his business on the weekend. After my arm healed, Coach Merritt needed me to pitch next season. There were just too many apple carts. I couldn't upset *all* of them.

Yet I couldn't help but think of Alma Martin.

She'd been a friend to me, my only friend the year my Pa had died, bringing her macaroons and sweetness, telling me with her French accent she was desolate when ordinary folks weren't even sad. Such a sweet person who, for some reason, had turned into an outcast.

"Why do they hate us?" I could still hear Alma's voice asking her question on her front porch months ago, mopping tears and asking why they had chased off her Uncle Raymond. *"Calling us bootleggers, and Frogs, and filthy Catholics, and telling us America's for Americans. They tell us we should all go home. This is my home. They blame the war on us. We're French. We didn't start it."*

I hadn't any clue who "they" were.

Until now.

And I didn't understand why they saw Alma as their enemy. She'd never said a mean word in her life.

But she was Catholic.

I made my way back to the party. Mr. Harris said they'd organized a blood drive, "just for Irwin, to make certain all the blood he gets is *white* blood."

"Nothing but pure blood out of red-blooded Americans," Irwin's wife said. To her, this evidently was important.

Alma Martin's blood was every bit as red as all the rest of ours. I'm certain she would donate all she could, had someone asked.

But I said nothing.

Tomorrow would be Decoration Day, and the men in Central Park were all wrapped up in flags and crosses.

They all enjoyed their deep-fried chicken.

I was too troubled to partake. I couldn't eat. I couldn't even finish off my Bubble-Up.

CHAPTER X

FRIDAY, JUNE 6, 1924

On prom night, driving Mr. Webber's Packard to our high school, I felt nervous in my Turton's Men's Wear combination suit. Skeeter Wilson and Colleen Harris rode along in the back seat. Helen sat beside me, looking as pale as the harvest moon that rose on the horizon as I parked behind the high school. Colleen and Skeeter had even thought to color-coordinate their outfits. The red in Skeeter's bow-tie matched Colleen's red dress and lipstick.

The school had lit up the gymnasium with searchlights on both sides like we were going to a motion picture opening in Hollywood. The doors were framed in colored buntings with the theme in big white letters:

ANAHEIM ALL-AMERICAN PROM
MUSIC BY GLEN OSWALD'S SERENADERS

The orchestra was tuning up inside.

I made my way around the Packard and helped Helen out the passenger door. It was misty out, but not so wet we needed an umbrella. I had this feeling in my gut the evening wasn't going to go well. It had started with the look I got when pinning Helen's corsage onto her dress only to learn she hadn't bought a boutonnière.

She wrote it off to being sick. Her ma had come to Helen's rescue with a faded red carnation she'd plucked out of an arrangement on their mantle. Her father glared at Helen like *he* was disappointed, and I braced, getting a look from Helen as cold as liquid nitrogen, while her mother pinned the flower into place on my lapel.

Still her prom dress was as stunning as her father had described. Pink satin, covered with more beads than any jewelry store in Hollywood, accentuated with a beaded purse and matching pink high heels. She was Marion-Davies-glamourous but Greta-Garbo-distant. It seemed her thoughts were somewhere else. She pushed her manicured bobbed hair off her forehead, twirled her rope of pearls in classic flapper fashion with one hand pressed against her hip as if it only lacked a cigarette. She glared.

"Are you okay?" I finally asked.

"Everything is copacetic," Helen said, her tone of voice making it obvious it wasn't. But it was not the time to press matters. Prom night was only getting started. I wanted to make happy and fun memories tonight if only Helen would cooperate.

We made our way into the gym.

Skeeter and Colleen seemed more enamored with each other than Mary Pickford and her swashbuckling heartthrob, Douglas Fairbanks. I'd landed in a different movie. I wasn't sure what I had done, but felt as welcome as Lon Cheney in

The Hunchback of Notre Dame with Patsy Ruth Miller playing Esmeralda offering me water.

Helen asked me, "Can we leave?"

Having seen her at the Bon Ton Ballroom chased by half of Hollywood, I understood that Anaheim, to her, was small potatoes.

"Care to dance?" I offered, shrugging.

Helen looked down at her watch the way her father did and acted like she hadn't even heard me. She twirled her pearls again. Glen Oswald's Serenaders serenaded. A cacophony of banjo strumming filled up the gymnasium.

In the winter, in the summer, don't we have fun?
Times are bum and getting bummer. Still we have fun.
There's nothing surer; the rich get rich, and the poor get children.
In the meantime, in-between time, ain't we got fun?

Alma Martin made her entrance on Boomer Corrigan's left arm. I felt good for them, excited, knowing both had lost their parents. Alma glowed, wearing a simple cotton dress she'd sewn herself. It wasn't beaded, but it sure made her look pretty in the crowd. Even though she'd worn her cheaters, their lenses reflecting red balloons, clearly Boomer was in love.

Another verse. *Ain't we got fun?*

Boomer waved at me. "Great prom. You kids look great."

I told him, "Thank you."

The school gymnasium was decorated with red, white, and blue streamers. Miss Elgena served as chaperone. She ladled cups of fresh-squeezed orange juice to the guests. I smiled at the beverage they had chosen.

Helen chortled. "What did you expect, Dean? This is Anaheim."

She popped open her compact beaded purse. It held a pint bottle of Hennessy's. She used it to add flavor to her orange juice. "Care for a small jorum of skee?" She winked at me.

I said, "No, thank you." I didn't remember Esmeralda serving liquor.

"Aw, Mrs. Grundy, you're no fun." Helen shot a sideways glare. "You're such a wurp. Have you been sent by William Burns to apprehend me. Are you an agent of the BOI to rat me out to the authorities?"

I shut my mouth. There wasn't anything, in fact, that I could say. Was I supposed to tell a teacher that my date doctored her drink? I sat by helplessly while Helen downed her cocktail in two gulps. She grabbed my arm. "Let's blow this joint."

"And go to where?"

"Laguna Beach."

I mentioned Skeeter and Colleen.

"We'll come back later," Helen said. "Give Skeeter time to get some nookie. Colleen's hot for him. She told me. There's a party in Laguna at Crazy Florence's tonight."

"This is our *prom*."

"Anaheim's boring. Bunch of rubes here. Flat tires. Dean, let's go somewhere exciting." She grabbed more orange juice, reenacting the same ritual. This wasn't Helen's first minuet, and she'd perfected getting snockered when she needed to, which seemed to be tonight.

Glen Oswald's Serenaders finished retuning their instruments. A drum rolled from a bandshell at the end of the gymnasium. Led by clarinets and trumpets, they played a song from Isham Jones. Colleen tugged Skeeter to the dance floor. She was singing with the lyrics. "It had to be you...the somebody who...." Couples circled, dancing foxtrots.

I stood in envy, watching Alma on the floor with Boomer Corrigan. I was thrilled to see her happy, but I swallowed back my jealousy.

Helen downed another cocktail, her third, if not her fourth, and I was wishing I had drunk some of her liquor to prevent her from consuming an entire pint of brandy by herself.

Helen had an edge. She was obviously tipsy. I stood beside her, held her steady while our classmates all had fun. The orchestra now played a Charleston, and everybody got out on the floor, except for Helen who complained that she was bored.

"Can we leave now?" Helen asked.

"This is our prom. Try to enjoy it."

"I'm out of brandy."

"Then perhaps we'll have to dance. I hear it's fun."

"Let's go find a pint of brown."

I draped my arm around my date. Nuzzled her neck. "Let's dance, okay? Shame to waste that gorgeous dress."

"There's a party in Labeana Gooch. I need you to chauffeur me."

"I'm sure all Hollywood will be there?"

Helen flashed a grin.

"Your dad won't let me. It's his car. For some odd reason, the man trusts me."

She staggered toward the exit door. "And it's starting to annoy me."

There was a drum roll. Glen Oswald's Serenaders sat with their trombones, trumpets, and tubas on the floor as the gymnasium went silent.

Mr. Cox, the high school principal, stepped quickly to the podium. He wore a too-tight dinner jacket. It looked old enough to vote. "And now the moment you've been waiting for." The microphone gave feedback. Mr. Cox took a step backward until the screeching finally stopped, then said, "Your prom queen." He had an envelope. He held it overhead.

Girls glanced at each other, at Mr. Cox, and then at Helen, as if everyone expected she'd be coronated as prom queen. I propped her up and felt her wavering. I panicked.

Another drumroll.

Mr. Cox opened the envelope.

"BARBARA BANNERMAN," he yelled.

"Jeepers creepers. That lousy quiff?" Helen glared at me in fury.

Somewhere inside of the gymnasium a cheer went out for Barbara, who blushed a shade of pink brighter than Helen's beaded flapper dress. Barbara was escorted to the dance floor by her date. We watched her cry as she was crowned with her tiara.

Helen turned white. I dared not say she was in no shape to be prom queen, but she wanted it. She seethed. She glared at me as if I somehow had betrayed her. She was shaking. Then she paled. Helen turned toward me and retched.

I had no chance to get out of the way.

Orange juice laced with Hennessy went all over my suit.

She broke away. I watched her stagger toward the exit.

People laughed.

I rushed to find myself a towel. Dashed toward the men's room. Threw cold water on my shirt. Tore off my coat and ran it underneath the faucet, hoping cold water would wash away the stench of Helen's puke.

It didn't, but it helped reduce the staining.

I staggered back onto the dance floor with my jacket on my arm, reeking of liquor. Glanced around.

Helen was nowhere to be found.

"Where'd she go?" I asked Colleen.

Skeeter pointed toward the exit.

Barbara Bannerman and Guy McCay were dancing by themselves. *Memory Lane* a song made famous by Fred Waring's Pennsylvanians. Somehow Colleen had Helen's purse. I raced outside to find my date.

Helen had disappeared into the mist.

A fog blanketed Anaheim. June gloom was right on schedule. I found my way out to the Packard, hoping Helen would be waiting. But she wasn't. I popped the trunk to lose my vomit-scented suit coat. It was ruined now. Besides it smelled as if I had been drinking.

Skeeter raced up with Colleen. "Look, Colleen found one of her shoes."

They were high heels. We found the other one. She'd dropped it in a trash can and had evidently taken off to someplace in her stocking feet.

"There she is!" I yelled. "On Center Street." Helen was so drunk she was teetering.

We piled into the Packard.

A Model T swerved to avoid her. Honked its horn.

I made a sharp left turn and pulled out into traffic, but the light turned red at Palm Street.

Helen padded down the sidewalk.

At Los Angeles Street, a bus stopped. Helen staggered up its steps and got on board.

"Crap," I said palming my forehead in despair.

She had managed to evade us.

My heart sank like a rock dropped into water.

What on earth would I tell Helen's father?

Stuck at a "STOP" signal with a traffic cop an inch from my rear bumper, and with a jacket in the trunk that reeked and smelled like a distillery, I watched the motor coach make its way south along Los Angeles Street, past Oak, Chestnut, and Broadway, to Ball Road.

Then it was gone.

At last the traffic signal gonged, and the "GO" semaphore popped up. But with that cop in my rear view, I had to drive below the speed limit. The motor coach Helen was riding disappeared into the night.

"Nuts," we said in unison.

"We have to find her." Colleen said. "She's my best friend. If Helen's drunk they'll make her spend a night in jail...."

I asked, "Okay, where do we find her?"

"How would I know?" Colleen snapped, her voice trembling with panic.

"That bus heads down to Santa Ana," Skeeter said. "To where the trolleys stop," "We're never gonna find her if she transfers to a Red Car."

"Did she say anything to you, Dean?" Colleen asked.

"Laguna Beach," I said. "She begged for me to take her to a party. I said no."

"Well then get going. There are no trolleys and no buses to Laguna."

"Where's the map?" I said.

"The glove compartment." Skeeter shoved the passenger seat

down and popped the glove box, leaning over the front seat.

A stack of business cards fell out onto the floor. He found the map.

"Look for a phone booth," Colleen said. "She'll have to call to get a ride."

I took Los Angeles to Manchester. We crossed the city limit into the county. Seeing no cops, I pressed my foot down on the gas. Farms and orchards along Manchester raced past us on both sides. Left on Chapman. We crossed the Santa Ana River past the hospital and finally made a sharp right onto Main toward Santa Ana.

"There's the bus," Colleen yelled out.

"Great. It's going the wrong way."

"Was Helen on it?"

"I didn't see her," Skeeter said.

"Did you look?"

"Of course I looked."

"Hey, there she is!" I yelled.

Cars honked. She was staggering down Main Street in her dress and her bare stockings where Colleen pointed her finger.

Just then, a motorcycle stopped, and she jumped on behind the rider, and the two of them sped off, turning down First Street.

They didn't see us.

The motorcycle whined and they sped off into the moonlight.

My chest closed up in panic.

I floored the Packard in pursuit.

It was a red Indian motorcycle, a 1924. I sped to follow it down First Street. Then we zig-zagged across Tustin. They were clearly trying to lose us, and that meant Helen had seen her father's Packard. East of Tustin, the motorcycle took the Coast Road.

They headed south toward San Diego. The motorcycle headlight blazed through the orange groves and the berry fields on both sides of the highway. At Irvine station they veered right, speeding south along Sand Canyon. Oak trees lined the roadway. The Indian climbed up toward the saddle where the road left Irvine Ranch and wandered down Laguna Canyon.

I slammed the Packard into gear. Luckily the road was paved, except I knew at any moment they might turn onto a side road to get rid of us.

And they did. A half a mile down Laguna Canyon Road, the motorcycle swerved and made its way around an iron gate and rumbled onto a trail down a slope through chaparral.

There was no way we could follow in a Packard.

The motorcycle shifted gears, like it was trying to climb a grade. We heard a load groan then a whine.

A blood-curdling scream. It flowed like ice throughout my gut.

"That scream was Helen!" Colleen shrieked. She was right, and thoughts of horror ricocheted inside my brain. I screeched the Packard to a halt.

For thirty seconds, we didn't hear another sound.

Three of us sat inside the Packard, knowing Helen and her driver were in trouble. We felt helpless. There were no cars on the road. I cupped my right hand to my ear and listened hard.

Silence.

I grabbed a flashlight from the glove compartment. I jumped out, followed by Skeeter and Colleen."

I waved the flashlight down the trail like a wig-wag. My heart hammered. We scrambled past the gate and we descended down the trail through chaparral into the canyon.

We followed motorcycle tire tracks along a brush-filled

hillside through prickly pear and laurel sumac. The trail descended into willows. I wagged the flashlight in the dark to find our way along a lakebed. The flashlight battery was dying. I turned it off for now.

I smelled gasoline.

"That's them."

Helen was groaning in the dark. "Ouch, my arm."

"Shut up, you bitch. I've had enough of your damn crap."

"I'm hurt, you sap. I think I broke something."

"Well, why the hell should I care? I just wrecked a seven-hundred-dollar motorcycle, dammit."

"Futz your lousy motorcycle."

SLAP.

"Ow! How dare you."

SLAP-SLAP-SLAP.

I turned the flashlight on.

Predictably, the slaps stopped.

I was staring at John Gilbert. His lips curled into a sneer.

Helen glared at us, terrified and obviously drunk. Her arm was bent at a weird angle, looking seriously broken.

I shined the flashlight toward the motorcycle driver. He jumped up. He staggered toward me, swinging fists.

I glanced at Helen.

"Duck," said Skeeter.

I was fortunate John Gilbert didn't know I was a lefty.

I smashed my gritted fist into his temple.

He looked at me. At Skeeter, eyes bulged out as big as golf balls, then he reeled and collapsed into the dirt.

Helen was sobbing.

"C'mon. Get up," I whispered, stretching out a hand to her.

"I'm staying here."

"You're drunk." I wrapped my arm around her knees and slung her over my left shoulder like a sack full of potatoes.

"Take me. To the party. With Crazy Florence. In Laguna."

She punched my back using her fist and then complained about her arm. She squirmed. I grabbed her tighter and staggered forward like a cave man.

After two minutes of screaming, Helen passed out.

Ten minutes later at the Packard, Skeeter helped me load her into the back seat.

Colleen sat with her.

Skeeter and I jumped in the front, and we sped up Laguna Canyon Road at forty miles an hour.

We hightailed back to Anaheim in 27 minutes. Skeeter was staring at his pocket watch. Colleen sat back with Helen. Luckily, Helen was asleep. Thank God, she couldn't moan or retch. I signaled onto Clementine and screeched into her driveway.

Jumped outside. Dashed to the porch. Rang the doorbell.

No one home.

It was past midnight. I rang the bell again and pounded on the door.

"Where the heck are Helen's parents?" Skeeter called out from the car.

I shrugged and hollered back I didn't know.

"We gotta get her to a doctor," Colleen called from the back seat.

"Without her parents?" Skeeter asked.

I made my way back to the Packard. "Her arm won't heal on its own," I said and jumped into the driver's seat. I fished the car key from my pocket and crammed it into the ignition, threw the Packard into reverse and backed the car out onto Clementine.

Helen moaned and groaned but remained unconscious.

I signaled right onto Los Angeles, left and onto Manchester, raced past the Anaheim city limits and those KIGY letters.

Left on Chapman. The silhouettes of Orange County General grew larger, like an antebellum Mississippi mansion.

The fragrance of Valencias still lingered at one a.m., as I sped through citrus orchards outside Orange County General. Skeeter sprang out of the Packard. Colleen cradled Helen's arm. Between the three of us, we managed to slide Helen from the back seat, propping her between Skeeter and me on both her sides.

Her eyes opened. She didn't seem aware of where she was. Colleen held open doors so we could carry Helen inside. She was still conked. Helen's bare feet floated an inch above the white hexagonal floor tile that led toward emergency admissions.

A shoe-faced nurse, old enough she might have served with Clara Barton, sat at a rickety oak desk reading a Willa Cather novel. She glared at me, lifting her eyeglasses. She gave Helen a look and scowled. "You scoundrels. You boys both should be ashamed."

"She broke her arm," I said.

"She's drunk. I have a mind to call the sheriff," said the nurse.

Colleen broke in. "We're just her friends. She needs a doctor."

"Fine friends *you* are. Where's her parents?"

"We tried to reach them," Skeeter said. "They aren't home. I found his card back in the floor well of the Packard." Skeeter reached into his shirt pocket. He stared down at the card. His face turned white. His eyes were wider than two super-jumbo marbles, and his jaw dropped like a Spittin' Bill Doak breaking ball in newsreels. "Holy sh..."

I looked over Skeeter's shoulder.

And I read:

YOU HAVE BEEN PAID A SOCIAL VISIT BY THE
KNIGHTS OF THE

KU KLUX KLAN.

DON'T MAKE THE NEXT VISIT A BUSINESS CALL.

I had seen the stack of cards without knowing what they said. They had dropped into the floor well of the Packard at the high school after Skeeter found the glove compartment map of Orange County. All along I had been thinking they were business cards, like Skeeter thought.

"May I see that?" asked the nurse.

"That's not his card, it's someone else's," said Colleen, who somehow managed to stay calmer than the rest of us.

"I'll need a phone number."

I swallowed, and my head spun with emotions: Helen's betrayal at the Bon Ton, getting drunk to ruin our prom, running off to see John Gilbert. She was gorgeous, but a handful. I felt awful that she had a broken arm, but I'd lost patience. Now Skeeter'd found that awful business card. They'd said it was a social club.

Clearly, there was more to it than they'd told me.

Colleen gave the nurse the phone number I knew. "Eighty-five L."

I smiled at Colleen. I was glad she'd come along.

Waking, Helen rocked her head. "Take me to Laguna Beach,"

she slurred, then dry-heaved. Thank heaven there was not much left to retch.

The nurse picked up the telephone.

"I've been a very naughty girl." Helen glared at me and muttered, but her voice cracked when she spoke. "Get me out of here right now." Her gaze was level, and it seemed she'd sobered up in a mere second.

"You broke your arm, honey," Colleen said, "when you fell off Johnny's Indian."

"Daddy will KILL me. Take me home," she shrieked and tried to wiggle free. She winced in pain. "Ouch." She glanced down at her arm, saw it was twisted, swollen up.

"Helen, I don't think you can leave," I said. "It's broken. I'm so sorry."

Helen acted like she hadn't even heard me.

She held her stomach with her good arm, eased into a chair and started sobbing.

Two orderlies emerged through swinging doors, bringing a wheelchair.

The nurse told us we'd have to wait outside the double doors.

My mind spun in confusion, but I quickly fell asleep on an antiquated sofa in the corner.

SATURDAY, JUNE 7, 1924

When I woke up, it was dawn. We were still inside the waiting room. Colleen was sleeping like an angel with her head in Skeeter's lap. My mind was whirling with emotions. Everything had come unhinged. All I'd done was what I'd promised, escorting Helen to the prom. But she was more than I could handle. Despite her beauty and her charm, I wished I'd never even met her.

The shoe-faced nurse walked my direction. "So I see you've woken up," she said. "'Bout time, big boy."

"Is Helen...?"

"Doctor McCay would like to speak with you."

"With me?"

"Says it's important." Her eyebrow lifted in contempt.

A man walked out wearing a suit, and he escorted me behind the double doors into his antiquated office.

"We need to have a conversation, son."

"'Bout what?"

"I think you know."

"I'm very sorry, sir. I *don't* know." I held my breath and swallowed hard. I felt my fingers fidget, stuffed in both my pockets out of sight. I looked away, wondering why I had been asked to see the doctor.

"Son, this is *not* a time for levity. No laughing matter whatsoever. You've been spooning with your girlfriend, and I'm sad to say there's been a complication."

"We've only kissed."

"Oh, come on. Damn it, Dean. The doctors did their best, but —" Doctor McCay inhaled deeply "— We found a lacerated cervix." He shook his head. "Badly infected, as if she'd stabbed her baby daughter with an icepick or a file. Helen miscarried last night. Her baby had been dead for several days."

"What? She was pregnant?"

"Don't get smart with me. Three months."

"But that's impossible. I never...."

"Son, I have no time for any more phonus-balonus."

I slid back into my chair.

The doctor shifted forward, every wrinkle in his brow accusing me of fornication. I had no words to prove my innocence. I hadn't known Helen was pregnant.

But dots connected in my mind.

The Bon Ton Ballroom. John Gilbert. Helen was sick the prior week, and she'd been moody. She'd put on weight. How could I have been so blind? I thought of Helen, and my heart seemed to implode in disappointment.

I got a hard look from the doctor like he'd never ever met a kid as stupid as I suddenly believed myself to be. But I would keep it to myself. I needed time to sort things out, and if I argued with a doctor that solved no problems at all.

I walked out through the double doors alone, hanging my head.

"Lucky for her she broke her arm," the doctor said. "It saved her life."

Colleen dashed my direction. She was sobbing like a baby.

"Did you hear?" she said.

"On Helen?"

"We just saw Alma leave the hospital."

"WHAT?" My pulse stopped in midbeat.

"Boomer Corrigan was killed last night. A car crash."

"Was she with him?" My mind flooded with dread. Two decent people, Alma and Boomer. *They'd been perfect for each other. How could* this *happen?*

"He dropped her off," Colleen whispered, swallowing tears. "Outside her house. Alma just told me Boomer never made it home. He flipped his truck. Front tire blew out on his old man's REO Speedwagon."

"Where?"

"A mile west of Anaheim on Center Street."

"Colleen, how awful." My words sounded as hollow as I felt, as if whatever heart I had had just been ripped out of my chest.

I wondered why people like Alma had to suffer so much hardship. She'd lost her parents, and her uncle had been driven out of town. Now Boomer Corrigan died on prom night. Boomer had lost his parents too. It was like Alma and Boomer Corrigan had been meant to be together. She'd looked so happy in his arms, arms that would never again hold her. It almost seemed like somebody had cursed them.

Numb, I steeled myself and tried to appear strong, leaving the hospital. But everything inside me felt as breakable as glass.

CHAPTER XI

SATURDAY, JUNE 7, 1924

I dropped Skeeter and Colleen off at their houses in the morning and drove the Packard back to Mr. Webber's house. He was pacing his front porch. The hospital had called him. He'd heard Helen was hurt, and he seemed anxious to go see her, now that I, at last, had come back with his car.

He checked his Packard up and down, as if surprised to find no dents. Then he said, "I don't understand. How did Helen break her arm? The doctor said there was an accident."

"She wasn't riding in the Packard."

"What?"

I inhaled shallow breaths, wondering how I would explain this. "Helen ran off on us. She had an invite to some party in Laguna."

"Hollywood types?"

I nodded, astonished Helen's father had believed me. I'd dreaded Mr. Webber thinking I had let him down.

What surprised me even more was Mr. Webber never spoke

of Helen's "miscarriage." I wondered if the doctor had even told him. Perhaps in towns as small as Anaheim, doctors kept their patients' secrets. Fueling gossip about Helen wouldn't do her any good. I kept waiting for the other shoe to drop.

It didn't.

And I felt no urge to mention it. I simply gave the keys to Mr. Webber who about-faced and dashed inside to find his wife.

Moments later, he emerged with Mrs. Webber on his arm. He helped her into the front seat, revved up the engine on his Packard.

They screeched off, without a wave.

I took a deep breath.

Held it in, watching the Packard signal right and speed away.

The morning sun seared overhead. Today was supposed to be a scorcher. I needed time to sort my thoughts out as I staggered north up Palm Street. Last night, everyone but Helen and I had been dancing in the gym. In less than half a day my whole life had unraveled, and I struggled trying to piece it back together.

Anaheim High was to my left. To my right, the four-edged steeple of Saint Boniface Catholic Church rose five stories toward the clouds. I'd heard Reverend Leon Myers call it the Catholics' "squared-off dunce cap." It was Alma's church. Four crosses guarded corners of their turret base. On their huge cross atop the spire you could crucify a giant.

I figured Boomer went there too, since most Irishmen were Catholics. The flag was lowered to half-mast, clearly in memory of Boomer. He never talked about religion. All Boomer cared about was baseball. He'd been a heckuva right fielder, had led our team in RBI's. I couldn't even think of playing baseball without Boomer.

Now he was *dead*. My eyes moistened. I always had admired how Boomer had honored both his parents in a town that called them drunks, the way he'd built that little shrine east of the river to remember them, the shrine we'd heard the Bolsheviks destroyed.

I turned left and walked down Center Street to see where Boomer had died. It was past the edge of town where Anaheim dissolved into a scattering of farmhouses and flowering Valencias, past the Five Points Service Station and the Anaheim Cooperative Orange Association. Stacked orange crates by their driveway showed a row of Helen's pictures like a filmstrip, with her photogenic smile.

The wheels of Boomer's toppled truck rose up on the horizon.

The crash site was past where Center Street turned into Lincoln Avenue. The car was in the ditch where it had flipped. The left front tire had been shredded and had blown off of its wheel rim. I hesitated, walking toward the wreckage.

The front windshield was shattered with dried blood around the edges. I imagined Boomer's face had punched its way clear through the glass. Blood ran from the windshield to the north edge of the asphalt where it stopped, marking where Boomer had been placed into an ambulance.

My heart hammered. I felt like a voyeur as I walked back toward the Speedwagon and reached my fingers through the shattered windshield. Beneath shards of broken glass sprayed on the ceiling of the toppled REO, I touched a small white strip of cardboard.

Bloodstained at one end, it must have fallen from the front seat to the ceiling, being buried underneath the shattered glass.

I raised the card where I could read it. The message made me shiver.

Boomer,

YOU HAVE BEEN PAID A SOCIAL VISIT BY THE
KNIGHTS OF THE

KU KLUX KLAN.

DON'T MAKE THE NEXT VISIT A BUSINESS CALL.

I think my blood froze. A hangman's noose had formed in my esophagus. I should have known better. The hateful language iced my very soul. Any innocence I clung to withered as I stood on Lincoln Avenue and stared at the remains of Boomer's wreck.

There was a dark side to the Klan that Mr. Webber hadn't mentioned. I wished somehow I could ignore it, but there it was, right in my face. The business card was worn and dirty. It had been there for a while. Someone in the Ku Klux Klan had something against Boomer.

But what? I'd never known Boomer to have a single enemy. I swallowed back my first instinct to contact the police. Most of Anaheim's policemen were inside the Ku Klux Klan. Helen had told me. So had Colleen's father.

That meant if *I* called the police someone might give me a card too or, being the cowards that they were, threaten my mother.

Especially now when Helen's father had enrolled me as a Klectikon, to be initiated in Anaheim July the 27th. Fifty-three days from now the Ku Klux Klan was holding their huge rally.

In Anaheim. At Central Park.

And I was on their dance card.

I was having big reservations now about the Ku Klux Klan. I felt uncomfortable joining them, but how could I bow out? They carried on like they were patriots, defenders of our values. Still I couldn't help but wonder why so few of them had served during the Great War where *my* father's service cost my pa his life.

Perhaps they'd joined the Ku Klux Klan to compensate.

I stuffed the card into my pants pocket and headed back toward town, wondering who I'd even talk to, wishing my father were still living.

It seemed my home town had turned evil while pretending to do good.

I felt as worthless as a compass with its needle pointing west.

Walking toward town with the Orange County sun baking my face, I racked my brain on who in Anaheim I dared to show the card to. I had evidence the Klan had played a role in killing Boomer. But the cops were in the Klan. The City Council were in the Klan, Boomer's *coach*, and Rollo Earnest at the *Orange County Plain Dealer*, and my *pastor* were in the Klan. To hear Reverend Myers talk, you'd think that Jesus Christ was in the Klan.

I just couldn't figure out why decent men would murder Boomer. The Klan needed a motive. Boomer had never hurt a soul. Sure, he was Catholic, but Anaheim was built by German winemakers who were Catholics, naming their church after the patron saint of Germany, Saint Boniface. And being winemakers, they probably all drank.

But unlike Helen, Boomer didn't drink.

The sun was almost at its zenith. The shadows of the pepper

trees grew short, circling the tree trunks on the lawn outside my high school. I wiped my forehead, ran my hand along a dress shirt soaked in sweat.

The church bells of Saint Boniface Church rang eleven times.

Antiquated benches built from wood planks and wrought iron looked out toward Center Street. On school days, students waited there to ride the school bus home. I took a seat, scraping a wad of Blackjack gum off with my jackknife, and then my gaze fell to the peeling olive paint embossed with hundreds of initials.

My focus zeroed toward fresh letters.

"BC ♥ AM"

I sat next to the carving.
And I wept.

Across the street, my favorite billboard with the lion in the center was remerging at the bottom underneath the pair of eyeglasses. The new message was still there, except the overlay was torn off near the bottom so the message on the billboard read as follows:

I TREAT BOTH CAUSE AND EFFECT STANDPOINTS
DR. LOUIS J. ELWOOD, MODERN OPTOMETRIST
106 E. 4TH STREET, SANTA ANA, PHONE 43-R
QUEEN OF THE ORANGE—LYON, KING.

That was where I'd first kissed Helen, right beneath our friendly lion, but like Anaheim, the message was becoming convoluted. I knew an orange queen here in Anaheim and scores of "lyin' kings," and I knew one of them had probably killed Boomer.

The more I thought about it, the only time I'd seen Boomer get mad was after Anaheim forbade him to replace the white-washed cross and flower shrine east of the river that the Bolsheviks destroyed.

Dumb question. Why would the Ku Klux Klan be siding with the Communists?

I didn't know. But it seemed like they were both on the same team. The question gnawed at me. I knew the Klan had something against Boomer, but what was it?

I also held a card inside my pocket that I might not want to tell people I'd found. I'd need to wait and see what happened. If someone in the Klan suggested Bolsheviks killed Boomer, I might have to watch my back. Perhaps the Klan committed crimes, then blamed the Bolsheviks and used them as an alibi.

I only knew I didn't trust the Klan.

A car pulled toward the curb, rolled down the window on my side and started honking.

Holy smokes. There was that V-63 Cadillac, lipstick red, the one I'd seen outside my house, the one I'd driven home with Margaret the night of the fiasco with John Gilbert at the Lick Pier Bon Ton Ballroom.

I felt as if I'd just swallowed a giant bag of ice.

"Willie, dahling, where ya been?" Margaret shrieked out from the driver's seat. She stepped out of her Cadillac and sauntered my direction.

I leaned so hard against my bench I felt wood splinters in my back.

She wore a rose flower-print flapper dress and tomato-red high heels that looked absurd supporting ankles that were uglier than mine. A raccoon stole covered her shoulders. Underneath it she wore pearls the size of jawbreakers.

"It's been ages, Willie. Gawd, it's really you."

"Yup," I said.

"What a co-inkee-dink."

"Amazing," I replied, taken aback she wasn't drunk. I'd never seen Margaret sober. Might make her harder to get rid of.

"You need a ride, Willie?" she asked.

I hesitated. Margaret reeked of cinnamon, like she'd just taken a bubble-bath in a tub full of *Lavoris*. But she was sober, and she knew about the Klan and didn't like them, and she was here.

I was upset. I needed somebody to talk to.

I said, "No drinking. Let's drive to Cypress. Then turn around and drive me home."

"How unromantic."

"I lost a friend last night," I said.

"Willie, how awful."

"Yeah," I said. "Do you remember when you talked about the Klan?"

"I hate those people."

"Drive east on Center Street, I'll show you where my friend died. Something about the car wreck doesn't smell right."

I jumped into the front seat. Margaret started up the engine, and her Cadillac roared west toward Lincoln Avenue.

We passed the Five Points Service Station and the Orange Cooperative. I glanced toward the horizon trying to pin down Boomer's car, but it was gone. Where hours ago, the ditch was littered with debris, a pair of workers in *sombreros* labored, hand-raking the roadside.

All signs of Boomer's accident had vanished.

I never thought of Anaheim as being that efficient. I ran my fingers through my pocket, touching the card I'd found this morning, my only evidence that Boomer's passing hadn't been an accident. It's just that I had nobody to talk to.

Except Margaret.

"Drive slowly."

She downshifted into second.

"Don't do anything suspicious." I glanced up into her rear view.

"This where your friend died?"

"Uh-huh. Looks like there never was an accident."

"Klan hit job? Amazing, how they cover up their tracks," Margaret deadpanned. "I ever tell you Hank, my ex, was in the Klan?"

"That Julian Pete guy?"

She nodded. "Now you're on the trolley, Willie."

"Did he hand out those little business cards the Ku Klux Klan prints up?"

"He was there the night they raided Fidel Elduayen's garage, the night somebody murdered Medford Mosher."

"So they covered that up too?"

"'Bout the time I started drinking."

She didn't speak much after that. She drove to Cypress and hung a U-turn at the trolley station, heading home the same way we had come. When we got back to the wreckage site, the Mexicans were gone, leaving no evidence but rake marks of how Boomer'd met his end.

"I had a talk with Father Browne the day you left me at Saint Boniface," said Margaret. She signaled left and turned into the parking lot.

I looked over my shoulder, hoping nobody was watching.

"He's a good priest. Helps me moderate my drinking. Thanks," she said.

"But I just dumped you in his parking lot. I didn't introduce you."

"If you'd like, let's go inside, and you can meet him."

"No, thanks." I glanced toward Center Street. Two policemen on the street corner were staring our direction, writing notes on yellow legal pads. I turned to Margaret and shuddered. "Let's get out of here," I muttered. "Look to your left at ten o'clock. Back on the corner."

"Klops?" she asked.

"You got it."

Margaret started up the engine. "You look upset."

"This is a small town, and the Klan runs the police. Boomer was Catholic."

"They don't *kill* people for being Catholic. Did he *do* something or *know* something?"

"Boomer never broke the law."

"Which means he knew something," said Margaret.

"The only thing he ever talked about was baseball, and Alma, Boomer's prom date. Alma wouldn't hurt a fly."

"You knew his girlfriend?"

"My neighbor."

"Can't you talk to her?" asked Margaret, "to learn whatever she and Boomer knew?"

"Not really. We've grown distant."

"Don't be silly," Margaret scolded. "These people stay in power by making everyone in town afraid of everybody else. Divide and rule. That's how they work."

Margaret's Cadillac pulled up beside my house.

I swallowed hard. I opened the passenger door and stepped out of her car.

"Thanks, Mrs. Hollingsworth."

"It's Margaret."

"Goodbye, Margaret. Stay sober."

"B'bye, Willie," she said, giving me a wink.

Margaret started up her motorcar and slowly drove away. She blew a kiss, screeched into second gear and laid tire tracks down my street.

I wasn't sure how to react. I didn't trust Margaret, or like her. But it seemed Margaret had first-hand information on the Klan. She was convinced Boomer had known something. But what had Boomer known? Unless...

If Boomer thought some men had wrecked his shrine and blamed the Bolsheviks, he might have caught the Klan doing the deed. Suppose it was the Klan. The City Council forbade Boomer to repair it. "Divide and conquer," Margaret had said. Play both ends against the middle. Her words made sense, gave them a motive for the calling card I carried in my pocket. But there was no way I could prove it when the Ku Klux Klan ran Anaheim.

Plus, I'd been inducted as a Klecticon.

I saw Alma through her picture window, reading in her living room.

I'd have to talk to her.

But how? I had no clue. I felt so bad for her. She'd carried a torch for me before I broke her heart, pursuing Helen. This was not the perfect time for me to show up on her doorstep.

Deep down, I was afraid to even try.

Except I had to.

I made my way toward Alma's porch steps, heart thumping like a drum, trying to think of useful words to defuse the situation.

I rang the doorbell, and I waited.

Two minutes later, Alma met me at her door, wearing her prom dress from last night, sleeves wet from tears.

"Hello, Dean," Alma whispered, clearly hoarse from all her grieving. She stepped outside, shutting the door behind her. Barefoot on the welcome mat, she faced me, hands on her hips. I think she wanted me to leave.

She examined one without saying a word and finally said, "Is there a reason you stopped by?"

I took a breath and then another. "To say I'm sorry. I'm sad, but not as sad as you are. I liked Boomer. I considered him a friend. We both played baseball. He was good."

"*Je suis desolée,*" she said, shaking her hair and dabbing her red eyes with a handkerchief. "Why would anybody kill a boy like Boomer?"

I took a step back, met her gaze. "You don't think it was an accident."

"It wasn't. It was your friends, but how am I supposed to prove that when it's almost open season here on Catholics in Anaheim." She looked up toward the sky, whispering in French before she finally got the words out. "*Mon Dieu,* I wish I knew."

She looked away, hiding her tears, and I wondered how long somebody could cry before their tear ducts wouldn't make any more tears. She wiped her dress sleeve against her face. It was wetter than a washrag.

"Alma, they cleaned up Boomer's wreck like there was evidence out there the Ku Klux Klan didn't want anyone to see."

"I'm not surprised."

"Did Boomer know something?"

"We all do, Dean. We *know* that we are hated by the men and the police who run our town."

"No one hates you."

She looked away again. "Well someone chased my uncle out of Anaheim for drinking." She turned her back and started sobbing. *"Français sans vin sont comme des pâtisseries sans sucre,"* Alma murmured. "A Frenchman without wine is like a pastry without sugar. They blame the Bolsheviks. They're lying. Boomer and I *saw* them. We know it was your friends who wrecked the shrine."

"Knew," I said.

To my horror, I realized what I'd just said.

She'd just confirmed they'd threatened Boomer to make sure he kept his mouth shut. But that's not how Alma took it now that Boomer had been silenced. I felt she was convinced I took the same side as the Klan.

She glared at me. Her jaw dropped. "Very funny. *Ce que vous pensez que c'est amusant?"* she said, clearly too upset to speak to me in English. Alma spun on her bare feet, opened her door, dashed inside.

Slammed it shut.

I heard her crying in her living room. Then she shot out the side door and down the street in her bare feet and ran away toward the Mercurochrome-hued sunset.

When I walked into my living room, Ma was sitting on the chesterfield, reading. She didn't even look up from her romance.

"Hi, Ma," I interrupted.

"Hi, Dean." She kept reading.

"Good book?"

"I'm almost finished. Then I need to go to bed."

"Big day tomorrow?"

"I'm just weary."

Clearly it wasn't a good time. After my father died, Ma seemed to have no interest in her life. She needed friends, but it was hard to make and keep a friend in Anaheim. Too political. Too polarized. I understood her pain.

She glanced at me and pasted on her trademark kit-bag smile.

I made my way back to my bedroom across our creaky hallway flooring. In my room, the pile of baseball bats and gloves had gathered dust after the playoffs. I had to keep my arm in shape, but I'd lost interest in baseball. After Mister Carson's accident the roofing jobs stopped coming. I was burning through my savings. Then there was Helen and her drama. She was more than I could handle with her movie stars, her drinking, those wild parties, her—promiscuity, friends she never introduced me to with names like "Crazy Florence." There was her father, and the Klan, their righteous pretense. Boomer's murder, Now I couldn't talk to Alma. My life careened at angles that I didn't want to follow.

Everything in Anaheim seemed crazy.

I wanted simple things like baseball season, kisses behind billboards in the orange grove, ice cream parlors, high school proms. It was all shattered. I wanted someone I could trust. I wanted someone I believed in. Not the Klan, with all their rituals pretending they were heroes, when it seemed so few of them had truly served in the Great War.

THE ANAHEIM BEAUTIES VALENCIA QUEEN

I moved my baseball gear aside. My gaze dropped to the floor. Beneath the dresser in the corner was the bare end of a rope. I tugged it toward me with my shoe. Several years of dust bunnies were starting to resemble dust opossums.

And then I recognized the bowline knot my father showed me how to tie the night before he shipped out to Fort Riley.

Where he died.

It seemed prophetic. Since then my life's been full of knots, hangman's nooses, Gordian knots too complicated to untie. I raised the bowline to my heart. I remembered my dad whistling. His troubles in his "old kit bag," he "smile-smile-smiled" down the hallway, and he sat down on my bed.

"You see, Dean, this end's the rabbit," I kicked a dust bunny. *Pa looked up at me and grinned. "The rabbit jumps out of his hole that I just made, and then he runs around the tree before he dives into the same hole he popped out of. Now you try it."*

I stared down at the knot I had tied years ago and wished that I could dive into the hole I had popped out of.

I missed my father. All these years I had been looking for a substitute. I'd failed.

I pulled the covers back.

Climbed into my bed.

Pulled them over me.

And wept like I had never wept before.

CHAPTER XII

SATURDAY, JUNE 21, 1924

The city flagpole had been moved from Los Angeles and Center Streets to Anaheim Central Park just in time for graduation. There we'd said goodbye to seniors who'd be heading off to college. I'd wished that I could leave Anaheim too.

My junior year had ended with a whimper, not a bang, with Helen cooped up with her elbow in a full-arm plaster cast. I saw her father every Sunday during church. He always waved, unlike his wife who believed Helen's broken arm had been my fault. I suspected she knew nothing about the "miscarriage."

Helen had now stopped coming to church.

I asked about her.

"Helen left for summer camp," her mother said.

"Up where?"

"Huntington Lake, at the foot of the Sierras. Quite exclusive," Mrs. Webber said. "Her bunkmate is a Jonathan Club debutante whose father does the books for Union Oil."

"How's she like it?"

"Helen says she's learning how to sail."

I wasn't sure Helen could sail with her arm inside a cast, although I sensed that Mr. Webber wanted Helen far from Hollywood.

I'd like to say I missed her, but I didn't.

I spent my summer doing odd jobs about town for various people in the Ku Klux Klan who passed around my name. It was piecework, but it paid, fixing door hinges and chopping weeds in orange orchards, or ditch-digging and setting up new standpipes.

Still, I felt like I was spiraling their drain.

I saddled up my newspapers and pedaled off to work for Mr. Earnest, delivering his *Orange County Plain Dealer.* I noticed now there was a pattern, a lot of *Plain Dealer* subscribers were the very families active in the Klan.

But there was little I could do. It was a job, and jobs were getting hard to find since Mister Carson closed his roofing operation. I needed work. I knew the Ku Klux Klan would not control my mind. But unlike Helen, whom I envied since she didn't have to work, the Ku Klux Klan controlled my purse strings. I relied on them for jobs to earn my living. Right now, I didn't want to bite the hand that fed me.

The Klan initiation was July the 27th, in five short weeks, I would no longer be a Klecticon.

I'd be promoted to a "Ghoul," their name for ordinary members.

I pedaled off to face the cloudy sunrise.

MONDAY, JULY 7, 1924

The last thing I expected after finishing my paper route was Helen on my porch rail wearing a low-cut sailor blouse. I was hot, sweaty, and thirsty. Helen's cast had been cut off. She twirled her pearls the way the gun molls do in Sunday matinees.

"Hello, Dean," Helen cooed. She waved like she was riding a parade route.

"What are you doing here?" I asked. "Weren't you at summer camp?"

"I got a ride from Crazy Florence. I'm playing hooky for the weekend. I was offered an audition for a role."

"Where? In Anaheim?"

"No, silly. In the San Fernando Valley."

"A real movie?"

"Kinda sorta." Elusively, she looked away. Perhaps she didn't want to jinx whatever chance she had at Hollywood. "Dean, I can't talk about it now. I need an escort to the petting pantry. Care to join me at the California Theater?"

I took her bait, if only out of morbid curiosity. I felt this surreptitious thrill my former girlfriend was a starlet. I told myself Helen's audition didn't mean she was a star, but I imagined Helen's name on the marquee.

Anaheim's California Theater did not show first-run movies. You had to ride the Red Cars up to Hollywood for those. If you couldn't ride to Hollywood, eventually their films showed up in Anaheim. Screening this morning—*Dorothy Vernon of Haddon Hall*.

That was Helen's choice, not mine. I'd hoped to catch *The Thief of Bagdad* with Douglas Fairbanks. But it only screened on Sunday afternoons. I was stuck with Mary Pickford who was right up Helen's alley.

At ten-thirty, the theater was empty.

"Hey, did you hear this movie ruined Mary's friendship with Marshall Neilan?" Helen asked.

"No," I said, my voice dripping with *ennui*.

"Well, I can tell you all about it." Only Helen would refer to Mary Pickford as just Mary, as if the two were bosom buddies. "Mary insisted he direct her, like he did in *Stella Maris* and *Daddy Longlegs*. But every day Mary and Marshall fought off-set. Mary tells me she was furious Marshall always showed up tipsy."

"No kidding," I deadpanned. "Hey, what's it like doing auditions? Did you try out at a studio I've heard of?"

"Nah, they're French."

"French like Pathé?"

"Mm, not exactly. A little place called Beaux Arts Pictures. God, I'm dying for some popcorn and a Coke, Dean." Helen said. She shooed me off, waving her fingers.

I indulged her for old times' sake. Five minutes later, we settled into the eighth row, right in the center, our prize for being there too early. Just in time for a cartoon, Koko the Clown. *A Trip to Mars.*

I was the only one not laughing. I sat next to her, bewildered, wearing my smile-smile-smile as I shivered to stay warm.

I wondered what Helen was here for. She didn't seem at all excited, as if movie work were no different than working an assembly line. She didn't share much. Said, "You wait a lot, and most of it is boring. Thanks for the popcorn and the Coke."

I hated being her valet.

Newsreel headlines flashed up on the screen.

"20,000 RALLY IN JERSEY KLANBAKE"

I sat up straight and watched while members of the Democratic Party all left Madison Square Garden at their National Convention. Hundreds marched in solidarity on a huge New Jersey field decrying the candidacy of New York's Catholic Governor, Al Smith.

"Threats of violence," read the subtitles "have revolved around attempts by non-Klan delegates, led by Alabama Governor Forney Johnston, to modify the Democratic Party Platform to condemn the KKK, alleging actions of brutality."

Helen glanced at me and rolled her eyes.

"Defenders of the Klan, prohibition, and fundamentalism rally in support of Treasury Secretary William McAdoo. Escalating floor debates turn into angry scuffles." Heavy men in suits bumped chests like bull elks during rut.

I glanced at Helen. She yawned and buffed her fingernails against her cotton sailor blouse. She frowned and took a long swig from her Coke. I was surprised the Ku Klux Klan was drawing national attention. I hadn't dreamed they were so active in New Jersey.

"McAdoo," said the subtitles, "stalwart Protestant proponent of prohibition and morality won't repudiate the Klan. This makes his campaign unacceptable to pro-immigrant New Yorkers, campaigning for Governor Al Smith."

After hours of raucous floor debates, moves to censure the Klan fail." Delegates walked briskly out from Madison Square Garden. "On Independence Day, to celebrate, 20,000 Klansmen don their pointed hoods and robes to reassemble in New Jersey. They blast Governor Al Smith, Catholics, Jews, Irish, and Negroes, and throw baseballs at their effigies. The night ends with a cross burning.

The newsreel showed a sea of men surrounding flaming crosses. I was disturbed at all the venom. People behind us clapped and cheered, leaving me nervous. In the dark, Helen used a compact mirror to fix her lipstick. I forced myself to stare up at the screen.

"This gentleman lambasts the 'Clownvention in Jew York,' A thousand daily papers mock their conclave as a "Klanbake." But the Democratic Party remains deadlocked after 61 full ballots between McAdoo and Governor Al Smith.

I swallowed hard. Helen dabbed her lips and capped her lipstick. She stuffed more popcorn into her mouth and used her Coke to wash it down. *She must be used to these theatrics.* Theater was in her blood.

But not in mine. I rolled my eyes and settled in for Mary Pickford, knowing Helen and I weren't meant to be together.

We took a stroll after the movie. It was 100 degrees out. We made our way across the orchard toward the J. T. Lyon billboard papered over with the eyeglasses of Dr. Louis Elwood and the words I must have read a thousand times.

I TREAT BOTH CAUSE AND EFFECT STANDPOINTS
DR. LOUIS J. ELWOOD, MODERN OPTOMETRIST
106 E. 4TH STREET, SANTA ANA, PHONE 43-R

Beneath the Elwood billboard, sun-faded orange letters were still exposed.

QUEEN OF THE ORANGE—LYON, KING...

Torn paper fluttered in the breeze.

Helen grabbed my fingers. She tugged me toward the fading billboard like a woman on a mission. What that was, I had no clue.

"Why did you come back here to see me?" I inquired.

"I can't tell you. Maybe someday, but I can't tell you right now."

Sweat was running down my neck, soaking the inside of my collar.

"Why not?"

We reached the billboard. Helen stepped in front of me. She stared at me the way girls do at dances, holding dance cards. She took both of my hands the way girls dance Virginia reels, swaying slowly like our dance was in slow motion.

"You know," she finally whispered.

A pit formed in my stomach. "I know what?"

She dropped my hands, tucking her pearls beneath her sailor scarf. Her head tilted. She stared at me. "You know about my baby."

I said, "Yes."

"It doesn't bother you?"

"Helen, I'm not the boss of you."

"You're the only man who treats me that way, almost like an equal. And I like that, Dean. A lot." Her voice choked with emotion. She stared through me as if she could see all the way to Hollywood. She sighed. Tears formed in the corner of one eye. I never dreamed Helen was capable of tears.

"But you said nothing about the baby, Dean."

"Didn't think it was my business."

"And you never told my father."

"Does he know?"

She whispered, "Nope."

I stepped in close. "So, who all knows?"

"Just you, me, and the doctor." Helen blushed. "Doctor McKay says it's the Hippocratic Oath. 'First do no harm.' We all know

Anaheim, and gossip can be hurtful. He's a good man for a Mick, Doctor McKay is."

I took a breath and held it in like I was holding Helen's baby, or helping Boomer, or my father. Every one of them had died. Our lives were wonderful but fragile, yet nobody seemed to care. I feared if I exhaled all our souls would blow away.

Helen stared down at the dirt, then at a mockingbird who'd perched atop the J.T. Lyon billboard. A quail called out from the orchard, and the mockingbird made fun of it. "Chi-ca-go," called the quail, and the mockingbird repeated it.

I smiled.

Helen poked a stick into the dust, and then she opened up her purse, fetched a tissue, and blew her nose. She shut her purse. For five minutes, we just listened to the bird. Helen paced, choking back tears, her chest in spasms, making faces.

"I don't deserve you. You're too pure." Helen turned away, now clearly sobbing.

I stepped back.

She reached to grab my hand, tilted her head. Tugged me toward her, slid her hand behind my neck. She shut her eyes while I resisted. I didn't understand what Helen wanted. She felt sweaty. Her lips encompassed mine like we were actors in her Sunday matinee. Her cigarette breath overpowered her perfume. Fingers reached behind my neck, pressing my lips against her own, as if she feared I let go she might drift away to sea. I got this feeling Helen coveted one final goodbye kiss. She was weeping. I tried to be as gentle as I could. I pressed my palm against the small of Helen's back.

Her eyes reopened. The terror in her pupils seemed to telegraph she knew where she was going. I sensed she didn't want to go there. But at last she let me go.

"Farewell, Dean," Helen whispered.

Something twisted in my stomach. She dabbed her tears away. Her smile seemed to harden like a fresh Venus de Milo's into marble, afraid someday she'd lose her youth, her arms, her beauty. She walked away through the Valencias without saying a word, swinging her lonely string of pearls into the glare.

I sat alone beneath the billboard.

I watched Helen walk away, knowing we would never kiss again.

SATURDAY, JULY 19, 1924

After 103 ballots at the Democratic Convention, the party compromised on West Virginia's Governor John Davis. Word was the South would vote for Davis. Northern Democrats would sit out the election, and Calvin Coolidge, the Republican, was favored. The incumbent in the White House had a lock on this election so tight Wall Street handed Coolidge all the money he might need. But Anaheim was as far away from Wall Street as it got. After two National conventions, local merchants set their crystal sets aside. They went to work doing what Anaheim did best, growing Valencias, and vegetables, and fighting in God's name.

It was all over the *Plain Dealer*. The Ku Klux Klan Kolossal Karnival—One Solid Week of Amusement was just six short days away. Twenty-thousand were expected at the "largest Ku Klux Klan event in Kalifornia history." The town and Klan prepared for it in earnest.

Every road entering Anaheim had a KIGY greeting embedded in the asphalt near the posted city limit. The Klan wanted to showcase Anaheim as a model Ku Klux Klan city. Sawdust, pony rides, and game booths appeared in Anaheim Central Park where rows of kewpie dolls and teddy bears hung from clothes pins overhead. A junior level Ferris wheel, a gasoline-fueled Karousel, a petting zoo, a circus train that ran between the parking lot and game booths had shown up after the sun went down on Friday. Signs on booths advertised vinegar fries, orangeade and fresh hot dogs. Posters promised fireworks you could see all over Anaheim.

All of this and more for only fifty cents admission, the cost to buy two tickets to the movies.

Sadly, I realized the reason they had moved the city flag to Central Park was unrelated to our high school graduation. That was the smokescreen. Central Park, I learned, was being reconditioned as parade grounds for a Konclave unlike any ever seen, Anaheim's 1924 Extravaklanza.

Klansmen were starting to arrive. I'd see them driving in their cars at night in sheets, six to a car, patrolling streets as if they owned all of Orange County. Some passed out flyers selling Klan paraphernalia. "How do Klansmen clean their sheets?" one dodger asked. The answer: "KLOROX, now in handy white half-gallon bottles with pointed tops."

Skeeter passed out literature condemning Catholics, and Mexicans, and Africans, and Marxists, and their communistic Jew-nions.

As the big event grew nearer, Colleen's father, Mr. Harris, was concerned I hadn't adequately memorized my Klankraft. It didn't interest me. Three issues of *The Cross and the Flag Magazine* lay unread on my bed table, making me feel unpatriotic. Skeeter read everything they gave him. He'd even learned their secret language and learned the names of all the months. July, in Klanspeak was "The Dreadful Month." The number 27 was spoken "startling" and "doleful."

It fit. And it was just a week away.

THURSDAY, JULY 24, 1924

Two days before the big event, I came down with a head cold. I was secretly delighted. My illness gave me an excuse to skip my "Naturalization into their Invisible Empire," a fancy term used to describe a person's Klan initiation. I would no longer be a Klecticon. I'd be a Klan member, a "Ghoul." But with Helen out of sight and mind, I had to figure out how I'd be telling Mr. Harris that I couldn't join the Klan.

Sadly, I failed to find the words. I racked my brain and came up empty. I was nobody in Anaheim, and these men ran the city. You didn't argue with such luminaries. Clearly they knew best. Who was I to lecture them on what was right and what was wrong? It stung, but there was nothing I could say.

Our doorbell rang. I peered out through Venetian blinds and shuddered. There was Coach Merritt on our doorstep with Mr. Harris and Mr. Webber.

"Dean, your coach is here," my mother called and peeked into my doorway.

"Ma, I don't feel too good. Could you...?"

"Already told him, but these men won't go away." She shut the door. I heard her padding down the hallway toward her bedroom in her tattered towel-cloth slippers.

Ma didn't know I was a Klecticon, so she didn't understand why three men stopped by for a visit when they hadn't been invited.

The front door opened and slammed.

Footsteps thundered down the hallway.

I threw my bathrobe on.

A rap against my bedroom door. Then, "Dean?"

"I'm sick."

The door flew open. Three men stormed into my bedroom. Mister Harris wore a poorly concealed sidearm beneath his suitcoat. They strolled into the center of my room, stopped at the foot end of my bed, shoulder-to-shoulder, towering above me.

My throat tightened. I sat up on my pillows.

My room felt colder than a meat locker. I looked up at Colleen's father. His lantern jaw was grinding on a chaw full of tobacco. He wore a pistol in a shoulder harness, just like this was Tombstone, Arizona, and I was staring down the Earps at their corral.

"What's goin' on, Dean?" asked Coach Merritt, crossing his arms across his windbreaker, the blue and yellow Anaheim Colonists one with "Coach" embroidered on it.

"I just told you, Coach. I'm sick." I blew my nose into a handkerchief, embarrassed that it hadn't yet been used.

"You don't look that sick to me. How many soldiers in the Army do you think can shirk their duties by pretending to be sick?" Coach Merritt asked in that loud voice he used to yell at us in practice.

I shrugged. "How would I know, Coach?"

Harris leaned over the bed so close he sprayed tobacco juice between his teeth. "Son, don't give us any lip."

I slid back.

"You're a man, Dean, and goddammit, most men have responsibilities. They keep their word. Your Ku Klux Klan

Naturalization is this Sunday. And you promised you'd attend. Mister Webber paid your Klektoken. It's wrong to ask an angel to front money more than once."

"If I don't go, the fee is forfeited?"

"Correct," said Mr. Webber. "All ten dollars. Boys with guardian angels shouldn't piss them off."

I looked at Mr. Webber, but he wouldn't meet my gaze.

I stammered, "I have money in the drawer to pay you back." It was enough to buy a suit, and I would pay it to walk free. But this seemed to be about more than ten dollars.

"Dean," Coach Merritt bellowed. "I know you're a team player. Or I thought so."

I held my breath, longing to say I didn't trust him. But they were standing in my bedroom. Mr. Harris had a *gun*. Coach could blacklist me. He'd make sure that I never pitched again. Helen had her dream of Hollywood, and mine was to play baseball. Walter Johnson, "The Big Train," had pitched for Fullerton ten years ago. I held onto my fantasy. I needed my big chance.

Coach Merritt cleared his throat and lowered his voice a half an octave. "Son, there are no second chances."

"I'm aware of that," I said.

"We're paying you a *social visit* to make certain you're prepared."

I choked as if a baseball were now wedged inside my throat.

My thoughts flashed back to prom night and the cards we found in Mr. Webber's glove compartment, the card I'd found in Boomer's REO, the one I still had in my wallet. In my mind, I saw my own name scribbled in where Boomer's name had been before:

Dean:

YOU HAVE BEEN PAID A SOCIAL VISIT BY THE KNIGHTS OF THE

𝕶𝖀 𝕶𝕷𝖀𝕏 𝕶𝕷𝕬𝕹.

DON'T MAKE THE NEXT VISIT A BUSINESS CALL.

I wondered what these men might do. Knew I couldn't call the cops. All the cops were in the Klan, and they would probably just laugh.

Mr. Webber checked his watch, looked up and straightened his lapel pin. I wondered just whose side Webber was on.

"Do y'all need help learning your Klankraft?" Mister Harris, folded his arms across his chest. I felt tobacco spray whenever this guy talked.

"No sir."

"Then Dean, Mister Webber paid ten dollars for your Klectoken. What's wrong?" Coach Merritt asked, steeling his jaw.

I sat up straight to summon courage. It seemed to me like Mr. Harris and Coach Merritt were both reading from some script the Klan had written.

Mr. Webber had said nothing. He just stared down at the floor.

I sucked my chest in, summoned courage. "B-Boomer Corrigan," I stammered.

The clock seemed to stop ticking. Mr. Webber checked his watch. Mr. Harris stroked the white scar on his chin and rubbed his jaw. Coach Merritt stood there with his arms crossed, like I'd given up a run to lose the ballgame, and he had no other pitchers in the bull pen.

Any last ounces of warmth inside my bedroom seemed to vanish. I felt like I was seated in the coldest pit of hell. I glanced at Mr. Harris' hand, saw his index finger twitching.

I bit my lip, felt a shiver and prepared to take a bullet.

Mr. Harris' gaze could freeze a man in place a mile away. But now he spoke matter-of-factly like a judge reading a sentence. "Did y'all know the man who killed President Garfield was Catholic? Did y'all know the man who shot Theodore Roosevelt was Catholic? John Wilkes Booth, the man who killed President Lincoln, was a Catholic. And in every single case when these men faced their execution, a Catholic priest was at their elbow to administer last rites to criminals unworthy of forgiveness."

I fired back, "Boomer was Catholic, but he never hurt a soul."

Coach Merritt seemed annoyed at me for rudely interrupting. He rattled off misinformation like a baseball statistician. "Over sixty-five percent of prison convicts are now Catholics. Less than five percent of Catholics are graduates of public schools. It's a national disgrace when only twelve percent of the entire United States claims to be Catholic, and yet they drink, and they cause sixty-five percent of all our crime. Dean, how on earth can you defend them?"

I glared back at Coach Merritt. "Coach, we're talking about Boomer."

Harris stepped in front of Merritt. "I was talking about decency. What facts do y'all have, Dean, having never gone to college? You're just a kid."

"Then I'm too young to join the Klan."

"You're too old not to," Mister Harris said. He leaned across my bed, fist in my pillow, his face so close I felt another spray of Mail Pouch. "And, Reynolds, let me state the obvious," said Harris. "Anaheim will be a model Ku Klux Klan city. The Klan controls this town. Your buddy, Boomer, crossed the line, claiming we vandalized that shrine he'd built to honor his dead parents."

I felt the wind being sucked out of me. Was Harris saying who'd killed Boomer?

Coach Merritt and Mr. Webber tugged on Mr. Harris' shoulder.

"You might see Boomer sooner than you think," blurted out Harris, his face turning radish red. He wagged his finger in my face.

Mr. Webber, glared toward Harris. "Harry, this is out of line."

I glanced up, swallowing that baseball. I looked away and felt my lip quiver, felt the weight of their contempt, their lack of empathy for Boomer.

"Twenty-thousand Klansmen are in Anaheim next weekend," said Coach Merritt. "Not including those who live in our fair city. That, and our Exalted Cyclops doesn't like being embarrassed. I know you're young, but is there something here you fail to understand?"

Coach Merritt didn't let me answer. It was like being back in hell week, when every player had to kiss his ugly butt to make the team. "You will be there on the twenty-seventh of the Dreadful Month," Merritt bellowed. "The Bloody Hour, six p.m. unless you want us as your enemies."

My throat tightened in terror as if *I* were being lynched. I knew what they had done to Boomer Corrigan.

My three guests lined up in formation. In unison they all right-faced and stormed out of our house, marching in military cadence.

My heart was rat-tat-tatting, and my temples thrummed in cadence. I had no choice.

Ma was standing in the kitchen, frying hash. "What did they want?" She waved at them and smile-smile-smiled.

I dared not answer.

She frowned. "Dean, are you okay?"

Shaking my head, I walked outside inhaling tears.

I made my way to the garage.

The kid next door was shooting crows with his new slingshot.

I picked my pace up. And then I threw up in the trash can.

FRIDAY, JULY 25, 1924

The next morning, I managed to complete my morning paper route. I'd been unable to sleep, and now my head was full of phlegm. Headlines of the *Orange County Plain Dealer* were all about the "HUGE EXTRAVAKLANZA" with photographs of Pastor Myers. He was grinning. It was the sort of smile I'd learned never to trust, a bit too wide, a man of God who was, in truth, a *wolf* of God. Something about him, those eyebrows, the way he didn't face the camera, left me nervous, especially with the threats I'd just received.

But as I pedaled through the neighborhood on my rusty yellow Schwinn, it seemed the biggest news in Anaheim had yet to make the papers. Someone had filled up all the outside locks of Saint Boniface Catholic Church with Elmer's glue and road tar. Today no one could get in.

Mister Bannerman and Father Browne were unbolting the hinges on the front doors of their church while other Catholics stood guard. Irish and Sonorans with shoulders wider than a Caterpillar tractor stood on guard with Colts in hand to scare off looters.

Cars were still leaving the parking lot. Word was the morning mass was cancelled. Three men were busy changing locksets out on all the classroom doors. A pickup truck bearing a license plate frame from Orange Empire Ford—San Bernardino sat full of strangers watching the episode with mirth.

There was no way to prove who'd done this, not when 20,000 Klansmen were descending upon Anaheim and started playing high-jinx. Even if someone had a photograph, the cops wouldn't arrest them or press charges. Not on *this* weekend. That newsreel from New Jersey had told me everything a man needed to know.

Any mischief that the Klan might choose to raise would go unpunished.

It made me sad. In the first grade, Mrs. Buist had taught us right from wrong in Sunday School in the basement of White Temple Methodist Church. But what we'd learned had been supplanted once the Klan had taken over. Boomer was *dead*. Alma was heartbroken. The Klan acted infallible, preaching Jesus had turned water into Welch's Concord Grape Juice. Since the Klan controlled our town, my opinion didn't matter. I'd even learned from Pastor Myers Mrs. Buist wasn't a Christian since her husband wouldn't join the Ku Klux Klan.

I set my jaw. Today was Friday. There were 20,000 Klansmen in our town, and they would have their way with Anaheim all weekend. Men were camping in their cars, carrying sidearms for protection, or for fun. They made me nervous. Outnumbered and outgunned, there was no way I could possibly fight back.

Feeling nauseous, I kept walking. Leon Myers had a Friday Morning Bible Brunch at Central Park. My presence was expected. I was a Klecticon. On Sunday I would change into a Ghoul.

It was so evil.

I understood why Helen had rebelled.

I wished I could find her now. I needed to take lessons. But where to look? She'd seemed so hesitant to tell me where she worked. My only chance would be to visit Beaux Arts Pictures where she filmed. All I knew was they were somewhere in the San Fernando Valley, a town called Lankershim, I'd found out at the Anaheim Public Library.

Making my way toward our bungalow, I found a ray of hope. The red Cadillac with Margaret in the driver's seat was parked outside my house. I wasn't sure if I could pull it off but had to take the chance.

She honked her horn.

"Willie, dahling," Margaret cooed.

I waved back, and I sprinted toward her car.

CHAPTER XIII

FRIDAY, JULY 25, 1924

It was the first time I had seen Margaret Hollingsworth looking healthy. She wore a jade-green cashmere sweater over pleated charcoal slacks. A gold-chain necklace enhanced her British Isles complexion, and the missing caked-on makeup said this was not the woman I'd met out at Lick's Pier.

I hated asking favors, but I needed one right now. If she was willing, I needed somebody to drive me up to Lankershim. I wanted to see Helen up at Beaux Arts Motion Pictures, learn her secrets, how she'd coped living among the Ku Klux Klan.

"You okay, Margaret?" I asked. Something about her said she wasn't. She sat as straight-faced in her Cadillac as a mask stolen from Tutankhamun's tomb.

She rolled her window down. "Git in, Willie," she said. She unlocked her right door and nudged it open.

I slid into the front seat of her car.

"I had to tell someone," she murmured, dabbing her forehead with a handkerchief.

I slammed the car door shut. "Tell what?" I asked.

Her face went white as Ivory Soap. "It's Hank," Margaret murmured. "Something told me you'd be here, and we could talk."

"About your ex?"

She touched her lips. "He turned up—dead."

"What?"

"Dead as a door hinge on a riverboat across the River Styx."

The way she said this sent a chill throughout the cabin of her Cadillac, as though Hank were stored on giant blocks of ice in the back seat.

We didn't say much for a spell. A yellow mongrel dog wandered south along the sidewalk. I sat by Margaret, half-numb.

"Do you have time?" she asked. "To talk."

"If you can take me up to Hollywood."

"Mind driving?

She handed me the keys to the ignition.

"Actually, north of there," I said as I traded seats with Margaret.

She settled in beside me, slammed the car door shut, and locked it.

"Let's go," I said at last. I turned the key. Margaret's 60-horsepower engine roared to life. She hadn't even asked me how far north. I didn't tell her. I just assumed that we could make it up and back in the same day.

Citrus-scented breezes blew through the passenger compartment as we drove west out of Anaheim down Center Street. We passed the site of Boomer's accident, where Center became Lincoln. I felt a second wash of winter.

We both rolled up our front windows.

"Can I talk now?" Margaret asked.

"You must be numb."

"I'm pretty certain Hank was murdered."

"Oh, how dreadful," I said, fearing that the deadpan of my voice needed to show a bit more empathy and sorrow.

"They found his body near the Tam O'Shanter Inn on Los Feliz, north of L.A., lying face down in his Buick," Margaret said.

"Was there an autopsy?"

"Found antifreeze, ethylene glycol, in his stomach. His last meal was Welsh rarebit. Wouldn't be hard to sneak it in."

"Did he have enemies?"

"Henry worked for Julian Pete. Need I say more? And he was also in the Klan."

"I see." I pursed my lips.

"You don't know half of what Hank told me," Margaret said.

I signaled right on Downey-Norwalk-Artesia Road and headed north through L.A. County through a maze of local farm roads. We drove through cow pastures and oil fields and had to hold our noses as we veered left onto Anaheim Telegraph Road toward L.A.

"So what'd he tell you?" I asked Margaret, piqued with curiosity.

"He wasn't working in petroleum at all. Hank was a loan shark, taking the proceeds from those Julian Pete stock issues and loaning them at interest rates the law doesn't allow." She lit a Marlboro.

"So someone poisoned him."

"That's a solution if a man can't pay Hank back."

"You know who did it?"

"Not a clue. Willie, not even an inkling. Hank made enemies like Sam Carter makes liver pills," she said. "He had hundreds of 'em, all owing him money. You cain't make that many enemies before one of them finds you."

"How are *you* feeling?" I asked, trying to notice her emotions. I glanced across the gearshift and I smile-smile-smiled.

"Okay, I guess. Hank's attorney says I made out like a bandit. Evidently our divorce papers had yet to be recorded."

Her lips flatlined after that. "Where north of Hollywood are you headed?"

"You know where Lankershim is?"

"San Fernando Valley west of Burbank. There's a road, Lankershim Boulevard that heads straight into town. It's not that big, more of a cowtown. Maybe half a dozen streets and not a one of them is paved except for Lankershim."

"Good," I said. "Because I need to find a place called Beaux Arts Pictures."

"Never heard of it."

"Me neither."

"Well I guess we'll both find out, Willie," she said. I made a left turn onto Stephenson Boulevard southwest of town. By noon, the L.A. skyline rose ahead of us.

We stopped for lunch. French dips and two cold lemonades inside Philippe's. Within an hour after lunch, I would see Helen at her studio. I suspected on our journey home we'd stop outside the Tam O'Shanter. Right now I wondered what I'd say to Helen.

I mopped my sweaty forehead and prepared my list of questions. First on the list. How to stay out of the Klan and not get hurt.

By two o'clock, the L.A. skyline sank down into my rear view, and we were headed north from Hollywood and toward Cahuenga Pass. The huge white "HOLLYWOODLAND" sign rose on the south slopes of Griffith Park. A lonely Red Car made its way north on the trolley tracks beside us toward the San Fernando Valley. It looked like no one was aboard.

I told Margaret about Helen, how Helen longed to star in movies, how she'd said she'd found an opening with Beaux Arts Motion Pictures. I'd never heard of them, but found out in the Anaheim Public Library they were in Lankershim. At Cahuenga Pass, the Red Car finally passed us, and the road north of the pass had only two lanes that were paved. The sign by the State Highway called the road Ventura Boulevard. It said:

SANTA BARBARA—90
SAN FRANCISCO—415

A signpost up ahead pointed to "Lankershim—3 miles." I signaled right onto what looked more like a farm road. To call Lankershim a boulevard required imagination. Two lanes of gravel and macadam with shoulders Lon Cheney would kill for were lined with telegraph poles and crooked rail fences. A herd of goats feasted on mustard flowers and weeds west of the fences. *What was the deal with Los Angeles and boulevards?* I mused. This was a city whose foundation was illusion, just like Hollywood, a land of big ideas afloat in lies.

Margaret interrupted. "Do you like me when I'm sober?"

"Yeah, what happened?"

"Father Browne."

"At Saint Boniface Catholic?"

"I've found religion."

"Good for you, Margaret. I'm glad to see you sober." I wasn't wild about religion but was glad to find out somebody had helped her, even the Catholics whom I'd been schooled to detest.

"When I woke up at ten o'clock outside the backdoor of their church, I went inside. Father Browne could clearly see I had been drinking. He said he'd listen to my confession if I had the time to make one.

"And so you did."

"Took me two hours."

"You must live one heckuva life."

"I did," she said. "You don't know half the stuff that goes on in the studios. They have these "fixers," so if someone winds up pregnant or on drugs, the studio fixers make it seem as if the whole thing never happened."

"How convenient."

"Except things *did* happen."

"You don't have to tell me what."

"Neither Hollywood nor the Ku Klux Klan are what they claim to be. I know plenty about Hollywood, its speakeasies and brothels. Seems to me the Klan and Hollywood are feeding off each other, providing sound reasons for each to feel righteous. But as Father Browne says often to me, 'Evil will not endure.'"

She snuffed her cigarette out in her ashtray.

There was the studio ahead. It looked more like a brothel from a movie set of Boot Hill or Dodge City. A palomino had been tied up to the fence rails, and two dusty Model T's were parked outside. One of the windshields was cracked.

I glanced at Margaret. "Let's go in."

She shook her head. "I'll wait out here. First, I need to find a gas station."

I handed Margaret the car keys. "You *will* come back for me?" I asked.

"Of course." She touched my hand, stepped out, and walked around her bug-encrusted Cadillac in her heels. "And I need to run an errand to the Tam-O-Shanter. I'll need a half an hour. Take your time."

I swallowed hard and made my way up concrete steps to Beaux Art Studios. Something in my throat warned me I might regret my visit.

Margaret screeched into the August afternoon to run her errands. Her Cadillac faded behind grit and clouds of dust.

I rang the doorbell, still rehearsing in my mind how I'd ask Helen how to steer clear of the Ku Klux Klan and not get myself hurt. I needed clarity, advice.

Helen understood their methods.

My throat tightened the moment I heard voices.

The door swung open. A flapper in high heels and a bathrobe looked up toward me. A bobbed brunette, she had two copper-tinted eyes that felt like daggers. They seemed too large to fit her well-proportioned face. Vaulted eyebrows rose like viaducts above her Roman nose. Her rosebud smile, pretty but thorny showed contempt. She asked, "Who are you?" glanced away, and lit a Pall Mall cigarette.

"Name's Dean Reynolds. I'm a friend of Helen Webber's."

"She's in Mexico, you know." The woman fanned her cigarette until it glowed. A line of smoke rose from its sterling-silver holder. "Come inside."

"I *didn't* know she was in Mexico," I said. Disappointed, I made my way into a room filled up with smoke and held my breath. *I didn't need to know*, I studied my surroundings and my jaw dropped.

Racy photographs of actresses I'd never ever heard of filled the walls. Their glossy 8 x 10's were stapled to the plaster. The girls were young enough for high school. Lonely faces, frightened faces; each made me wish there was a way that I might hold them in my arms and somehow comfort them. They stared toward me like puppies in a shelter when I realized that none of them were wearing any clothes.

This was the sort of "den of sin" I'd heard about from Pastor Myers in his sermons. I got this feeling he had actually been here. My gaze landed on a photograph that seared into my soul, a perky blonde with pouty lips I had once kissed beneath a billboard in a citrus grove in Anaheim. My heart sank like a brick.

There was her stage name. "Valencia Larue." Her gaze was tilted. A naughty swirl of errant hair seemed to sweep above one eye, like she was winking at me, even though her eyes were frozen open. There wasn't any doubt that it was Helen.

A fat man stepped onto the staircase. He stood and overlooked a room that looked like nobody had swept it since the day the guy'd moved in. It even smelled sleazy. Tobacco scents masked odors reminiscent of a locker room but somehow even worse.

The woman puffed her cigarette. "Helen's filming at our ranch in Ensenada, doing art films. We make oodles of 'em, don't we, Russ." She glanced up toward the fat man who wore a scally cap to cover his bald head. "By the way, my name's Lucille. Lucille La Sueur. Grew up in Texas, Oklahoma, Kansas City. Where do you come from?" she asked.

My stomach tensed. "Anaheim, but born in Brooklyn."

"You look like someone we could use here. What do *you* think, Russ?" She wagged her cigarette toward the stranger. "Look at me. Gimme a smile."

My gut twisted up tighter, and I froze but smiled back. This whole establishment felt dicey. I thought of Helen, gulped revulsion back. Small wonder she'd been cagy. These guys apparently made *stag films*.

Their cigarettes were bothering my eyes.

Lucille eyed me like my work shirt was transparent, touched the muscles in my arms. Her rosebud smile lifted.

"Come inside," said Russ. "Siddown. You need a cigarette? A soda?"

"No thanks, sir."

The fat man sauntered down the stairs into the parlor and plopped down into a sweat-stained leather swivel chair behind a huge oak desk. Most of the lacquer was worn off of it. "Whatcha doin' here?" he asked.

"Says he knows Helen." Lucille turned toward him, grinning while she smoked.

"You tell him Helen's out of town?"

"We were sweethearts, sir. In Anaheim," I said.

The man inhaled his cigar and blew a smoke ring. Then he chortled. "Sweethearts, eh? Lucy tell ya what we do here?"

"No," I said. I took a breath. "But I can guess."

"You like art films, son?" he asked.

I gave him a blank look.

"Stag films. Naked women. Do you like films with naked women?" I couldn't stand how this guy pushed people around like they were stupid.

"Sir, I don't think they show those films in Anaheim."

The man's face scrunched like a prune. "Poor town sure ain't what it used to be," he said. "We call it Klanaheim up here. Like Klanta Ana. Helen tells me Ku Klux Klan members are all over Orange County like barnacles on buoys in Newport Harbor."

"It's true," I said.

"I know it's true. That's why I have a proposition."

"What?" I said.

"I'm sensing Lucy likes you." He looked up.

Truth was I didn't care for Lucy.

Russ bared his teeth, the sort of teeth you see on tree saws, only sharper. And his eyes were different sizes.

Lucy spun around to face me. I caught her sly kittenish smirk.

"I think she'd like to make a film with you. 'Zat right, Lucy?" he said. A vapid smile spanned his cheeks.

I blushed and looked away, clasping my hands. "Sir, I'm afraid I might be somewhat—inexperienced."

"Virgin, huh? No problem, kid. We can fix that in a jiffy. You're not a fag, are you? An Ethyl?"

"Not exactly, sir," I said.

"You're not a killjoy, a wet blanket?"

"That might be closer to the truth."

The man mashed his cigar stub down, submerging it in ashes. "You're more naïve than Helen Webber. Thinks she's gonna be a big bright star in Hollywood. 'Zat right, Lucy? 'Cept every lady's gotta pay her dues,"

Nodding, Lucy flashed a sly lascivious grin.

"Everybody got to pay their dues to climb the ladder. You know that, Lucy. Helen thinks it's all about her looks."

A surge of anger rose inside me, but I managed to contain it.

Lucy fired a glance at Russ. It was a glare that might leave exit wounds. A look worthy of a cripple locked upstairs or in a straightjacket. I grieved for Helen. The heels at Beaux Arts were only using her.

I'd find Helen, someday, and tell her everything I'd learned.

Russ opened his top desk drawer. I spied a firearm near the top, A Colt 1918, black, semi-automatic pistol. He wagged his cigarette toward the door.

"Kid, git outta here," he said.

I dropped my gaze, swallowed my terror, and I took the man's advice, my pulse pounding in my head like a machine gun.

Heartbroken, I held my head up and descended concrete steps back to the street, feeling my heart race. I was hoping to find Margaret. She hadn't come back from her errand. A quarter block away I found an orange crate. Helen's face was on it. Ironic, I supposed.

I flipped the crate over and sat on it, wondering where I might find Helen after Mexico. I clearly wasn't welcome at her studio. What they did here was illegal. They were using Helen, scamming her, promising her stardom while they pocketed the proceeds. There was no difference between Hollywood and Julian Petroleum. They promised you the moon while they scammed everything they could. Except now Margaret's husband, Henry Hollingsworth, was dead.

I surmised she'd gone to revisit the crime scene.

But lots of movie stars had died. Olive Thomas, Bobby Harron, Wallace Reid, Virginia Rapp, and even William Desmond Taylor. Everybody up here made the rules up as they went, using those fixers Margaret talked about to clean up dirty laundry.

If the way of life I'd grown up with in Anaheim was dying, in Los Angeles and Hollywood, those ways were long-forgotten. Here, it was each man for himself. There was no chivalry or honor. Amidst a vacancy of virtue, opportunity had knocked, and opportunists like the Reverend Leon Myers had arisen, letting the specter of their Ku Klux Klan expand into the vacuum.

Again, I saw that wall of photographs, stapled to the plaster, frozen in Kodak immortality, and seared into my memory. Naughty girls with star-struck eyes longing for somebody to care about them, worship them and love them, kiss them, make them feel they *mattered*. I shut my eyes, but I saw Helen or Valencia Whoever's image staring from the wall. They hadn't even framed her picture. She had run away but had nowhere to go.

Outside the Klan I didn't have a friend that I could count on.

I stared across the dusty streets. Tears dampened my eyes. I felt alone and wiped my face onto my sleeve. Longing to be strong, I felt deserted and abandoned. I was scared. But so was everyone in Anaheim I reckoned.

I heard a car horn. "Willy?" Margaret shrieked out from her car window. She honked again. She screeched up to the curb. Unlocked the passenger door.

I ran to jump inside.

Margaret shifted into first, spun up gravel, and made a right turn onto Lankershim. We sped south out of town.

I didn't even look in the rear view.

I must have conked out before we even made a left onto Ventura. When I awoke I was on Center Street and headed east from Cypress. From moonlit Anaheim horizons, strings of incandescent bulbs, silhouettes of circus tents, and a Ferris wheel glistened.

Margaret gave me a quick glance. "So you finally woke up."

I yawned. "Uh-huh," I said. "Learn anything more about your ex?"

"Everything was covered up, just like it was the day your friend died," Margaret reported as she braked behind a stop sign.

The KIGY monogram was glistening in her headlights as we passed into the Anaheim city limits.

And I was home. Not in a perfect world, but one I understood. I'd learned more things about Helen than I ever cared to know. I understood now why the people here in Orange County were frightened. There was a scary world out there beyond the Orange County limits. Hollywood was creepy, and Los Angeles corrupt. I wanted safety. I'd heard soldiers who had fought in the Great War talk of the world. I wasn't ready for that world. At least not yet.

Margaret was telling me, "There are no perfect people." She'd been talking about Hank.

I answered, "Margaret, you're right."

She said, "I'll miss Hank." She was no longer the Margaret I'd met out at Lick's Pier. She lit a Marlboro and shifted down to second.

"I'm very sorry about your husband."

"Thank you," Margaret said.

"I admire you for getting off the sauce."

"That means a lot, Willie."

She pulled up to the curb outside my house.

I stretched my arms, opened the door and made may way out of her bug-stained bright red Cadillac.

She put the gearshift into park, unlocked the car's front door and opened it. Margaret made her way around the car hood to my side. "You're a sweet lad, Willie," she said. "What did you say your real name was?"

"Dean," I answered.

I met her gaze. Margaret kissed me on the cheek. She clasped my hand between both hers. She squeezed. "Good-bye, Dean. *Adios.*"

"You act as though you're leaving."

"Forever," Margaret said. "I'm packing up for Oklahoma."

"Good luck."

"Thank you, Dean. Gal like me needs all the luck that she can get."

I smiled back. "Thanks for the ride."

She sauntered back around her car, opened the door, jumped into the driver's seat, and started the ignition. She revved the engine. A cloud of gasoline fumes spurted out the tailpipe.

She shifted into gear, and she was gone.

But as Margaret drove away, I was still thinking about Helen. An awful vacuum filled my gut. I was reminded how I felt the night my father died. I shut my eyes and Helen seemed to sail off a cliff, all in slow-motion. I could only hold my breath, swallow numbness and pray someone might help Helen like they'd helped Margaret.

I never did see Margaret again.

CHAPTER XIV

SUNDAY, JULY 27, 1924

R iding my paper route the morning of my Naturalization, I felt the thrill any man feels when a circus comes to town. There were those silhouettes of big-top tents, a Ferris wheel, a carousel, the whinnies of distant horses and the bellow of an elephant.

The weekend of the Ku Klux Extravaklanza had arrived. The headlines of my *Orange County Plain Dealer* sang its praises. It gave me lots of mixed emotions. I was happy to be home where I felt safe from the corruption of Los Angeles and Hollywood. But that corruption was infecting my home town.

Two Catholic employees of the Anaheim City Water Department carried shotguns in their trucks. They claimed some men were trying to kill them.

Smoke rose from the orchard across Center Street from Anaheim Union High School, where the billboard was, where Helen had first kissed me. I felt a sadness that my memories were somehow being erased. Tractor engines moaned among the trees.

I crossed the street and headed toward the orchard.

Stunned, I froze in my own tracks. A bulldozer had taken out twelve trees. The engine crawled toward the billboard, belching exhaust. Smoke ascended toward the sky amidst a steamy summer morning.

Moans of a calliope were toodling in the distance.

A backhoe showed up, scooping up the earth behind the footings on the posts that held the billboard up and setting dirt aside. An operator raised the steel blade up on the dozer. It pressed against the billboard face. The gears shifted and groaned. The bulldozer blade pressed against the lumber.

I heard a CRACK!

The billboard snapped and toppled to the earth.

My heart imploded, as if a piece of me had vanished with that billboard. Workers in overalls brought chainsaws and reduced the thing to kindling. Although I'd gotten over Helen, sadness washed into the void left in my heart. She might be gone, but I had nothing to replace her.

The Briggs and Stratton roar echoed so loud it made my head hurt. I was trespassing, I didn't dare edge closer to the workers as they sawed up fading memories and stacked them by the roadside where a group of workers loaded up their flatbed trucks with firewood. I recalled sprinting here after baseball practice, eager to meet Helen, see her smile, smell the fragrance of Valencias and Helen's floral lips pressing on mine. I could still taste her flirty breath. Her nimble fingers tiptoeing up and down my neck to launch that soft electric kiss. For one brief moment we felt safe, believing everything in Anaheim was going to be okay.

Except things weren't okay. Not now. While men might kiss Helen in stag films, no one cared about her, not the way that I had. A cloud of loamy dust rose from a grove of toppled citrus trees. Upended naked root balls lay by craters in the dirt. Workmen ran chainsaws through the branches, spewing discs of airborne sawdust. The Anaheim I'd loved was being bulldozed, making room for future subdivisions, gas stations, and storefronts.

So many things I'd loved were gone. Pa had died during the War. Helen was gone. Within eleven months, I'd graduate from high school. With no job on the horizon I'd be forced to leave the town I had grown up in. The idea terrified me. Young men needed mentors and it seemed the Ku Klux Klan was all I had.

I swallowed heartbreak. A man needed some sort of a foundation, something unchanging and eternal, and not fleeting like the Great War or that billboard I'd seen bulldozed only twenty minutes ago. Its faded paper image fluttered, and for one last glance the eyes were staring back at me through butt-ugly black eyeglasses:

I TREAT BOTH CAUSE AND EFFECT STANDPOINTS
DR. LOUIS J. ELWOOD, MODERN OPTOMETRIST

And then the billboard's broadside rose up, fluttering kite-like, above citrus trees. Its paper eyes glared down at me as if they disapproved. The message plummeted behind a redwood fence with weeds behind it. There were no eyes left to look out for me (or down on me), deciding whether I measured up against their shifting standards.

I recalled the day I'd wept in my Ma's arms the day my Pa had died and praying to a God who hadn't listened. I wanted God, except there wasn't any God I could believe in until Mr.

Webber came along and actually called me, "son," and Mr. Carson gave me work, and Coach Merritt let me pitch.

And now the only God I knew about was in the Ku Klux Klan.

But there were times I feared their god wanted me dead.

The afternoon of Sunday's Ku Klux Extravaklanza bustled past me with more frenzy than a mob of Keystone Kops chasing a flapper. Boys in dungarees ran ring tosses and hammer-bell arcade games watched by pig-tailed little sisters inhaling kones of kotton kandy. Aeroplanes buzzed overhead, flying noisy loop-the-loops. Ingenues in bright cloche hats and patent-leather Mary-Janes hung on the arms of men in boater hats and dandy pinstripe sport coats strolling to loud John Philip Sousa marches booming from the bandshell.

Hot winds from Santa Ana Canyon, dried my mouth and made the hairs on both my neck and arms rise up like little radio antennas. Events whirled past me like a carousel got jammed into high gear. I was on it, and I wanted it to stop and let me off. Within hours I'd be ushered through my Naturalization and would cease to be a Klecticon, elevated to a Ghoul.

The orchestra stopped playing. The arcade games had shut down. All the ponies and the elephant were led away to feed pens. Summer sun set on Valencia orchards rolling west of Anaheim. The evening felt unseasonably weird.

"Dean, you ready?" It was Skeeter. "Jeepers creepers, I can't wait."

It was 95 degrees, but I shivered.

Skeeter was flanked by Colleen Harris and her arrogant old man, E. Norbert Harris, the Klavern's Klabee, a fancy word that meant their treasurer. He rubbed the white scar on his lantern jaw. He looked at me with scorn and then ejected a wad of Mail Pouch the size of an old golf ball.

"Y'all ready, Reynolds?" *There was that pistol Harris hid beneath his suitcoat.* "Truth be told, don't know what Goblin Webber sees in ya. Be warned. Y'all came *this* far. There cain't be no turnin' back. Lest you wake some morn and find that pretty mother o' yours hangin' from an orange tree wearin' a 'Mississippi necktie' round her neck."

I looked at Skeeter. At Colleen. They were evidently used to this. I wasn't. I resented any threats against my mother, but since Harris had a sidearm there was nothing I could do. His gun gave him a license to be mean.

Skeeter Wilson and Eddie Harris gave each other looks as crazy as a pair of pet raccoons underneath a kid's red wagon.

"Git goin'," Harris ordered.

Skeeter and I got in formation. Two-hundred Klecticons formed lines outside a ten-foot wooden fence. It enclosed several thousand Klansmen. Dozens of Klaverns were assembled from the Province of Kalifornia, and a few from Arizona. This was "The biggest Naturalization ceremony in Kalifornia history."

Several faces looked familiar. Mr. Carson was reassigned to be our Kladd, the Klan's conductor who would lead us through their gates into their ceremony. He wore a suitcoat he had bought for this occasion. Odd seeing Stubby in a suit. I'd only seen him working roofing jobs before that awful accident had cost the man his hand. He pointed toward the portal with his stump and said, "Get ready. I promise you a night you won't forget."

I feared that Mr. Carson wasn't lying.

Behind the fences, I heard murmurs. Mr. Harris made a pass between our ranks and questioned Skeeter why the Ku Klux Klan burned crosses.

"That's how Klansmen show the Aliens that Jesus lights the world," Skeeter fired back.

"Attaboy, Skeeter," Harris said. "I'm mighty proud of you. A fine Klansman you'll be after tonight."

I shuddered.

Skeeter, though, was beaming with delight.

"At-ten-hut," bellowed Stubby.

We all snapped to attention.

Our degree teams had assembled, wearing suits and flag lapel pins. A cop I recognized stood just inside the gate.

Skeeter jabbed my ribs. "He's the Klexter, Skeeter whispered. "Their outer guard between us and our Naturalization."

Another man wore a black hood, with skull and crossbones on his robe across his chest. He carried a gleaming steel sword, and he looked scary, like a castoff from a Halloween fiesta, but with hands so white he looked as if he wore a pair of gloves.

"That's the Night Hawk," Skeeter said.

The rangy Night Hawk clasped a clipboard. He looked like Death did in the comic strips. I managed not to laugh.

"Men, I need each of you to sign a blank petition begging permission to become citizens of our Invisible Empire," said the Night Hawk.

We complied.

After the Night Hawk collected all our signatures he rapped three times against the gate.

"Who dares approach this Klavern?" asked the Klexter, placing himself before the entrance, holding one hand on his scabbard.

"I, the Night Hawk of the Klan,"

"Advance with the Countersign," thundered the Klexter.

Our Naturalization had begun.

The Night Hawk whispered toward the gate.

"Pass," the Klexter bellowed.

We were left outside alone, several hundred of us lined up in formation in four rows. Behind the fences, men were whispering. I wanted to skedaddle. If outsiders couldn't trust these pompous fools, then why should I? But I remembered Mr. Harris. I had to stand my ground, lest I find my mother outdoors with a Mississippi necktie. I smelled candles from their ceremonies far behind the gate.

Mr. Carson wagged his stump at us as, gave us the glare boys get in church for misbehaving.

We straightened up, like soldiers too afraid to breathe.

After ten minutes the Night Hawk reemerged.

"Worthy Aliens," said the Night Hawk. "His Excellency, the Exalted Cyclops, the direct representative of His Majesty, our Emperor and chief guardian of the portal of the Invisible Empire, has informed me it is the constant disposition of a Klansman to assist those who aspire to things noble in thought and conduct and to extend a helping hand to the worthy."

Who didn't hunger for nobility? Maybe this wasn't so bad. My mind raced to the evening Mr. Carson had his accident. Members of his brotherhood had come to lend assistance, men whom Mr. Carson knew and counted on as friends.

I'd been told that Leon Myers would be serving as the Klokard. There he was with his assistants, the Klaliff and the Kludd.

"Raise your right hands," the Kludd commanded.

Reverend Myers read aloud: "Each of the following questions must be answered by a loud and emphatic yes."

I braced. Swallowed hard and steadied myself.

Reverend Myers cleared his throat. He shined a flashlight on his clipboard. "Is the motive prompting your ambition to be a Klansman serious and unselfish?"

"YES" we said in unison.

He cleared his throat again. "Are you a native-born white, gentile American citizen?"

We all were. "YES."

"Are you absolutely free of and opposed to any allegiance of any nature to any cause, government, people, sect, or ruler that is foreign to the United States of America?"

"YES."

"Do you believe in the tenets of the Christian Religion?"

I did.

"Do you esteem the United States of America and its institutions above any other government, civil, political, or ecclesiastical in the whole world?

Like the Pope? I recalled the Klan didn't trust Catholics.

"Will you, without mental reservation, take a solemn oath to defend, preserve, and protect same?"

"YES."

"Do you believe in Klanishness and will you practice same faithfully towards Klansmen?"

"Do you believe in and will you faithfully strive for the eternal maintenance of White Supremacy?"

No, I thought. But surrounded by policemen in plain clothes, I kept thinking of that Mississippi necktie.

"YES," answered several hundred voices.

I moved my lips but spoke no words.

"Will you faithfully obey our constitution and laws and conform willingly to all our usages, requirements and regulations?

"YES."

"Can you always be depended on?"

"YES."

I held my breath. Pastor Myers lined us up in single file,

and placed our hands upon the shoulders of the Klecticons in front of us. He said, "Follow me. Be men," and led us through the outer gate toward the Klavern.

The Klexter drew his sword. "Who and what is your business?"

He locked eyes with Mr. Carson who replied, "I am the Kladd of this Klan, acting under special orders of His Excellency, our Exalted Cyclops. I am in charge of a party."

"What will be the nature of your party?" snarled the Klexter.

Mr. Carson took a breath. "Worthy Aliens from the world of selfishness and fraternal alienation, prompted by unselfish motive, desire the honor of citizenship in the Invisible Empire and the fellowship of Klansmen..."

My mind began to wander. Mr. Carson lectured on, giving a speech it must have taken him at least a year to memorize.

My throat tightened. I was shifting on my feet. My head was nodding...

"...What if one of your party should prove himself a traitor?" barked the Klexter.

I snapped back to attention, eyes wide open. It was brought home to me that I didn't fit in here. Eventually, someone would find out.

Mr. Carson raised his chin. He bellowed loud so we could hear. "He would be banished in disgrace from the Invisible Empire without fear or favor, conscience would tenaciously torment him, remorse would repeatedly revile him, and direful things befall him. All this they now know, have heard, and must heed," hissed Mr. Carson with a strange look on his face.

"Advance with the countersign," roared the Klexter.

Mr. Carson passed through the wicket, whispering to the Klexter.

The Klexter threw open the gate. "With heart and soul, I the

Klexter of this Klan welcome you and open the way for you to attain the most noble achievement in your earthly career. Be faithful and true unto death, and all will be well and your reward sure. Noble Kladd, will you pass with your party?"

We passed the outer door, marched in, and stopped.

The Klarago, another Anaheim cop and inner guard announced, "Your Excellency and Klansmen assembled, I hear the signal of the Kladd."

A man wearing a white robe with fancy black embroidered trim I took to be the Exalted Cyclops roared, "My Terrors and Klansmen, one and all, make ready!"

Each Klansman now put on his hood, both aprons down, with every robe completely buttoned. Candles were snuffed out, leaving the Klavern dark as night. We stood among them in the stillness, eyes adjusting to the dark.

"Sirs, the portal to the Invisible Empire is being opened. Your righteous prayer is answered, and you have found favor in the sight of the Exalted Cyclops and his Klansmen assembled. Follow me, and be prudent."

Behind the inner gate, the voice of Pastor Leon Myers thundered out. "God give us men." He was speaking as their Klokard.

"Men who serve not for selfish booty.

But real men, courageous, who flinch not at duty,

Men of dependable character, men of sterling worth,

Then wrongs will be redressed, and right will rule the earth,

God give us men."

The policeman serving as Klarago interrupted. "Will each of you as Klansmen always earnestly endeavor to be an answer to this prayer?"

"YES," we all murmured.

The Klarago right-faced toward the Cyclops. "Your Excellency and fellow Klansmen, just such men are standing in the portal of the Invisible Empire, desiring the lofty honor of citizenship therein, ready and willing to face every duty that may be imposed."

The Exalted Cyclops rose. "Faithful Klarago and Klansmen." His voice echoed toward the sky. "Let them enter the Klavern, but keep a Klansman's eye upon them. If one of them should flinch, show up as a coward or a scalawag in the future, it is your duty to eject him from the Invisible Empire. Be thou not recreant to duty's demands."

"Thou?" What, were we living in Elizabethan England?

The Night Hawk lifted a gasoline-drenched cross up from the altar. He struck a match and let the flames light up the Klavern. He made his way toward the Klaliff, who took and held the fiery cross.

The Klarago stepped aside. "Pass," he told the Kladd.

There were Klansmen all around me, hoods with points as sharp as icicles. We marched toward the cross of fire all in lockstep. The assembled in the Klavern gave a sign and faced the altar. We paused.

I heard a signal, and the Klansmen walked in file.

Each member slowly passed in front of us. Each looked me in the eye like they were judging me in search of any trace of insincerity. Coach Merritt glared at me and offered me a frown that could burn toast. Mister Harris shook his head. Leon Myers looked right through me, then Mr. Webber passed and didn't even glance in my direction. It seemed the only smile I got was Mr. Carson's.

Once all this was over, we sat down.

"Faithful Klaliff," said the Kladd. "These are men like the Invisible Empire and the times demand, men of strong minds and great hearts, true and faithful with ready hands, worthy Aliens known and vouched for on orders of His Excellency."

"Pass," the Klaliff ordered, but I longed to turn around. These men made pretenses of honor while conspiring in secret. I remembered Boomer Corrigan and how he had been murdered.

In line, we circled around the Klavern and then halted before the Cyclops.

We got a lecture from the Cyclops. I was starting to lose interest. We got a lecture from the Klokard. I fought to stay awake. We got a lecture from the Klaliff. I was bored out of my mind. And then the Kludd rose, and I think I fell asleep right on my feet.

Something jarred me back awake. The Exalted Cyclops stated. "If you have any doubt as to your ability to qualify either in body or character, as citizens of the Invisible Empire, you now have an opportunity to retire from this place with the good will of the Klan. I warn you now, if you falter or fail now or in the future..., you will be banished from the Invisible Empire..."

"...Do any of you wish to leave?"

He was looking my direction. Coach Merritt fired me a glare. So did Eddie Harris and Skeeter. I longed to walk away. If I left now, never again would I play baseball on their team. Plus, they would gossip, even if they didn't lynch my mother.

"Faithful Klokard, you will direct the way for these Aliens to the sacred altar."

The Night Hawk stood before us holding the fiery cross aloft between the Klavern's sacred altar and the Exalted Cyclops' throne.

The Klokard rose, approached their altar. "Your excellency," he said. "The Aliens in our midst from the world of selfish and fraternal alienation forsake the past and are now ready and willing to bind themselves to the Invisible Empire, the White Knights of the Ku Klux Klan of Kalifornia. Raise your right hand. Repeat I, and pronounce your Christian name."

The oath the man administered dragged on for twenty minutes. We repeatedly pledged ourselves to uphold Christian civilization, the Holy Writ, the Constitution (as originally written), the Constitution of the White Knights of the Klan of Kalifornia, the lawful orders of our Klan officers, to the brotherhood of the Klan, to the Almighty, as if all of these were somehow interchangeable. We pledged to resist Satan and the Satanic force of evil, but I feared my new companions more than I'd ever feared Satan.

"I do hereby bind myself to this oath unto my grave, so help me, Almighty God."

At last, the oath had ended.

The Exalted Cyclops lofted up a vessel filled with fluid. "With this transparent, life-giving, powerful, God-given fluid, more precious and far more significant than all the sacred oils of the ancients, I set you apart to the great and honorable task you have aspired to as citizens of the Invisible Empire. You will kneel."

Four hooded Klansmen hummed in barbershop, the tune, "Just as I Am.

The Exalted Cyclops stood. "Sirs, 'Neath the fiery cross...I dedicate you...to the holy service of our country, our Klan, our homes, each other, and humanity."

He sprayed a few drops of his oil on our backs and said, "In body", he placed a few drops on our heads and said, "In mind." He placed a few drops on his hand and tossed it upward, saying, "In spirit." He let his hand circle above, saying, "And in life."

The Kludd offered a prayer.

"Stand," bellowed the Cyclops. "You are no longer strangers

or Aliens among us, but are citizens. I on behalf of our Emperor and all Klansmen welcome you to citizenship in the Empire of chivalry, honor, industry, and love."

He raised his hood.

I was shocked. That half-blind umpire, Ace Clarkson, was the Cyclops.

The other Klansmen raised their hoods, but I was choking back my laughter.

"By authority vested in me by our Emperor, I now declare and proclaim you as citizens of the Invisible Empire, the White Knights of the Ku Klux Klan, Realm of Kalifornia, the most honorable among men."

"A Klansman," roared hooded people all around me.

I stood spellbound.

Several hundred wooden crosses had been stacked beside the gates outside the Klavern. Citrus aromas filled the Orange County skies along with scents of buttered popcorn, cotton candy and the faint whiff of manure from the Karnival's events.

Crosses were lashed up by the picnic benches, crosses made from orangewood I'd seen bulldozed from the orchard only fourteen hours ago. There were those paper billboard LOUIS J. ELWOOD eyeglasses some Klansman had retrieved, had torn in half, and set aside to light the fire, along with sawdust they had raked in from the midway.

Men buttoning Klan robes were assembling, packed into Anaheim Central Park, pulling hoods over their faces. Klansmen glared out through the hood slits. Panic filled me. I felt as though a mob were being assembled. A pit formed in my stomach as the mob become unruly.

Hundreds, even thousands of men covered in white sheets had come from distant towns like Bakersfield and West San

Bernardino. They came with gasoline, and kerosene, and lighter fluid in cans, waving their flags, and singing hymns that left my bones colder than ice.

The pleasant citrus scent was drowned out with the stink of gasoline men poured across the orangewood crosses, a stench so strong it hurt my eyes.

"Down there," hissed a Klansmen. East of Anaheim Central Park beyond the bandshell and the picnic tables the steeple of Saint Boniface Catholic Church rose in the night. There, hooded Klansmen marched toward the lawn in eerie silence.

Twenty Klansmen drenched the church front lawn with gasoline.

Oh God!

The lights were on inside the building.

We made our way toward the church, where I heard singing and an organ playing Bach's "Saint Matthew Passion."

Knowing Klansmen hated Catholics, I swallowed back my dread.

With people inside?

Really?

From the church rang women's voices.

Glancing up, I froze in horror.

Klansmen bellowed outside, "Mine eyes have seen the glory of the Lord."

Skeeter Wilson and Eddie Harris looked on like a pair of rabid hound dogs smelling flesh for the first time. Thousands of Klansmen had assembled. They were passing around crosses, sticks and torches. Behind us came their giant fiery cross.

My heart was battering my chest. Revulsion thudded through my temples. This was not what I signed up for. I fought back an urge to retch.

Ace Clarkson drove up with a pickup truck bed stacked with orangewood kindling. Men stacked the branches on the lawn. Someone doused the sticks with kerosene and wrapped the billboard paper into a three-foot paper cylinder so one big billboard eyeball circumscribed the roll.

The fiery cross arrived and dipped to light the kindling.

Fire roared up like a dragon toward the moon, twenty feet high. Robed men lit crosses in the bonfire, held them up like torches. Flames were passed from cross to cross. Gasoline gathered in our throats until the crosses were all lit and held aloft against the sky, making the night so bright I thought it was still daytime.

Heat from flames seared all around us. I mopped hot sweat from my forehead. Klansmen circled stained glass windows, throwing rocks, screaming "Come out you filthy Catholics." Their gasoline fumes left me dizzy, and smoke made it hard to see who drenched the front doors of the church with lighter fluid.

The music *inside* had gone silent.

I shut my eyes and prayed nobody might get hurt.

Outside the Klan pounded the doors, then lit the wood.

A pine tree lit ablaze. Its flames shot skyward though dry needles.

The front door smoldered in the night beneath a fireproof stone wall. And then the flames went out. The August night filled up with oily smoke. I stood in horror on the gasoline-soaked lawn and saw the silhouettes of Klansmen pass the stained glass toward the rear doors of the church.

Girls in choir robes were scrambling outside to save their lives.

Two girls turned and sprinted toward me, Barbara Bannerman and her friend, Ethel. Like rabbits herded toward the center of a ring of men with hunting dogs, they shot toward us in terror, at full sprint.

Shrieking.

Screaming.

I saw a third girl.

My gut felt like I'd just swallowed a thirty-five-pound biscuit

Alma! Alma Martin, the neighbor girl who'd always been a friend, who'd gone to prom with Boomer Corrigan. She'd baked me macaroons after my Pa died.

She was screaming out my name.

"NO, GOD NO, DEAN. NOT YOU TOO!"

I longed to melt away in shame.

Barbara tripped, lost her footing in the gasoline-soaked grass. She splattered like a broken doll one-hundred feet in front of us. Her chin sported a gash. She wiped her arm across her eyes. Her hair was soaked in gasoline and mud.

Alma skidded to a stop, tugging Barbara to her feet. Both girls faced us.

Glared.

Klansmen perambulated forward. They lifted torches overhead.

"Run." shrieked Alma. "For your life."

Alma sprinted my direction toward the darkness as our eyes locked.

Alma dropped her gaze and sprinted faster.

I watched her heart break.

Felt my soul implode with shame. I had betrayed her.

The flames from fiery crosses seemed to char through my insides as though I'd damned Alma to hell.

And damned myself.

She galloped past me, terror singed into her face, pumping her arms, not looking back, with Barbara Bannerman a few paces behind her. Blood poured out from Barbara's jaw.

Quick as does, they sprinted past me disappearing into darkness and the night, making it clear never again could we be friends.

Her terror seared into my thoughts.

The echoes of their footsteps thundered eastward along dirty asphalt streets. I watched them zigzag toward Central Park and down dark streets of Anaheim, reflecting back the cruel light of our torches.

Then I felt silence, save for the roaring of our kerosene-flame crosses as they crackled in the dark, lighting night up with their stench until I wondered if we'd filled the sky with hatred or with brimstone.

Someone in the Klan gave out a piercing Rebel yell.

I heard another crack, but this one sounded loud, like a report heard from a hunting rifle.

"Sniper," yelled a Klansmen. "To the west."

Shouts arose.

A flashlight pointed toward a tree. And then another tree. Another.

"Where's that bastard?" yelled Ace Clarkson. He wagged his flashlight toward a pine tree. There was no finding Ace's sniper, for we couldn't see each other through the haze.

"Anyone see him?" Ace's flashlight now blinked out.

Murmurs grew louder.

Someone lit another flashlight, but it couldn't pierce the smoke.

The Anaheim cop who'd been the Klarago fired back toward the tree.

No return fire.

Mr. Harris shot six bullets.

No reply.

Maybe the sniper had been hit.

No one seemed eager to find out. Then again, if he'd been hit he should have fallen from that tree.

The crowd dispersed through sooty fog, leaving the church structure still standing, minus front doors, and a tree, and a lawn soaked in gasoline. My lungs were aching from the fumes of all the fuel we'd been inhaling. Several thousand angry Klansmen, backed by Anaheim's police force, disappeared into the balmy summer night.

The crosses burned more distant as we scattered through the streets until at last the angry flames had flickered out.

Tonight I knew I wouldn't sleep. Alma's words spun through my mind, a broken cylinder repeated on a never-ending Victrola:

"NO, DEAN. NOT YOU TOO."

I kept seeing Alma's tears, and the ceremony words from Stubby Carson echoed back. "If one of them should flinch or show up as a coward..."

I was a coward.

And so was everybody else I'd seen tonight.

Except for Alma. She had turned around to rescue Barbara Bannerman.

I was in the Ku Klux Klan with all their rights, titles, and honors.

I was a Ghoul.

I wondered if I'd ever sleep again.

CHAPTER XV

MONDAY, JULY 28, 1924

The shadows from the moonlight crept between the blinds into my bedroom, pasting narrow slats of light against the plaster. My bed felt hot, so hot my cotton sheets were marinated in sweat. My bed pillows were drenched. I kicked the covers to the floor.

I couldn't sleep. The horror I had seen on Alma's face kept me awake. To think, I used to be a decent guy. Or so I'd thought. Now I knew different. Sadly, I was not alone. My whole town was infected with a virus just as cruel as the wave of influenza that had carried off my Pa.

The alarm clock by my bedside seemed to tick at the wrong speed. Bars of moonlight pendulated up and down the wall. I pulled the blinds up, glared out through my dusty bedroom window toward Alma's house. I wondered if she sat in there and wept.

I wiped sweat out of my hair, wishing I could weep as well.

Three a.m. Too soon to start my paper route, I thought. But still, I left the house peddling my rusty yellow Schwinn. I hoped my neighbors wouldn't see me. In thirty minutes, Rollo Earnest would be setting out his *Orange County Plain Dealers* and we'd fold and wrap them up in rubber bands and cram one-hundred morning editions into our ink-stained denim bike bags. I pedaled off to work at double-time.

And I was glad when Mr. Earnest showed up early to his office.

Three stacks of *Orange County Plain Dealers* felt hotter than the pepper fields east of town in summer. Headlines burned above the fold beneath a line of fiery crosses:

ANAHEIM FOR GOD AND COUNTRY

The irony appalled me.

I scanned the paper for the truth.

It wasn't there.

My heart sank, and my hands felt as cold as winter frost on oranges.

There were photographs of Klansmen shaking hands outside their Karnival. There was the Reverend Leon Myers with his patronizing smile, baring teeth sharp as a whiskey bottle smashed to start a fight. There were no photos of Saint Boniface or girls fleeing in terror. The winners wrote the history books. Lies bled through the headlines. I felt heartsick. This morning I'd deliver only lies.

But who on earth was I to point a finger?

I kept secrets of my own and lacked guts to speak the truth. I felt alone, pedaling past memories of Anaheim, past bungalows and ballfields, past city parks and orchards. *This is not the town that raised me*, I kept thinking. But perhaps it really was, a town where small-town sensibilities masked big-city enigmas.

I prayed I'd never have to live in paradise again.

There was a note beside my bed when I returned after my paper route. My mother said she'd answered several calls from Mr. Webber. Said there was something at his house he thought I needed to pick up. She queried me how Helen was.

"Helen's fine," I lied.

Within five minutes I was out the door and halfway toward the house where Mr. Webber lived, where Helen used to live, but didn't now. I sensed from half a block away, the Webber house wasn't the same.

Once I set foot inside the living room my fears were all confirmed.

The pictures of Helen had been removed. Only picture hangers remained inside fresh squares of floral wallpaper the sun had yet to fade. I thought of asking what had happened, but I knew.

And Mr. Webber knew.

He wanted to know more.

"When was the last time you saw Helen?"

Nervous, I stepped back.

"We saw a movie at the theater. *Dorothy Vernon of Haddon Hall*. Three weeks ago," I said.

It was the truth. I was lucky I'd been asked an easy question. I didn't need to talk about my journey north to Lankershim.

"I understand Helen's in Mexico." Webber lit a Lucky Strike. Inhaled. Blew a smoke ring. It drifted off into the curtains.

My heart sank. He exhaled again and stank up the whole living room. He knew more than I'd hoped, and I fought hard to keep my mouth shut. A cuckoo clock went off inside the kitchen. *Eight a.m.*

I asked, "Is Mrs. Webber still asleep?"

"Emily's heartbroken. Helen takes a lot after her mother, just like Bert took after me before he killed himself at Stanford."

Bert didn't kill himself, I thought. *It was an accident. A fall when he'd been drunk.* I didn't argue. I only knew now Webber's stories didn't match. He seemed to make things up to suit the conversation the way you do when something hurts so bad you can't express the truth. I felt bad enough his daughter had run off, but I was holding back my own truths, her failed pregnancy, our prom fiasco, my excursion up to Lankershim.

Thank God, Webber hadn't asked about those matters.

"Dean, to be honest..." Mr. Webber frowned and hitched up his suspenders with his thumbs.

My heart stopped. I swallowed. *Here it comes.*

"Emily's back in Iowa for a spell," said Mr. Webber.

I exhaled.

"We had a fight." Mr. Webber tore the cover off his matchbook. "She insists that I take out a second mortgage on our house to buy some oil stock her father's pushing. Julian Petroleum. Says we'll finally be rich." Webber shook his head. "I have my doubts. I believe in working *hard* to make a living. These modern women have *ideas.* They believe in easy money. I like old-fashioned women, gals who show a decent man respect."

"I'm sorry, sir." *Their fight must have been one lollapalooza.*

Webber sailed off on tangents like I wasn't in the room. "Have you noticed how modern women kiss like movie stars?" he said. "Their kisses telegraph a working man don't matter anymore. Like something's *wrong* with us. They're colder than Pacific Fruit Express cars."

"I don't think that's the reason, sir, you asked me here," I muttered.

Webber puffed his cigarette. "That's right. We have some business."

He gestured me into the extra bedroom. He pressed the light switch in the closet. Moved aside a bag of golf clubs. Kicked the rug away beneath it. I was looking at a trap door.

"What's this?" I asked. "A secret entrance?"

Beneath the trap door was a staircase. Mr. Webber struck a match and lit a candle. He led me underneath the footing and outside beneath those tennis courts I'd seen them putting in the previous May. Redwood boards, holding back dirt were built on both sides of the stairwell like a set inside a gold mine in an old Francis Ford Western.

There was a small room at the bottom lined with masonry block walls. Two shafts of light came through the ceiling through a pair of iron vent pipes. The floors were made of the same redwood that had lined the hidden staircase. A wall calendar showed photographs of fully naked women.

No wonder the man's wife didn't trust him. There were stacks of magazines, some from the Klan, like *Dawn* and *Kourier*, others with awful illustrations of nude women, bound and gagged. Next to the calendar a frame held a certificate:

HERBERT WEBBER SR.

This proclaims to the world that the above-named person has stepped forward and distinguished himself through his quest for citizenship in the Invisible Empire and has fully met the qualifications required by the Invisible Empire and has expressed his desire to serve the Empire and the White Race for the betterment of both

on this date, this person of honor, before God and man has been
duly appointed to the rank of

GHOUL

I hereby command all Klansman of the IKA Empire to show due
respect to this person. At the same time, I command this ghoul
to obey all laws and orders given him by all senior officers. This
citizenship is valid until revoked.

WITNESS IMPERIAL WIZARD

August 1923

The fading signature below was now illegible.

Beneath a cartridge box of Smith & Wesson 0.38 special bullets lay a stack of several envelopes. One with *my* name was on top.

"This is yours," said Mr. Webber. It was a plain manila envelope. No writing. "You're gonna need to find a safe place you can store this."

I peeked inside. My new certificate looked just like Mr. Webber's. There was a membership list, mimeographed and reeking of fresh ink. It had been cut from an old stencil. The letter "e's" were filled with ink, and there were faint lavender creases where the stencil had worn through.

I was fighting back my nerves.

"Well, there you are," said Mr. Webber. "Remember 'Klansmen deal with Klansmen.'" He quoted this like it was scripture. "Any money Rollo pays you should be spent in Klan establishments. We put the flag in the front window so you'll know we're in the Klan. Rollo Earnest pays attention. And you know he runs the press."

"You mean the *Orange County Plain Dealer*."

"Only paper we read or need."

Mr. Webber snuffed his Lucky Strike butt out into an ashtray. His secret room was filled with man stuff, a Smith & Wesson single-action, a hip flask, ashtrays, girlie magazines, Cuban cigars, Movie-star photographs. The top one had the bottom half burned off below the shoulders. She'd been naked.

It was a photograph of Helen.

I tried not to look surprised and shot a glance toward Mr. Webber. His weary gaze was hard as granite. His face bore no trace of a smile. He looked hard-boiled like a man who had been knifed and healed over without scars. I understood now why the Ku Klux Klan was fixated on aliens. They'd been wounded. They understood alienation.

But they were taking their revenge against the innocent.

And I knew who was in the Klan now. All of Rollo Earnest's customers. *My* customers. I'd been pedaling past their houses every morning. It never had occurred to me they might be in the Klan.

Or that they drank.

Or collected naked pictures of young girls, or somehow came into possession of nude photos of their daughters.

Maybe that was why he trusted me. He knew that I was "safe" and would watch out for pretty Helen when she ventured up to Hollywood. She'd gotten pregnant. I wondered if John Gilbert was the father.

Or?

It was a thought I didn't care to entertain even though Helen had said Daddy was a lecher.

But I knew the Klan kept secrets. Secrets I didn't want to know. I climbed the stairs two at a time, somehow keeping a straight face. I thought of Webber and his daughter, wondered what Helen hadn't told me. Had someone tipped the old man off about his daughter's occupation, or had he mail-ordered pictures, found his daughter's in the package, and had the "decency" to burn the lower half?

"Rollo Earnest will be in touch with you next time we meet in Klavern." Mr. Webber shook my hand. It felt like holding a dead snake.

I clutched my stomach, rushed outside, shaking off the heebie-jeebies and stepped out into a postcard-perfect California morning with flag-lined streets, a lemonade stand, canopies of jacarandas. A pair of girls in bloomers were playing hopscotch on the sidewalk.

Nice to know that the façade was still intact. I tried to smile. But my kit-bag was overflowing now. The smile never came.

CHAPTER XVI

SATURDAY, AUGUST 3, 1924

At nine o'clock I made my way toward the ballfields at Anaheim Union High School where Coach Merritt was assembling us for practice. It was the start of a new season. Coach wanted everybody there. He'd told us this year our opponents would be ready.

The empty hole where my orchard billboard was demolished made me sad. The steady eyeglasses and eyes of Doctor Louis J. Elwood and the lion underneath it had been torched to set the fire at Saint Boniface. That had happened just last week. It seemed a century ago. The searing kiss I'd shared with Helen had grown colder than the ashes of the burnt and blackened tree stump that still stood outside Saint Boniface.

But today I had to focus on my pitching.

I walked down Center Street. My baseball glove, my autographed Joe Jackson on my right fist had, until now, made me feel like a champion. I remembered how Ace Clarkson, aka

"Exalted Cyclops" had made a bad call on a pitch that let us win in the ninth inning.

I'd written it off to his bad vision. But it wasn't about eyesight. All of Anaheim seemed more fake than an eighteen-dollar bill. We shouldn't even have been champions. Santa Ana should have won. Ace had called strike three a ball right before Skeeter's clutch home run.

Our win had felt good at the time, but the veneer had been scraped off.

"How's that arm, son?" yelled Coach Merritt.

He was standing in the dugout. Skeeter Wilson stood beside him, acting like the Ku Klux Klan had made him special.

"Time to show us how that arm feels," Merritt said.

Eddie Harris and his twin sister, Colleen, had both shown up. Colleen was holding Skeeter's hand while he grinned wide.

"It's feeling better," I replied, pasting on a smile.

"Throw some pitches, Dean," said Merritt.

I made my way toward the mound. Skeeter tossed me out a baseball. Eddie stepped into the batter's box, knocked red clay from his cleats.

I threw a fastball.

Eddie lined it into center field.

It seemed my fastball had no zip today. My curveball wasn't curving. My change-up wasn't changing, and my slider wasn't sliding.

Coach Merritt glared at me. He spat tobacco, shaking his bald head. Everything I threw across the plate was getting hit. "Your arm okay, son?" Merritt asked,

"Hurts a little bit." I lied, feeling my arm ache.

"Well ice it down, son," said Coach Merritt. "And go home. Maybe try again tomorrow."

My arm was throbbing. I grabbed my baseball glove and walked out through the outfield to Center Street and gravitated west along the roadside. Up ahead, the orange packing house appeared to need some work. A wall of Helen's picture crates was stacked along the driveway. They were fading in the sun. A truck pulled up into the rutted gravel driveway, and three workers loaded crates into its truck bed.

Morning glared into my eyes. I pulled the bill down on my ballcap and kept walking several blocks up to the spot where Boomer Corrigan had died. I thought of Alma. She was probably at home now and still heartbroken.

I wished that I could speak with Boomer Corrigan.

He'd lost his father, just like me. He'd liked Alma. I had too. But Boomer recognized the good in her while I'd been selling out, and to the Klan, hoping somebody would come to my assistance. But the people in the Ku Klux Klan were messed up worse than I was. I'd been seduced into their whirlwind. I feared I'd lose my soul if I continued. I pitied them but felt too weak to fight them.

Glancing up, I saw a Cadillac the same bright red as Margaret's.

It was the first time I wished Margaret hadn't left.

I missed her. She'd moved away to Tulsa, Oklahoma, which I'd heard made Anaheim look like a picnic. They'd had race riots in 1921, and several hundred blacks were murdered in the aftermath by uniformed police. Still that wasn't in the history books. It wasn't in the newspapers.

Margaret had told me it was true.

We'd told ourselves that Anaheim was different.

Was it really?

But Margaret had escaped. First she'd slipped into a bottle, but she'd managed to crawl out. And she'd told me how she'd done it. Wanting out too, I prayed to any higher power who might listen. I steeled my jaw and turned to face the sun.

I ran home at a slow jog, past the packing house, the orchard where the billboard had been torn down, past my high school, past Saint Boniface, past Helen's house, past Alma's.

I knew who had helped Margaret.

Perhaps there was a chance they could help me.

I made my way up my front steps, dashed to my bedroom, threw off my t-shirt, put on a collared one and sprinted north up Palm Street.

Reaching Saint Boniface Church, I stooped to finally catch my breath.

Its burnt-out doors were boarded over. A canvas sack covered the charred corpse of a tree stump, and the dying lawn still reeked of gasoline. A Model T was parked outside of the back door. The car belonged to Father Patrick Browne, who'd been ordained in Dublin, in Great Britain, back before the Irish Free State was created.

I'd never met him.

I shut my eyes and prayed that he might listen to me, help me find some clarity, perhaps even forgive me.

In one fist, I held the envelope I had from Mr. Webber. The other held the baseball glove I'd put on for my practice.

There was a line by the confession booth.

I slipped in at the end, letting people cut in front of me who showed up after I did.

I felt more alien than ever. Plaster statues filled this huge cavernous sanctuary, and Jesus statues stared down from the wall beneath fourteen Roman numerals between the timber trusses.

The line in front of me had gotten shorter.

After an hour a tiny Mexican *mujer* I'd let in front of me made her way out from the wooden door and whispered my direction. *"Toca a usted."*

There was nobody behind me.

She looked at me and gave a toothless grin.

I stepped away.

She wrapped her shawl around her face, turned on heels the size of horseshoes. She moseyed out the door tying her red and green *mantilla*.

I held my breath and made my way into a lacquered wooden booth, holding my baseball glove and envelope in front of me.

My heart was pounding. *I shouldn't be here.* I blushed, forced a grin, straightened up against my chairback. I looked above the metal screen and stammered. "Bless me f-f-father."

No answer.

I tried to think of what I should say next. I glanced down at my feet. "For we have sinned."

The breathing of the priest came through the grille of the confession booth. I didn't want to be here. I wasn't sure why I had come.

"Yes, my son."

I cleared my throat. "Sir, I'm not Catholic," I said.

"I know that," said the priest. "But you've come here for a reason, and I'm willing to listen. It's entirely your choice."

My pulse throbbed in my ears. Catholic churches felt so foreign. I wasn't used to seeing Mexicans in church, even on Saturday. I reminded myself lots and lots of Mexicans were Catholic. Signs on Protestant church lawns still read "No Mexicans or

Dogs." We weren't used to sharing churches with Hispanics.

"So you play baseball?" Father Browne asked, trying to penetrate my silence.

"Yes, sir," I muttered.

"What position?" I was surprised the man had asked. Evidently he was trying to find a way to break the ice. I couldn't fault the man for that. "Um, I'm a pitcher for the Colonists."

"Do you have a favorite player?"

"Joe Jackson," I replied.

"Interesting," said Father Browne. The priest's shadow leaned back.

I popped open the door. "Aren't there more people outside?" I asked. I glanced outside and prayed for an excuse so I could leave.

There was no one else in line.

Nervously, I pulled the door shut. I was stuck here in confession. No one else could take my place, and Father Browne seemed well aware of this. He wasn't in a hurry.

"Why Shoeless Joe?" asked Father Browne. I shot a glance down at my envelope, the reason I was here. *Why were we talking about baseball?*

"I met him once," said Father Browne. "When he was playing with the White Sox, in 1920 in Chicago, the year after the scandal."

"Did you like him?"

"I felt sad for him. The man had played his heart out in the Series. Batted three-seventy-five against the Reds. And then they kicked him out of baseball when he didn't rat his friends out. How do you feel about that?"

"I haven't thought about it much, but I am wondering why we're talking about Joe Jackson."

I peered up at the ceiling. There was a water spot above

me where the lacquer had peeled off. The naked wood looked white like leprosy.

"Shoeless Joe said he was innocent. Are you innocent, my son?"

"No," I whispered.

"Is there something I should hear?" The priest leaned forward.

My throat constricted so tightly I feared I wore a noose. I raised the hand holding the envelope and shoved it his direction. "We torched your church. In my hand I have a roster of the Klan members." My face went white. I'd just betrayed a trust, even an oath. I'd been told I might be banished from the Invisible Empire like Joe Jackson was from baseball. But then Joe Jackson never squealed on his friends. Either way I had a problem but didn't care.

Or did I? Coach Merritt would never let me pitch again. Skeeter, Eddie, and Colleen would never speak with me again. Stubby Carson would never hire me. Rollo Earnest would surely fire me. The Webbers would all turn on me. Leon Myers would excommunicate me. All of this would happen within days if they found out.

The thought of losing all my friends sent a jolt into my chest. I'd be a traitor, someone nobody in Anaheim could trust. I didn't care about their Empire, but I cared about my life.

"So you are in the Ku Klux Klan?"

I sucked in a giant breath and stammered, "Yes."

"Do you understand why people join the Klan?"

"To hate?" I asked.

"I have a theory." The priest's shadow leaned forward.

So did I.

"Well son, suppose a simple man feels betrayed by those he cares about. His boss, his wife, his children don't appreciate his efforts. They let him know. Or say his country sends an army to his state and burns it down, like General Sherman did in Georgia."

"What about it? Is there some reason you defend the Ku Klux Klan?"

"I'm simply trying to understand them, son."

"What's there to understand? Sir, I can give you all their names. I have them right here in this envelope. Here take it."

"Can't do that, son."

My jaw dropped to my shirt. "You can't...?"

"There's a seal on the confessional."

"Are you saying you don't even care who tried to burn your church down?"

"I've been listening to confessions from parishioners all day. I can't tell you what I've heard, but I believe you can imagine."

I exhaled.

"Think about it."

"I have been, and I'm sorry, sir," I whispered.

"I believe you, son. But some things are complex."

I realized there might be shooting as my thoughts returned to Saturday, the sniper, screaming girls, guns in window racks in pickup trucks. Catholics weren't stupid. The Klan had fired the first shot, but I had a sinking feeling the war the Ku Klux Klan had started wasn't over.

"Some very angry people have made confessions here," the priest said. "Being from Ireland, I've known Catholics who've warred against the Protestants. People died. Died by the thousands. I don't want any more violence. Son, your sins have been forgiven. God be with you."

"Good day, Father."

"I will ask almighty God to find a way for you to rise above your circumstances."

I rose and stepped outside of the confession booth.

The lights were off inside the church. There was no one else in line. I made my way out from the sanctuary, guided by the light from stained glass windows.

I dreaded violence I feared might take more lives.

CHAPTER XVII

SUNDAY, AUGUST 4, 1924

On Sunday morning outside the parking lot of Saint Boniface Catholic Church, I got the feeling I had walked up to the edges of Dodge City. My baseball glove I'd need for practice after church hung from my belt while I clutched onto the envelope I'd offered Father Browne. Remorseful, but bewildered, I had no clue what to do with it. So many Catholics were armed. I was afraid and kept my distance.

Men bore more sidearms than Bat Masterson and Wyatt Earp combined. Their families glanced over their shoulders to make sure no strangers followed. Dark-haired pigtailed girls in dresses and their ragtag little brothers sprinted from weathered Model T's into open guarded entrances where boards had been removed to let parishioners inside. Behind the children marched their mothers, gazes as focused as Annie Oakley's, followed by fathers strapped in bullet belts like freshly armed *banditos*.

I glanced down at my baseball glove and hurried across Palm Street. Making my way a half-block northeast, I watched more pickup trucks arrive, sporting gun racks in their cabs. Every pickup had a shotgun. The trucks were herded toward the church inside a makeshift roped corral where Irishmen the size of steam boilers sat guard on folding chairs with Springfield rifles lying ready at their sides.

Armed men guarded every entrance, Germans, Irishmen, Sonorans. The incident last week had brought them new-found solidarity. It seemed their anger at the Ku Klux Klan had bonded them in wariness. I recalled what Father Browne had said. Parishioners were fuming. I'd had no idea how angry people were until right now.

Alma entered the church alone. I dared not meet her gaze. My heart felt heavy, filled with sorrow. Poor girl probably felt orphaned.

Barbara Bannerman was wearing a huge bandage on her jaw. She must have gashed it pretty bad. I had to turn away.

You go through life thinking you're good, only to learn you've no more conscience than the Cavalry at Wounded Knee or Germans mustard-gassing Ypres. I used to think I had more scruples. Mine were easily short-circuited. I sat alone across the street, face in my hands, squeezing my glove and saying prayers that the Anaheim I loved saw no more hatred.

Catholic mass lasted forever. I'd never sat through one before, yet here I was, sitting outside amidst the mourning doves and crows, biting my lip, fighting an anger I had turned against myself. I wished somehow I could weep, except I couldn't find the courage. I pounded on my glove like I was punching my own soul.

When church was over I wandered south, hoping nobody had seen me. New black Ford pickup trucks were showing up for mass at nine o'clock. I still felt guilty. I walked down Center

Street and kicked a rock in front of me, due west, toward where Boomer had been killed.

I was more convinced than ever Boomer Corrigan had been murdered. I could understand why Catholics were coming to church armed. They were on-edge, and sad they'd all been forced to act like *vigilantes*. Since the cops had turned against them, there was no one to protect them when their families were threatened, or in Boomer's case, were murdered.

Scents of citrus smoke still lingered from last week's Extravaklanza. Another orchard had been bulldozed, making way for more development. Two blocks away on the main diamond north of Anaheim Union High my baseball teammates were assembling for an unofficial practice on a Sunday. I didn't join them. I had too much on my mind. Even thinking of Coach Merritt tied my stomach up in knots.

Coach Merritt blew his whistle. His pink cheeks bellowed on both sides. He wasn't looking my direction. I crossed the street, while ducking down.

He hadn't seen me.

I glanced at my old Joe Jackson glove.

I thumped it. It felt hollow, as if my baseball days were over.

And yet I didn't have a plan. Within a month my senior year would start. I'd drifted off from everyone I'd counted as a friend. Surely no Catholics would talk to me, especially Alma Martin. I didn't dare speak to Coach Merritt, or Eddie Harris, or Skeeter Wilson, who only cared about the Ku Klux Klan and went around now bragging about last Saturday. Pa was dead, and Ma was living as if Pa had never died, thinking our town was like some Norman Rockwell painting.

I made my way beyond the packing house. Another row of orange crates with Helen's glowing face on them was stacked beside the driveway. I longed to cry, but I still couldn't. I thought of Helen and her father. I choked, knowing why Helen had turned out the way she had. Her father used her. She used me. It was a never-ending cycle. The Ku Klux Klan was only window-dressing, giving people somebody to hate, so in the end they wouldn't need to hate themselves.

The way I hated myself now.

Somehow I needed to break free. I had no plans, but playing baseball wasn't going to get me out of this.

I shut my eyes and wished I'd never heard about the Klan.

A car horn honked.

Startled, I jumped off the unpaved roadway.

Gravel sprayed up from the tires against my dungarees and stung.

The truck veered to the shoulder.

The rusty orange pickup truck belonged to Barbara Bannerman's old man. There was a shotgun in the rack.

Mr. Bannerman sat alone. He rolled the window of his truck down, spat tobacco onto the asphalt, poked his head out toward Center Street. He pointed my direction.

Boomer Corrigan had died almost right here.

I gulped hard.

His finger motioned my direction.

"Git in, Reynolds."

My heart rattled like a Thompson submachine gun.

Mr. Bannerman shoved the passenger door open near the roadside. He was drumming on the steering wheel and gesturing me forward. "I didn't drive out here to hurt you, Dean. Just git inside the truck. Father Browne sent me. Couple of people from our church have plans to kill you."

I glanced over my shoulder, slid inside the truck and ducked, closing the door so quick I barely yanked my foot inside ahead of it.

He'd left the engine running. Now he shifted into second gear. We jerked and hightailed out of Anaheim at thirty miles an hour. I glanced toward his hip, saw his gun and held back panic.

Bannerman took us through a maze of gravel roads and herds of dairy cows and then into the oilfields northwest of Buena Park. I was reminded of the rides I'd taken once with Stubby Carson, or Mr. Webber before the Ku Klux Klan had gotten in the way. Now I rode with the other side, grateful we were outside town. It was more than just confusing; I was frightened for my life.

We entered L.A. County, speeding beside a string of telegraph poles stretching from the county line for miles toward Los Angeles. Signs pointed right toward Pasadena, and Frank Bannerman veered north. I wished I had a clue where we were headed.

He rolled the window up and glanced at me. "That tree your friends burnt down last week." He lit himself a cigarette, wagged it in-between his teeth. The San Gabriel Mountains rose above the valley floor. Bannerman swerved to miss a jackrabbit and sped along the asphalt, letting the truck cab fill with smoke so thick my eyes began to water.

He cleared his throat. "The first Christmas tree was planted by Saint Boniface, the patron saint of Germany, to reflect the Tree of Life. We planted our Christmas tree your friends burned down clear back in 1880. Thanks to them, our cherished Tree of Life is now 'The Stump of Death.'"

I dared not ask about his daughter, but he seemed to read my mind. "You hear my daughter just got 27 stitches in her chin?"

"No," I said, swallowing hard, glancing back down at his pistol.

Bannerman shifted into third. "You probably reckon I'm your enemy."

I nodded, saying nothing.

"I'm the only friend you have right now. I wouldn't trust the Klan." Bannerman signaled to change lanes.

"I know. I don't." I glanced over my shoulder at the road.

A red Ford pickup and a dirty yellow Oakland drove behind us.

"A pair of Anaheim police killed Boomer Corrigan," said Bannerman. He drummed his fingers on the dashboard. "Christ, Dean, don't you even know? Our whole parish knows, but nobody in Anaheim will listen. Couple of Anaheim police learned Boomer's parents were providing competition, bootlegging liquor."

"You're saying *cops* killed Boomer's parents?"

My mind veered into overdrive. If that were true, it meant the Klan had wiped out Boomer's entire family. My stomach churned. And right in Anaheim. But who would ever know, given the cops would surely take care of each other? And what jury in Anaheim would send a cop to prison?

Mr. Bannerman changed lanes. "Dean, that's what everybody thinks."

"Everybody in your parish?"

"Well, we can't go to the police. They're in the Klan with all your friends. What are we Catholics supposed to do? Move away from our home town because we're threatened?"

He downshifted into second and made a right turn onto San Gabriel Boulevard.

I sucked my cheeks in, feeling big dry gobs of cotton in my mouth.

I exhaled. "Where are we going?"

"Mountains north of Pasadena. Mount Lowe Tavern. Dean, you're gonna need some time to sort your thoughts out. So that's where *you're* going." Bannerman looked at me and snuffed his cigarette out. "As for me, I'm driving home. I told your mother you'll be safe. Your pa and I used to be friends. But all the Catholics know your name now. Seems you're the only Dean in Anaheim, and Alma called your name out. Every Catholic in town knows who you are."

I shuddered.

"And I'm afraid two of our church members are threatening to get even."

"You mean they're coming after me?" I looked over my shoulder. A black Dodge, the red Ford pickup and yellow Oakland were behind us.

"Hard to say. Not every Catholic in town is in agreement. Some like me are pretty scared. Some have already left town. But there are two angry parishioners who want to send a message."

"You mean get even. Murder a Klansman." (*Which was evidently me.*)

"I'm just repeating what I've heard."

"Wipe out my family, even the score. So first you drive me out of town." My heart surged into high gear amidst this whirlwind of vendettas.

"Only you, Dean. I have yet to hear a threat against your mother."

"She's innocent." I grabbed my baseball glove and pounded it in rage. Then I stared out through the windshield, toward mountains in the distance, now aware two guys in Anaheim were looking for revenge. Somewhere up there was Mount Lowe, slightly lower than Mount Wilson. It wasn't where I'd planned to spend the weekend.

Or get murdered.

The black Dodge made a right on Valley Boulevard.

"This is complicated, Dean. It isn't safe to stay in Anaheim. And nobody quite knows whose side you're on after the fire."

I was fed up with the Ku Klux Klan but knew I couldn't say so. "Are you absolutely sure my ma is safe?" I glanced toward Bannerman.

"She is for now, Dean. She'll be safer if you lay low for a while. That way no one can put you and her together."

I kept my mouth shut. This was a stupid war, and one I'd never wanted. But the Catholics and Ku Klux Klan were at each other's throats, and I was stuck right in the middle. I didn't want Ma dragged in with me.

The red Ford pickup and yellow Oakland were both still in the rear view.

Bannerman glanced my direction, signaled a left turn, cleared his throat. "I was led by Father Browne to understand you have a list."

Again I looked over my shoulder. The Ford pickup had gone straight. The yellow Oakland remained two cars behind us.

A lump inside my throat burned like an ember. I glanced down to see that list right on my *lap*, only Bannerman didn't know it. If I kept looking there I'd tip him off. If he *knew* I had his list he just might kill me on the spot.

I kept my eyes glued to the mirror. My temples pounded like the truck tires thumping asphalt. I wiped my forehead, sighed and quieted my breathing.

We rode another fifteen minutes to a train station just north of Altadena near the foothills of the San Gabriel Mountains.

Bannerman stepped out of the cab. Shook my hand. Gave me five dollars.

An enormous granite wall of rugged mountains rose before me.

The Oakland drove on past but parked a quarter mile ahead.

Ravens perched on telegraph wire cawed toward Rubio Canyon.

I heaved a slight sigh of relief. Bannerman had let me live. He seemed to want to be my friend, and at a time I truly needed one.

"You're a good kid, Dean. But it seems you've waded in over your head. We're only praying that you'll make the right decision, what's best for Anaheim."

And do what? Betray the Klan after what they'd done to the Corrigans? They'd be watching me. They weren't the sort of enemies I wanted.

"My wife booked you a room at Mount Lowe Tavern for two nights. Let's let things cool down in Anaheim. Maybe call me in three days."

I exhaled. *So many loose ends. Would they ever come together?*

I asked, "You'll come and get me? Are there telephones up there?"

"So call one of your friends if you prefer." Bannerman shrugged.

His voice tone sent a shiver up my spine.

Two men walked toward us from the Oakland. They wore olive gabardine suits and slouch hats. The shorter one carried an Army-issue duffel bag. The taller one looked at his pocket watch and turned his face away. He spat tobacco onto the gravel and continued our direction.

And now I realized there was no Ku Klux Klan here to defend me. The Catholics knew where I was, and they could kill me if they wanted. Except my only other choice right now was sleeping on the streets of Altadena, or catching a Red Car and riding off to God knows where. I wished I had a father I could call.

I felt upended. I hadn't had a bite to eat since Friday night. There was a tavern near Mount Lowe, and I was starving.

I turned and caught Bannerman's gaze, somehow managing to whisper, "If I call, will you promise me your friends won't start new violence? Defend yourselves, just don't start nothin' new."

I brushed my hand against my forehead. It was filled with beads of sweat, as were my palms. One of the gabardine guys stopped to snap a photo with his Eastman Kodak Brownie. The other man set down his duffel bag. Padlocked shut. Then they picked up again and wandered toward the station.

Bannerman turned toward his truck. Muttered, "I'll try." He met my gaze, and I believed that he would do the best he could to help my ma. Still, I feared his good intentions weren't enough to solve the problem.

I stepped out into the cold and watched an antiquated trolley make its way down from the mountain and descend through Rubio Canyon.

Bannerman screeched off in his truck. His taillights vanished down Lake Avenue.

I stood alone in Altadena on the street corner of Lake and Calaveras. A half block north, I spied the red roof of the Mountain Junction Station. Its faded flag snapped in the breeze, tattered and worn. I set my chin, swallowed my weariness and soldiered toward an old cobblestone structure. Fighting back hunger pangs, I climbed its concrete steps onto a weathered wooden platform, facing out toward the orchards. My empty stomach twisted up in hunger.

A dilapidated Red Car emerged from Rubio Canyon. The sun was sinking in the west. The groaning trolley turned its light on. The edges of the sky were tinted cotton-candy pink.

I breathed in deep and tried to find my bearings.

I wiped my forehead and my eyes. Tried to think about my family. Why did my father have to die? I'd done my best to raise myself, take care of Ma and earn some cabbage, but my life had been upended by the Reverend Leon Myers and his band of angry Klansmen.

It seemed bizarre. The Klan seemed even more scared than the Catholics, which probably explained why Klansmen hid beneath their sheets, little men longing to be big men. I made my way inside the station, hoping I'd find a stove fire to stay warm.

I pushed open the door and froze

It couldn't be.

I gulped down air, except it seemed like all the air had just been sucked out of the room. Helen was sitting on a peeling lacquered bench next to a well-dressed man who looked a lot like Charlie Chaplin's Tramp but more disheveled.

Breathing shallowly, I bought myself a ticket at the counter, watching reflections of the odd man in the mirror next to Helen. He wore a bowler and a monocle. I sensed the man was English, but I couldn't place his accent since he muttered but three words. "Chin up, deario."

Helen raised her chin and straightened up her skirt.

She stared ahead, straight out the window. I'd never seen

Helen so frosty. I wondered why. Venturing forth, I pushed myself to say hello. But Helen acted like we'd never met.

I smiled.

Helen didn't. Instead, she looked away.

The Brit and Helen's lady friend smiled back.

One olive-suit guy took a walk and bought a *Pasadena Star*. When he returned both hid their faces behind newsprint and slouch hats.

To Helen's left a homely woman whom God forgot to give a neck was telling stories about aeroplanes and Mexican banana boats. The woman, aged in her mid-twenties, wore a battered leather jacket and a greasy pair of overalls like those worn by mechanics. Somehow she wrenched Monocle-Man's face into a smile. I was enchanted.

Clearly Helen wasn't.

The Mount Lowe Red Car groaned and braked, rolling toward the station. The car looked old enough to be considered an antique. It wore so many coats of paint that flake marks masked over the wood grain. Several panes of window glass were missing.

The car stopped.

"All aboard," muttered a grizzled old conductor.

I made my way up wrought-iron steps and took a seat facing the San Gabriel Mountains. Helen walked past me. She didn't even bat an eye. I could smell the same perfume she'd once seduced me with. Its orange-blossom scent triggered old memories. I'd been passed by, not just by Helen, but by everyone in Anaheim. I breathed in deep, shrugged hard, and faced the jagged foothills up the tracks.

Helen found a seat toward the back with Captain Monocle or whatever the man's name was. The Red Car felt as cold as winter. They flipped the trolley seat, ensuring it faced forward as they both sat down to ride the winding tracks up Rubio Canyon toward Echo Mountain. *Who was the stranger?* I was sure I hadn't seen his face in movies. Was he her escort or her john?

I felt a warm touch on my shoulder.

"May I join you?"

I glanced up. It was Helen's homely woman friend. She grinned. She wrapped a scarf made out of wool around her non-existent neck.

"Have a seat," I offered, glad I wouldn't have to ride alone. I smiled back, gave her the window seat and slid toward the aisle.

The olive-suit guys took a window seat on the trolley way up front. The tall one's Brownie was still out, and he snapped photos of the landscape. *I've seen him somewhere. In Anaheim*, I thought but wasn't certain. Right now, he seemed busy snapping photographs.

"Name's Reynolds," I told the woman who had settled in beside me. "From Anaheim. Dean Reynolds, Junior. Pleased to meet you." I smiled wide.

The woman looked me over and began laughing out loud. "Well then, I've heard a bunch aboutcha. Helen told me you play baseball."

"Played," I said, glad for a companion I could talk to. It ensured the olive-suit goons wouldn't bother me in public.

"That's a damn shame." The woman slid onto the varnished seat so close I smelled her lipstick and rogue scents of chaparral from off her jacket. She tossed a tattered leather zippered overnight bag toward her feet. She seemed exuberant and smiled like a pit bull full of play. I got the sense that she was rich but tried to hide it.

"What have you heard?" I asked.

"From Helen? Helen and I travel all over, so quite a lot."

I muttered, "Uh-oh."

"My name's Florence, by the way. Florence Lowe Barnes." She smiled wide. Her skin was rough like Western leather. She shook my hand. Her grip felt stronger than a carpenter's or plumber's.

"Lowe?" I asked. "You mean like *Mount* Lowe?"

"Man, *you're* as sharp as a coyote. I'm Thaddeus Lowe's one and only granddaughter," she bragged.

"So then how do you know Helen?"

"Honey, how do you think Helen gets around? You mean to tell me you don't know?"

"I...apologize," I said.

I have to say this was a question I had wondered about often. She'd be at summer camp in Huntington Lake, clear up in Kern County. Then she'd stroll right into Anaheim as if she'd just crossed the street. She'd been in Mexico, but here she was today.

In Altadena.

"Okay, then. How?" I asked and paused. "You mean to say you're...?"

"Crazy Florence."

My jaw dropped. I had heard the name of Crazy Florence often, but I have to say she didn't match the image in my mind. I'd pictured Florence as being beautiful, and elegant, and rich. She wore a motorcycle jacket. A pair of bug-smeared goggles dangled from her purse strap. She wore pants and leather boots like caballeros. She wasn't pretty but she seemed to fill a room with personality. She was not what I'd expected, but she was one of a kind.

The car lurched.

"Lookee there," she said and pointed toward a hawk.

It was a red-tail. It seemed to catch a wind and soared up higher, making its way toward Rubio Canyon in a wide and sweeping circle. The Red Car rolled past Newkirk Station and veered west toward a stretch labeled the Poppyfield. The hawk returned and soared up even higher.

"Don't mind Helen," Florence whispered from the corner of her mouth. "She's worked herself into a lather."

"Over what?" I muttered back.

Florence answered *sotto voce*. "Lord Fancy-Pants there on her left." She met my gaze and gave a wink before she slapped me on my knee. "He's the Eighth Baron of Flintshire and as broke as Casper Milquetoast on a budget. Got a two-by-four shoved sideways up his tusche."

I blushed.

Florence didn't. "She's lining up to be a baroness. Nasty business Helen's in. Hollywood men taking advantage."

"Ain't that the truth, Florence." I sighed. The red-tail hawk dive-bombed a meadow and emerged bearing a rodent in its beak and sailed off.

"He's Helen's ticket out of misery. Me?" Florence pointed toward a second hawk still circling. "Honey, that's what I dream of becoming."

I cocked my head.

She said, "Don't look at me that way. I'm an aviatrix. I've flown with Helen twice. Last night I flew her here from Mexico."

My jaw dropped.

"We stopped for fuel in San Diego," Florence deadpanned. "Then March Field, and then Arcadia."

I turned. "The Ross Balloon School?"

Florence chortled. "I'm still not rated. One of my cousins has this plane we used to fly up north of Palmdale. You don't need to have no license if you're wealthy and you know folks. Ain't no cops up in the sky."

Florence laughed at me and pointed at my face. "You think I'm joshing?" She looked at me again and touched my knee a second time. "Stay with me, Dean. I'll show you more fun than a man deserves to have." Her voice was earnest. She didn't seem crazy at all. She looked dead serious.

The train began to slow, approaching Rubio Pavilion. Both of the olive-suit boys rose, and one took photos of the platform. Florence mentioned that her grandfather had built it in the Eighties. A white funicular, the "Echo Mountain Incline" waited on the lower platform. Its tracks ran 35 degrees straight up the mountain.

Florence grinned. "We only look crazy," she said and gave a wink.

My heart ricocheted with random fears and unsorted emotions. I didn't know what to expect. We were far away from Anaheim.

I swallowed back my nerves and told myself that I was ready.

At the top of Rubio Canyon we changed trains to the funicular.

The white car of the funicular ascending the Echo Mountain incline looked like an opera box on rails being cabled up the hillside. There were three boxes in each car in a staircase configuration. We crossed the old MacPherson Trestle standing one-third way up the slope. Steel wheels groaned against three rails anchored onto redwood truss frames.

The sister car was coming down. *"ECHO"* was painted on

its front. The three-rail track split into four tracks so the cars could pass each other. The falling "Echo" and rising "Alpine" cars both passed at the tracks' midpoint, each suspended from one cable balancing weights of the two cars.

Helen was in the box below us as we stared down well-worn rails to Rubio Canyon and the wood pavilion spanning a dry creekbed. The third box below Helen contained both the gabardine guys. I racked my brain. I'd seen them somewhere, probably outside Saint Boniface. One glanced upward toward me sideways.

Something tightened in my gut.

I ached with disappointment watching Helen with someone else. She was a complicated woman I had never quite deciphered.

I called her name. "Helen," I said.

She didn't even turn around. She bristled slightly, enough to make it clear she'd heard her name, knew who I was, and was choosing to ignore me for the moment. The empty echo of her name bounced off the mountains and returned.

Florence touched my shoulder. Whispered, "We'll talk about her later." A barrenness inside me was beginning to implode. I could speak Helen's name again but didn't want to draw attention to myself with both those olive-suit men sitting right below us. For now, I'd bide my time. I hoped Florence would enlighten me on what was going on with my ex-girlfriend.

I wished Monocle Man luck. I hoped Helen would be happy, and the time had come to let her go for good. Helen, I had concluded, wore men like she wore jewelry, as accessories to focus more attention on herself.

She'd been my first kiss, and the first girl I had ever fallen in love with. She had a smile so infectious it was hard to turn away. I'd been befriended by her father. He'd had big plans for my future. But his plans for me were mixed with his allegiance to the Klan. I imagined all those plans now being smashed on rocks below.

The car kept climbing higher. Higher, until the hawks were at eye-level, soaring upward on warm thermals that ascended Rubio Canyon. I felt us braking toward a stop. I heard a groan and smelled asbestos. A whirring flywheel in the powerhouse now coasted to a standstill.

There was a platform at the top beneath the remnants of what once was called White City, when these ruins had been the gem of the San Gabriels. The 40-room Echo Chalet, a stately 70-room white Victorian hotel, the Echo Mountain House, had been visible from all of Pasadena, lined with gas lanterns and a searchlight wagging beams across the Southland. All were gone now, the chalet, the Echo Mountain House, the zoo, and the observatory had burned down in a 1900 fire. All that remained were wooden platforms to change trolleys at the summit, a gasoline generator station, decayed foundations, and a half a dozen "echo-phones" of flaking rusted steel.

White City was a ghost town, scorched to bedrock like my soul.

To the south and far below, were the orchards of the San Gabriel Valley and the grids of Pasadena and Monrovia. Further south, beyond gray silhouettes of the distant Puente Hills was Anaheim where Helen and I had both grown up.

We couldn't even say goodbye, for that would interrupt her acting. Helen's life seemed like a motion picture interspersed with nightmares. I wondered why we'd met again when she was flirting with her baron. Coincidence, perhaps, for surely none of us would plan this. Helen treated me as if I were a stranger.

I smelled her orange-blossom perfume. *Goodbye, Helen.*

Farewell. May you find happiness in England with your baron and your castle. I wasn't sure how they would manage. I'd heard nobility found ways.

The Englishman held Helen's hand.

She smiled back at him. She laughed. Everything in her demeanor shouted "baroness." *Or barrenness.*

I stared across the canyon, far beyond them, toward Mount Lowe and toward Mount Wilson on my left. I smeared a tear across my cheek and glanced toward Helen and her baron. Stared at my own work-battered hands. I glanced at L.A. in the distance and thumped my worn Joe Jackson baseball glove. It didn't feel right today. Up here, things seemed so different.

Life was spinning out of balance in a dozen different ways. My life in Anaheim made sense, although I'd been both boy and man, under eighteen, but still required to earn enough to help pay bills. Now I felt as though my last tethers to youth had come unraveled.

The sun sank beyond the mountains to the west.

A blue-uniformed conductor unlatched doors onto a weathered wooden platform. Florence exited the funicular to my right. We both watched Helen and her baron mounting wooden steps behind us, huffing past us, up the hillside toward the "echo-phones" and power house. I heard Monocle Man panting. Altitude did not agree with him. Reportedly the platform stood at 3200 feet.

I pulled my chin up off my chest. Florence briefly spoke with Helen, then Florence tugged on my right arm. "C'mon," she said. "Best part's ahead." A second Pacific Electric trolley car awaited at the platform. The words "Mount Lowe" rolled into place on the car's destination scroll.

Monocle Man held Helen's hand. Both of them hollered through their Echo phone.

"HELLO-O-O-O-O..."

An echo ricocheted off canyon walls.

"HELLO-O-O-O-O."

Both of them laughed.

"I LOVE YOU..."

"I LOVE YOU-U-U..." echoed back, but rather weakly. Most likely, Helen didn't notice. She seemed a woman on a mission and not easily distracted. Her attentions seemed consumed with courting her real English baron.

Florence and I both showed our tickets to a sleepy-eyed conductor. He tipped his cap. We flipped a trolley seat, and both of us sat down, facing the mountains and the trolley tracks that snaked among the Echo Mountain ruins. Three seats ahead of us the gabardine boys whispered, still snapping photographs. In those suits they looked like BOI enforcers.

The car jerked forward. Only eight of us would ride up to the tavern. Florence told me Helen had decided to turn back.

"Where will they stay, Florence," I asked.

"Hotel Raymond or Hotel Green back down the hill in Pasadena. They were gonna spend the night here. Helen had a sudden change of plans."

Helen and Monocle Man had yet to finish playing with the echo-phones. The conductor began his spiel. Helen faded out of view.

"Friends, you are now starting the last three and a half miles of this trolley trip, on which you will cross eighteen bridges and pass around one-hundred and twenty-seven curves..."

Telegraph poles shadowed the trolley tracks. We ascended along the hillside. Florence pointed out the sights where Echo Mountain House had stood before a kitchen fire had burned it down a year before her birth. "Damn, I wish I could have seen it." Florence frowned and shook her head.

One of the olive-suit boys turned and spat tobacco out the window. He had wax paint on his face, like an extra in some movie. Odd I thought. Men masquerading as a pair of BOI agents, but why? Then it occurred to me that Bannerman had warned me. The Catholics might send out vigilantes.

Crazy Florence mopped her brow while cold washed over me in waves. We left Helen and the Monocle Man standing near the wreckage of the burnt down Echo Mountain House. Florence had already moved on.

I was watching men in olive suits and trying to do the same.

The tall one dipped tobacco into his cheek.

Something about him seemed disturbing. Too much makeup on his face, more theatrical stick greasepaint than Lon Chaney ever dreamed of. I could smell it. It disguised their facial features like masks of wax. Still their whispers and their movements looked distressingly familiar.

"There's Castle Canyon." Florence pointed toward a canyon full of jagged granite cliffs. Toyons and California buckwheat sprawled below. We crossed a trestle that transported us across Las Flores Canyon, into a grove of coast live oaks that stretched above us in a canopy.

The trolley roped along the mountainside up toward the Cape of Good Hope. There the trolley tracks looped out and overlooked all Pasadena and the Raymond or the Green Hotel where Helen would be staying. I managed to push Helen from my thoughts.

The conductor pulled the brakes, and I could smell the burnt asbestos. "Will you now have your tickets ready, please?" he said, slowing the trolley. "We are approaching the Cape of Good Hope where we will cross…into Millard Canyon…."

Florence turned to me. "Nifty view, eh?" She tilted her head sideways.

I said, "Yeah."

She grinned, "Most outdoorsy men enjoy it."

"Florence, you hardly even know me."

"But I know Helen. Or I *knew* her." Florence frowned and seemed to stare across the valley clear to Anaheim. She spat outside onto the ground. "You think she's making a mistake?"

"Yes. Yes, I do."

"So do I."

Both the men in gabardine stood up.

The trolley stopped. It was a chance to see a spectacular view. I tailed the men in suits to get a better look, but neither lingered.

"Is Helen moving to Great Britain?" I asked Florence, hearing sadness fill my voice. And then I wondered why I'd even brought her up.

"England won't suit her. She'll find out rich people are boring," Florence said. "But does she listen?"

I shook my head. "She thinks small towns invented boredom. We're from Anaheim. Nothing there except the Klan for entertainment."

"Honey, Helen talked about your father. Said he died."

I glanced across the valley. "During the war," I said, "I miss him."

Florence frowned and winged a rock into the canyon far below like a big overgrown kid inside the body of a woman. She didn't have a pretty face but she made up for it with fun.

Her eyes were brown, big as a puppy dog's awaiting new adventures. She'd seemed gruff at first. It shocked me Crazy Florence could be tender. "Dean, you're lucky." She touched me on the shoulder with concern. "You had a *good* father. Not many modern women get good fathers. At least I knew my grandfather adored me."

"Thaddeus Lowe?" I met her gaze.

A smile spanned between her cheeks. Florence straightened. She looked up, as if a child once again. "Professor Thaddeus S. C. Lowe." Florence beamed and cleared her throat. "This trolley we're both riding on was Grandfather's idea. But he lost it 'round the year that I got born. Business reversals. My lucky break. That let *me* become the son he'd always wanted.."

The conductor rang the trolley bell.

Most of us reboarded.

"Took me to every aviation meet in Southern California," Florence said. "In 1910 he took me to Dominguez Airfield. Crazy biplanes and balloons ascending over California. Just then I knew right what I wanted, but I lacked the guts to say so. Wasted ten years tryin' to please everyone else."

The olive-suit boys climbed the trolley steps and took a seat behind us. The bell rang, and the trolley car lurched forward with a jerk. My baseball glove fell off my lap. I bent down to retrieve it, hiding my list of Ku Klux Klan members where nobody could see it.

I glanced at Florence's chapped hands, and I was left with the impression her life contained enough adventure to make Douglas Fairbanks jealous. She placed both palms against my knees and looked straight at me, saying, "Dean, don't make the same mistake as Helen."

I looked away without replying.

Florence looked into my eyes, "When you have a choice, choose happy. Helen never understood that."

Florence stared toward Mount Wilson. Her face creased into a frown. "I'm a tough broad. It's a side of life that Helen hasn't mastered. I doubt merry old England will suit Helen."

I studied the south slope as the Mount Lowe Trolley wandered up the hill toward Horseshoe Curve. Coveys of quail fluttered off. I wondered why I had allowed the Ku Klux Klan to wreck my life, and now I wondered if those guys in suits were sent up here to tail me. Were they heavies for the Catholics whom Bannerman had sent, hiding weapons in that creepy padlocked duffel bag?

The trolley rounded Horseshoe Curve and the long Circular Bridge that wound its way along a promontory, rising toward the sky. "As we come out of this grove of live oak trees into the open, we can see the city of Long Beach," came the voice of the conductor, "and other coastal areas more than thirty miles away. Looking beyond may be seen the Catalina Channel with Catalina in the distance, nearly sixty miles from us."

The guys in suits stared at their newspapers and faced toward the window. We were handed slips of paper. "There is a souvenir newspaper printed daily at the Mount Lowe Alpine Tavern. If you will print your name and address on the slips of paper being passed out to you, your names will appear in today's issue of the paper."

The last thing that I wanted was my name in someone's paper after Bannerman had warned me about Catholic vigilantes. I printed the name, "Warren G. Harding," who had died the prior year.

The Granite Gate loomed half a mile ahead.

Its marker gave the elevation, just above 4000 feet. Behind

a pair of bedrock crags, the tracks continued through an oak forest and into what a trackside marker pointed out as the, "The Grand Canyon." The forest became thicker as we climbed.

It was dark now. Florence told me she'd be staying overnight at Alpine Tavern. Up ahead, kerosene lanterns lit a platform in the forest. I knew we'd reached our destination.

The conductor gave his spiel. "There are several places of interest in the vicinity of Mount Lowe Tavern. There is a fox farm where silver foxes are bred and raised for the fur market. There is also a small zoo where a few of the small animals native to this area are on display. About a ten-minute walk from the tavern is Inspiration Point where there are a number of sighting tubes pointing out numerous places of interest in the valley below. From Inspiration Point is operated the OM&M Railway, One Man and One Mule, a narrow-gauge railway which runs the along the side of a scenic canyon of inspiring views."

"Look me up tomorrow morning. I'll fill you in more about Helen," Florence said.

"Maybe breakfast?"

"Sounds like a plan, hon," she fired back.

The trolley braked into a crawl. "And now friends, we are arriving at the Tavern. Cars will leave from here this evening at seven-thirty. Make yourselves at home and may your visit be a pleasure and a memorable one."

The brakes shivered. Our trolley trip had ended.

Florence grabbed her bags. She made her way toward the exit. One olive-suit guy was in front of her. My eyes locked on the second, and I froze.

He chewed tobacco. I smelled his breath. *Eddie Harris' old man!*

Harris elbowed ahead of Florence. His partner's coat was oversized. Sleeves hid both his partner's hands. His duffel bag contained a rifle. Its barrel protruded against the canvas. Their trolley seat still reeked of wet tobacco.

"Last stop tonight," called the conductor. The man gestured toward the inn.

Harris and his companion made their way into the lobby.

I glanced down. My hands were freezing. Heavy thoughts swirled through my mind. What to do? I wasn't sure. Perhaps I'd know tomorrow morning. Tonight I'd sleep on it. I didn't want my path to cross with Harris.

I shuddered.

Tonight I'd make sure all my doors were locked.

I'd had Florence at my side. She'd been my witness to prevent any attacks. But now I was aware I was alone. Inside the lodge at Alpine Tavern I was told that I would sleep in Cabin 8, where Mr. Bannerman had made my reservation. I worried somebody might find me there if someone tipped them off. For once I wished I'd brought along a gun.

The desk clerk handed me my key.

I made my way outside the lobby down a boardwalk to a trail and up a flight of concrete steps.

I found cabin number 8. I clutched the key inside my hand.

A Coleman lantern on a nail lit a rustic mountain porch.

I placed the key inside the lock.

Something slipped out from the doorjamb. It fluttered like a falling leaf. Fell face-up on the doormat.

I bent over. Picked it up. Held it closer to the lantern.

The cabin door was already unlocked.

I made my way into my cabin, struck a match and lit a candle.

I read the words.

My nervous heart froze like an iceblock. I gulped and swallowed half the air remaining in the room.

Dean:

YOU HAVE BEEN PAID A SOCIAL VISIT BY THE
KNIGHTS OF THE

𝕶𝖀 𝕶𝕷𝖀𝕏 𝕶𝕷𝕬𝕹.

DON'T MAKE THE NEXT VISIT A BUSINESS CALL.

CHAPTER XVIII

SUNDAY, AUGUST 4, 1924

On the bed inside my cabin room I tossed and turned, awake, feeling a bedspring poke my back every time I changed position. My mind coursed with adrenaline as if preparing for the playoffs.

I kicked my blankets to the floor, got dressed and stepped outside, locked the door, and made my way down concrete steps toward the trolley and the platform.

I had to sort my thoughts so I could sleep.

Frogs and crickets echoed from the creek.

A wooden sign over the doorway of Mount Lowe's Ye Alpine Tavern banged against the windows of the day room. Moonlight reflected off the glass. Embers still glowed inside the fireplace.

From the Crystal Springs below echoed cascading mountain water, tumbling its way into Grand Canyon.

I made my way toward the creek, down a flight of wooden stairs. I knelt beside the ripples, drinking in cool mountain water in the moonlight.

I shut my eyes, wondering what I'd do tomorrow.

But now I glanced up at the night, and it occurred to me tomorrow was today. I still hadn't decided what to do. My baseball glove was in my cabin right beside my list of Klansmen. What on earth did Shoeless Joe and Ku Klux Klansmen have in common?

Odd combination.

Or was it?

A frog croaked near the shore. He splashed away.

I glanced toward the full moon and had a thought.

Behind admirable veneers both hid their secrets from the public. Shoeless Joe covered up the Black Sox Scandal back in 1919. In the World Series he had thrown he'd batted .375 but didn't dare rat out his teammates. His fate was not an easy call after he claimed he'd been rebuffed while trying to contact Charles Comiskey, owner of the 1919 White Sox.

But I was doing the same thing, covering up the Ku Klux Klan. I'd even sheltered Helen's secrets and her back-alley abortion. Boomer was dead, Klansmen had tried to set Saint Boniface on fire. Even the cops were in the Klan. Anaheim had no chance for justice.

I shut my eyes. Thoughts ricocheted all around my head. I'd seen many sides of evil, but I didn't want to tattle. Even Reverend Leon Myers could excuse the Klan's behavior, often reminding us how Judas was a snitch who'd fingered Jesus.

Still, someone told me once that sunlight was the world's best antiseptic. Thanks to me and people like me, Ku Klux Klan members could hide behind their sheets. If one couldn't perform actions in broad daylight, there were reasons. At daybreak, I could do something about it.

Behind the tavern was a trail sign. It pointed toward a trail up a ridgeline toward the "Switzer-Land" resort, one canyon over. It was six miles, round-trip, but I could hike there in ninety minutes if the mile-high elevation didn't sap me.

Moonlight reflected off the waters of the glistening Crystal Springs. I stuffed my hand into my pocket, feeling the card I'd found outside my cabin door. It wasn't Catholics who'd followed me up here.

It was the Klan.

An owl screeched through the forest.

Moonlight glared between the oaks, casting long and crooked shadows. The barn owl screeched a second time. I made my way back up the steps and found a can of gasoline left on the front porch of my cabin.

That can hadn't been there when I'd left.

I'd locked my door. To my horror, it appeared to be unlocked. Inside, the candle was blown out.

I shut the door, fumbled in darkness, and found a matchstick. I lit my candle.

Scanned all corners of the small room.

Called, "Hello?"

I raised my candle. Its light crawled up the dusty cabin walls. Its flame flickered. I heard something.

Like breathing.

A gust of air blew through the cabin window, rustling dusty curtains.

I slammed the sash down. Its noise rattled the cobweb-laden walls.

Someone coughed.

I spun around.

I held my candle at arm's length, listening for breathing. Heard a heart beat. A second cough echoed from underneath my bed.

I kicked the bedframe to one side.

A muffled shot rang out, tearing all the covers off my bed, shredding a crater through the mattress.

Yikes! I bounded back.

I glared at the intruder, making out features from the shadows on the wall. And a smell. *Tobacco breath from Old Man Harris!*

Holy crap!

He staggered to his feet and sneered my name.

He wagged his 0.38.

I was unarmed.

I stood frozen.

Our gazes locked, but it seemed Harris' gaze was loaded. He looked as feral as an angry mountain bobcat in a corner.

Harris lifted up his pistol. A scowl creased through his makeup.

Without a glance I made a dash and crashed out through the cabin window.

Shattered glass tinkled around me.

A second shot rang through the night.

"Dammit," Harris bellowed.

A dull pain ripped through my right forearm. Blood was all over my shirtsleeve. Stunned, I staggered to my feet.

The front door flew open, cracked against the wall, and out ran Harris with a Coleman lantern, yelling, "C'mere you goddamned coward." He waved the lantern in the night.

Someone else stumbled from the forest.

The cut on my right arm stung like a thicket full of nettles. I moved my palm to touch my cheek and felt a painful shard of glass.

I tiptoed north around the cabin wall and found a good-sized rock, a perfect stone, shaped like a baseball in the weeds behind the cabin. I held my breath. Hid in the shadows.

"Stubby?" Harris called. "Stubby, you seen that Judas piece o' crap?"

"No, sir," he answered.

Holding his lantern on his hook, Stubby staggered toward the porch. It was clear he hadn't seen me. I held my rock and didn't breathe, observing both men moving closer.

I fired a prayer in Boomer's honor.

Cocked my arm.

Lantern light came arcing my direction.

"There he is." Harris called out.

I threw a fastball.

It seemed to linger in the night, like it was moving in slow-motion. If it didn't take down Harris, I'd be deader than the nails in Boomer's coffin.

Harris lifted up his 0.38. He pointed it straight toward me.

My heart leaped up my throat.

I heard a thud.

Harris bellowed, staggered, and folded to the floor.

Squirts of blood flowed from his temple. Red streaks oozed in lengthening streaks across the dirty cedar porch.

Elation overpowered my heart.

I raised a fist. "Steee-rike!" I yelled.

Stubby sprinted toward Harris.

I had to reach the gun first. I catapulted over the porch rail. Harris was out cold on the planking. The still-hot pistol was in his hand. I grabbed the gun to fire a warning shot.

Click.

The gun was empty.

My heart sank.

The barn owl bellowed from the woods.

Stubby hurtled toward me, swinging his glass lantern toward my face.

Just in time, I ducked beneath it. He careened into my chest knocking me flat against the porch, leaving me breathless and still bleeding.

Pain stabbed at my torso. Stubby's knee gouged in my lung. Something was wrong. A busted rib perhaps. He raised the lantern high and slammed it down toward my face.

I moved my head away in time.

The Coleman shattered into pieces, and the gaslight was no more. The stench of kerosene filled up the chilly night.

Flames ignited on the porch. Stubby forced his weight on top of me. His knee pressed on my lung. Pain stabbed from my ribs and up my chest till breathing hurt.

Stubby panted like a freight train.

Warm blood dribbled through my eyes. I touched my face and felt more glass cuts than before.

The kerosene flames inched toward the can of gasoline.

Stubby raised his hook. He took a swipe toward my throat.

I caught his forearm. Twisted. Hard. The hook dislodged from Stubby's stump.

A howl of wrath engulfed the canyon.

Somehow, I found myself on top of him.

We rolled into the flames.

Shrieks from Stubby. "*Aaaaagh. Ouch. Aaieee!*"

I grabbed his hair and smashed his head against the threshold, knocking him cold. I dragged his legs out from the flames and saw the fire was near extinguished. I banged his head against the porch another time.

The night lay still.

Stubby wasn't moving.

I tore the blankets off my bed, suffocating remnants of the porch fire.

Harris groaned.

I kicked his solar plexus, dreading he'd wake up. I found a water pitcher, emptied it extinguishing the last remaining embers.

I recalled there'd been a rifle in their duffel bag.

The porch reeked of kerosene. If I slept, and they woke up, they'd start a fire or find some other way to kill me.

I dragged both men inside my cabin. I tore more bedsheets from my bed, ripped the sheets into long streamers and tied up both the Klansmen's hands behind their backs and to my bed, one to the headframe, one to the footframe.

I couldn't stay. I grabbed my ball glove, Harris' pistol and his holster. The list of Klan members was still beside my bed. I took it with me.

I touched my face. It was crusted up with blood, as was my forearm. My ribs roared out in agony with every breath I took.

I poured the gasoline into the dirt.

Daylight would break in several hours. Weary, I knew I had to find a place the Klan would never look for me, far away from Mount Lowe Tavern. I had to keep on moving. The trail toward Switzer Land would get me out of camp, and if the Klan had reinforcements, they'd be far enough below me I could ambush them the same way I'd just ambushed Mr. Harris.

I grabbed myself another rock. Thumped it deep into my ball glove for safe-keeping.

I hiked uphill. The grade was reasonably gentle. Winds made their way across the ridgeline before gusting down the hillside, swaying branches on the oaks and rustling pines.

Pain throbbed from my chest. Blood still oozed out from my

facial cuts. I staggered up the trail to Switzer's Camp, gritting my teeth, knowing there were no cops or firemen responding to the gunshot, only the barn owl screeching loudly up the canyon.

CHAPTER XIX

MONDAY, AUGUST 5, 1924

From the chapel above Switzer's Camp I stared toward the sunrise that lit up the summer morning in tints of lavender and beige. I'd left my baseball glove behind. Laid it gently at the altar by a rugged oakwood cross someone had hewn out from the forest.

I hadn't cried since Pa had died. I'd packed my troubles in my old kit bag the way my Pa had taught me. I had kept them to myself. Once I'd said goodbye to Joe Jackson and everything he stood for, just like baseball had banished Shoeless Joe, my town would banish me.

I tried to weep. I wanted to, but tears refused to come.

My very presence back in Anaheim would place my ma at risk. I couldn't take that chance. There was no way I could go home, not with the Ku Klux Klan in charge, running a validation racket that ensured no matter what they did, they still controlled the town beneath a thin veneer of counterfeit morality.

I'd been misled by obscurities, ignoring what was obvious.

Ace Clarkson couldn't win a Purple Heart. He only had one eye. He'd be 4-F. And Helen's claim about her father and the Navy now rang true. Inside his house I'd found no evidence he'd served, no mothballed uniforms, no honorable discharge, no citations, ribbons, medals. Not a single scrap of evidence suggested Herbert Webber had spent a single lousy minute in the Navy.

They were false patriots masquerading behind rituals and sheets. I couldn't name a single war hero who'd joined the Ku Klux Klan. They were the draft dodgers, the cowards and 4-F's, who'd never served. They had no voice for they were echoes, had no wings, only their strings. They were liars and imposters.

I'd been lucky to escape them.

It felt great to turn from secrecy and cover-ups and lies. Call me a Judas, but last night their Ku Klux Klan had tried to *kill* me. Since there were no cops in Anaheim who weren't inside the Klan, I had no remedy. The baseball glove, my gift from my late father, my Shoeless Joe Special Edition, I had placed beside the altar. Soon as I reached the Mount Lowe Tavern and their post office had opened, I'd mail Bannerman my roster of the Ku Klux Klan in Anaheim.

I hoped for once I'd make my father proud.

In twenty minutes, I ascended from Switzer's Canyon to the crest. I stared along the ridgeline. The sun peeked over the horizon like a giant glowing California lemon on a fruit label.

Dawn brought a kaleidoscope of light into the forest.

Near the crest, there stood a silhouette more regal in the sunrise than anything I'd ever seen. I stood in awe, heart in my throat.

On the ridgeline stood a stag.

His antlers rose above the hilltop like a tribute to the wilderness and purity. I stood in wonder. The huge buck stared across the canyon looking past me, standing tall. For a moment I believed he knew my father.

The sun rose higher, and the stag sauntered away.

This majestic animal had set my mind at ease. I couldn't return to Anaheim Union High School and complete my senior year. The Klan would kill me, kill my mother, burn our house the way they'd tried to burn Saint Boniface. They'd kill us like they'd murdered all the Corrigans.

I oddly felt a peace I can't explain.

As my trail crossed the saddle and switchbacked into the Grand Canyon I had confidence some new pathway would open up before me. I resumed my daybreak journey through the sagebrush down the slopes, hearing turbulence from the tumbling Crystal Springs.

Smoke ascended from stone chimneys. My side was tender when I touched it. Two of my ribs were bruised with swollen lumps the size of tangerines. I staggered forward, toward cabins and old structures built from river rock. I smelled bacon and the sweet vanilla scent of lodgepole pines along the trailside for several hundred yards. I looked up from the trail and was shocked that Crazy Florence and a friend had come to meet me.

I don't remember ever being quite so glad to see two strangers.

Florence wore the same old leather jacket she'd worn yesterday. She said she'd brought a friend, a teen from Glendale named Duke Morrison. He looked too old to be in high school, but he said he was my age. Said he had driven to Altadena and had hiked up to the Tavern.

Florence studied me. She frowned. Her over-six-foot-tall companion looped his thumbs around his beltloops. "So, what happened?" He glanced down. "You look as though you just went nine rounds with a grizzly in the ring."

"Ku Klux Klan members." I looked over my shoulder. "In my cabin."

"Well, that don't sound too good."

"I heard gunshots," Florence said. "Found two men roped to your bedframe screamin' louder than coyotes. Found two shells on your front porch."

I handed Florence Harris' pistol. "For the cops, in case they need it."

Duke shook his head. Spat in the dirt. "Well you're a braver man than I am, fightin' two armed men alone. Either that or there's a screw loose."

"Take your pick." I volunteered.

I tried to laugh, except my sore ribs interfered.

Florence and Morrison grinned wide. It made the pain stabbing my chest and my cut face hurt slightly less. I had to stop and catch my breath.

"Good thing we found you, Dean," said Florence. "We gotta talk sense into Helen."

"But..."

"I'm supposed to fly her out this morning to meet her baron in San Pedro. They're both sailing for Europe on the *Empress of Great Britain*."

"You gotta talk to her," said Duke.

"You *know* Helen?" I fired back

Looking down, Morrison shrugged.

I swallowed. "Okay, Duke, you know her, but then how did you find *me?*"

"Followed your footprints from the camp. An' I know Helen from Flo's beach cabana down south in Laguna. Helen's a vamp. Surprised you know her, but you need to talk some sense to her."

"Right now?"

Duke shrugged. "Well, Florence doesn't have all day."

For some reason, that seemed to settle everything.

As we hurried down the hill, Duke kept telling me how Florence Barnes had taught him to ride bareback at her ranch in San Marino. "You ain't tried nothin' till you've ridden beside Florence on a stallion. That gal's crazy, but even Tom Mix can't ride horses the way she can."

We made our way into the campground. I saw no signs of the Klan, but I was nervous any moment Stubby or Harris might show up. On the grill I smelled a fragrant slab of bacon with our name on it and plates of scrambled eggs.

We scarfed our food down in ten minutes.

"We need to hurry," Florence said, pointing south toward Pasadena. "Helen's meeting me at nine o'clock outside the Ross Balloon School."

I was eager to get out of camp before the Klan awakened. I mailed my last item of baggage from Ye Alpine Tavern's post office to Bannerman in Anaheim. I wrote inside the envelope and begged there'd be no violence. I sighed with sad relief.

Anaheim's playing field was level.

I'd given Bannerman the baseball, my list of Klan members in Anaheim. He'd be pitching in relief to finish off the Ku Klux Klan.

I knew I wasn't going back.

Right now, we had to saddle horses and race down to Ross Balloon School to find Helen before the Ku Klux Klan found out I had returned. I hoped to somehow talk her out of one last terrible mistake. But with the Klan up here, I couldn't hang around.

It appeared since Mount Lowe Tavern had been named for Florence's grandfather, she still carried some influence with tavern personnel. The Lowes had sold out to the Pacific Electric Railroad years ago, but the wrangler at the horse barns let us borrow three young geldings.

We saddled quickly.

"Giddyup." Florence shot off down the trail. The best rider of the three of us, she ran us at full speed along the Mount Lowe Trolley roadbed. Duke ran 50 yards behind, and I hung on for my dear life, fighting terror at every turn, keeping pace with my companions, while my ribs screamed out in agony. Sweat seared through my face cuts. I wondered how I'd stay alive, keeping pace with Crazy Florence as we rocketed downhill.

The mountain trail zigzagged south. We raced at a full gallop, and the hour-long uphill trolley ride compressed into thirty minutes. Heart in my throat, and like some rodeo cowboy bouncing on a bronc, I somehow hung onto my saddle as we ricocheted down the slopes.

Duke had parked his battered pickup truck at the mouth of Rubio Canyon, beneath an oak grove with an old corral beyond it.

He unsaddled our three horses, led them into the corral, and tossed our mounts into the pickup bed behind a bag of footballs.

Gasping for breath, I was bent-over. Florence sauntered to my side. "Hurry," she said. "We can't let Helen leave for Europe with that baron."

Florence vaulted with one leap across the tailgate into the truck bed.

In pain, I cranked the engine. Then I crawled up front with Morrison.

The Chevy's engine roared to life while I was still catching my breath.

The pickup raced out of Rubio Canyon leaving a swirling cloud of dust. Morrison floored the truck. It fishtailed. He shifted into third, stuck out his arm, signaled left.

We shot down Altadena Drive, which became Santa Anita Avenue next to Eaton Canyon Wash. We braked at Foothill Boulevard at the stop sign.

We swung left. A signpost pointed toward Ross Balloon School.

A giant airfield spread before us beyond Southern Pacific tracks which made their way up toward a battered yellow station for "ARCADIA." There, the Southern Pacific Railroad intersected Santa Fe tracks.

A mile west an old red trolley chugged our way from San Marino. Its headlight glistened through the morning, winding east behind a row of Curtiss Jennies, aeroplanes parked in the sun beside the runway. Morrison pulled up behind the trolley station.

Florence leaped out from the truck bed.

I jimmied open the shotgun door and jumped out onto the turf.

"Good luck," Morrison yelled, tipping his ballcap in his hand, throwing his pickup into gear. "I gotta take back all them ponies."

Before I'd mouthed a word, the truck was rolling toward the roadway.

"Florence thinks she's gonna teach you how to fly," Morrison yelled. "You wouldn't catch me *dead* in one of them crazy-fool contraptions. But you know Florence."

"She's an unusual woman," I yelled back.

Morrison roared north onto the avenue.

Florence tossed her head back. Gave a laugh that echoed halfway up the San Gabriel Mountains and left me in good spirits.

Along Huntington Drive, the Pacific Electric Red Car trolley braked. Its white dash sign read "Arcadia, Monrovia, Glendora." Its headlamp dimmed. The brakes squealed as the car groaned to a full stop at the platform for the Arcadia station.

On the Red Car, I saw Helen, with the baron in her tow.

She wore a sailor dress, a cloche hat and a yard-long string of pearls the size of cherries like a poster girl promoting the Cunard Line. A velvet purse hung from her shoulder, lily white to match her pearls, a scarf, and matching leather gloves she'd buttoned halfway up her arm.

Florence blocked the pair off at the trolley steps, and her gaze locked onto Helen. "Honey, just where are you goin'?" Florence asked, shaking her head.

"You're gonna fly me to San Pedro," Helen ordered. "Like you promised." Helen slurred her words like she was snockered.

"Helen, you're making a mistake," I called while Florence blocked her way, folding both her arms across her chest.

Helen glared at me. Then at Florence. She bulldogged past Florence toward *me*, wearing a look to freeze a man at forty paces.

Two feet away from me, Helen halted. I smelled brandy on her breath. "You ruin everything, Dean. Don't you?" Helen's angry eyes were bloodshot.

"Excuse me?"

"I had a reservation last night at Mount Lowe till *you* showed up, the way you *always* show up, ruining my life. You're such a wurp."

"Helen, we never..."

She tottered toward me, wound up, and slammed me with her purse. My face and forehead stung like scorpions. I swallowed back the pain. "You bastard," Helen shrieked. She swung her purse again. Connected.

I staggered back. Blood from the cuts above my eyes clouded my vision. Helen was drunk and seemed as crazy as a bedbug who smoked opium.

I stepped back, mopping my brow.

Helen glared at her new purse. "Damn," she muttered. "This new purse just cost me seventy-five dollars in I. Magnin's in San Francisco. You have *some nerve* to bleed all over it. How crass. How thoughtless. I just have a mind to mail you the bill."

Monocle Man followed behind her, "Deario," he said. "Come here."

"What did you say to Russ and Lucy at Beaux Arts Studio?" Helen stammered.

"Nothing."

"What did you say to my old man?"

"Nothing," I said. "Helen, you've had some bad stuff happen, but you *can* turn things around. You're a good girl, Helen. You still don't have to throw away your life."

Her face twisted into hatred. Her hair flung wildly like Gorgon's hair. She screeched. "You goddamn liar. Hurt him, Stanley. I detest him. He's the evil boy who raped me at that party in Laguna."

Monocle Man stormed up to her side.

He tried to soothe her. "Chin up, Helen. I'm afraid you're slightly zozzled, but we need not waste our time on any Orange County riff-raff."

Startled, I took a step away.

The English baron stepped between us. Met my gaze "Oh

my, those *are* some nasty cuts, old boy," he muttered. "You really ought to see a doctor." He yanked Helen toward the trolley. "Come, deario, let's take you shopping. We shall buy us a new purse, and find our own way to San Pedro for the sailing."

Whatever energy had lit up Helen's visage seemed to vanish. Her face seemed to deflate like a flat tire losing air.

They both made it to the trolley just in time before the doors closed, and the Red Car rumbled east toward Monrovia.

I never saw Helen again.

For that, I'm rather grateful.

I know I got the best end of the bargain.

CHAPTER XX

MONDAY, AUGUST 5, 1924

A line of red dripped from my chin. I stood startled, wiping blood onto my shirtsleeve for five minutes until Florence found a towel to stop the bleeding, and I felt better.

Florence grabbed me by both hands, shaking her head. "To think I promised Helen I would teach her how to fly. Her loss," said Florence. "Damn shame Helen is shackled to her beauty."

Wincing, I smiled at Florence, although I, too, felt sad for Helen. But I was angry at her father and her too for all their lies. The Ku Klux Klan was drunk on hatred. Helen's drug of choice was brandy. I knew of no way to retrieve her. She had made up her own mind to sail away with Captain Monocle. I wished them lots of luck.

I grinned at Florence the way I'd smile at a crazy older sister if I had one. Florence seemed perfect for the role and full of fun. "Wanna fly?" She winked.

"Of course."

I couldn't believe I'd actually said that, but it didn't seem as dangerous as going back to Anaheim.

"There's our biplane." Florence pointed.

Next to the runway stood an aeroplane, a Curtiss Jenny JN4 two-seater trainer with a boxy frame and double wings with lightweight wooden struts. Pairs of cables strung from ailerons no thicker than a shirtbox.

At once, I understood Morrison's wariness.

Florence leaped into the pilot seat. She yelled out, "Yank the crank."

I tugged it hard and heard a clicking.

The aeroplane engine roared to life. "Jump in," yelled Florence. "The seat behind me. We're gonna have ourselves a blast. More fun than Klan weenies will see in their whole lifetimes."

I clambered into the rear seat.

I grinned and held my breath.

"Buckle up, buttercup," yelled Florence.

I clipped my harness into place and felt a jerk. We were moving. The engine howled and shook the plane. We taxied from the apron to the airstrip.

The aeroplane trundled down the runway, gaining speed, catching the wind. I felt us lift, and within minutes we were passing through the clouds and gaining altitude. The wind tussled my hair and chapped my cheeks as we soared high above the San Gabriel Valley.

"Pull that joystick back," yelled Florence.

"You mean *me?*"

"Is Helen here, honey? Tighten your leg muscles. Dean, you need to keep the blood up in your brain or you'll black out. We're gonna fly a loop-the-loop. You're gonna thank me."

I pulled the joystick back and felt as if I weighed three-hundred pounds, but we were climbing, overturning. Cold wind whistled past my ears. I glanced up from my seat to see the grid of Pasadena streets directly overhead. I was pinned against the cockpit.

I held my breath, hardly believing I was flying upside down. My heart soared even higher than the aeroplane we flew.

"You like it, Dean?"

"I love it."

"Pull out. Let's try a barrel roll."

I did. I've been hooked on aviation ever since.

We flew an hour toward March Field. Over Anaheim, she let me buzz the church where Leon Myers would be teaching folks to hate. I pushed the joystick forward, dove, and then I pulled out just in time. The engine roared so loudly Leon Myers raced outside, made a gesture and screamed epithets no pastor ought to use.

I learned right then and there what Florence meant.

We had more fun in one hour than Leon Myers and his Klan weenies will see throughout their hate-infested lifetimes.

CHAPTER XXI

DECEMBER 1930

I was welcomed at March Air Field by a man named Happy Arnold and his assistant Reuben Fleet. They told me Florence wasn't rated. But the thing was, she'd brought Happy Arnold six flyboy recruits. I soon learned I was conscript number *seven*.

That's why Happy doesn't bother Florence. *She's* his best recruiter.

And me? Pa tried to tell me once what everyone who fought in Europe knows. There are no heroes; the closest thing are folks who take pride in their *missions*. Pride in oneself will destroy everything it touches.

The Klan still hasn't learned that. Nor has Helen, I'm afraid.

Alma used to say pride was a sin.

But I'm living the best years of my life.

I finished high school up in Riverside while flying afternoons for the US Army Mail Service in Southern California. I got rated on the same day as I graduated high school. Ever since then, I've been living in the clouds and taking courses. Once I graduate from college, I'll be Lieutenant Dean Reynolds, Junior, an officer for the U.S. Army Air Corps and the Mail Service, making enough to keep supporting Ma and have myself some fun, although there aren't too many things more fun than flying.

Still the highlight of my senior year, in 1925, occurred in February, the month the Ku Klux Klan got voted out. Special election. Using my list, Frank Bannerman's Knights of Columbus exposed the Knights of the Ku Klux Klan and voted out the City Council. They fired all but one policeman. Shut down the *Orange County Plain Dealer*. The City Council and Leon Myers were invited to leave town. Made me proud to be from Anaheim. With the Klan removed from office, I could go home. The only problem was the skies were my new home after Ma married a judge and moved to Colorado Springs.

Helen's father died a suicide. Lost his wealth at Julian Pete, sold his house, moved up to Glendale and drank like Helen's brother. He took a jump off Suicide Bridge and blew his brains out halfway down. Guess he wanted to make sure he didn't make it.

Helen's mother is still alive. Word is she doesn't speak to anybody. Baron Monocle divorced Helen. She landed back in Hollywood. She changed her name to Helen Flanigan and starred in several movies before the talkies ruined everything. Her face outshone her voice.

And Alma Martin? She's a nun. She learned about me from Frank Bannerman and mailed me a package I just opened up this morning. Fact is, I'm eating one of Alma's macaroons this very moment. I still love eating anything she bakes.

I mailed an offering in gratitude to her Sisters of Saint Dominic. They plan to buy the Flintridge Biltmore where they'll open up a high school.

Alma writes she's having fun.

I have to smile.

So am I.

Poor Ku Klux Klan weenies and Helen have no clue how much they're missing.

THE END

DRAMATIS PERSONAE

Characters in *italics* are fictitious. Characters in **bold** were real people.

Arbuckle, Roscoe Conkling "Fatty"—1887-1933—Pioneer Hollywood silent movie actor who was tried and acquitted for the rape and murder of actress Virginia Rappe. The 1922 trial effectively ended Arbuckle's career in Hollywood and helped trigger implementation of the Hayes Code of decency.

Arnold, General Henry Harley "Happy" (later "Hap")—1889-1950—Aviation pioneer instructed in flying by the Wright Brothers, one of the first three rated pilots in the U.S. Army Air Corps. After overseeing the expansion of the Air Service during World War I, Arnold rose to become commanding general of the U.S. Army Air Forces, becoming the only Air Force five-star general in U.S. History.

Baisden, Harry—1893-1926—Bandleader of Harry Baisden's Orchestra, a West Coast Orchestra that frequently played the Bon Ton Ballroom in Santa Monica.

Bannerman, Frank—1888-1948—Fictitious Catholic building contractor and leader in the Knights of Columbus.

Barnes, Florence Lowe "Pancho"—1901-1975—pioneer aviator, and founder of the first movie stunt pilots' union. In 1930, she broke Amelia Earhart's air speed record. Founder of "Happy Bottom Riding Club" resort located south of Edwards Air Force Base and featured in *The Right Stuff*. Reportedly Pancho Barnes became rated in 1928, I've taken the liberty of assuming she flew solo before gaining her pilot's license.

Bow, Clara Gordon—1905-1965—One of the 1924 WAMPAS (Western Association of Motion Picture Advertisers) Baby Stars. Brooklyn-born Hollywood film star and sex symbol known as "The It Girl."

Browne, Father Patrick—18xx-19xx—Dublin-born priest of Saint Boniface Catholic Church in Anaheim during the 1920's and 1930's.

Carnegie, Dale—1888-1955—1920's public speaking guru and subsequent author of numerous self-help bestsellers, including *Public Speaking: a Practical Course for Business Men* (1926) and *How to Win Friends and Influence People* (1934.)

Clarkson, Ace—Fictitious Anaheim baseball umpire and Grand Cyclops for the local Klavern.

Coolidge, John Calvin, Jr.—1872-1933—Vermont-born Republican 30th President of the United States from 1923 until 1929.

Corrigan, Boomer—1907-1924—Fictitious Anaheim Union High School student murdered in 1924.

Davies, Marion Cecilia—1897-1961—1920's Hollywood silent film star known for being mistress of William Randolph Hearst and being associated with murder of millionaire producer Thomas Ince on Hearst's yacht.

Fidel Elduayen—18xx-19xx—Basque bootlegger in Inglewood whose moonshine barn was raided in 1923 by Ku Klux Klansmen in an incident resulting in murder of Inglewood policemen Medford Mosher, allegedly by a fellow Klansman.

Elgena, Ianetta "Miss Elgena"—1890-1968—Fictitious Anaheim High School history teacher.

Elwood, Dr. Louis J.—18xx-19xx—Santa Ana "Modern Optometrist" known for advertising billboards in Orange County similar to the T. J. Eckleburg billboard in F Scott Fitzgerald's *The Great Gatsby*.

Fairbanks, Douglas—(nee Douglas Elton Thomas Ullman)—1883-1939—Early film star and cofounder of United Artist Studios married to Mary Pickford.

Fleet, Reuben Hollis—1887-1975—West coast aviation pioneer and U.S. Army officer. Founded Consolidated Aircraft Corporation in San Diego.

Gilbert, John—(nee John Cecil Pringle)—1897-1936—Hollywood silent movie star known as "The Great Lover." An alcoholic, he went through four marriages and divorces in his brief life and had a reputation as a womanizer.

Glover, Warren—18xx-19xx—Fictitious owner of a restaurant in Anaheim.

Goldwyn, Samuel—1879-1974—Polish-born Hollywood studio pioneer whose studio Samuel Goldwyn Pictures was later merged into Metro Goldwyn Mayer, and whose trademark roaring lion at the beginning of features became the MGM trademark.

Griffith, David Wark D.W.—1875-1948—Kentucky born movie pioneer and director and producer of *The Birth of a Nation*, based on Thomas Dixon Junior's novel *The Klansman*. The movie, which President Woodrow Wilson praised saying "It is like writing history with lightning, and my only regret is that it is all so terribly true."

Harding, Warren Gamiliel—1865-1923—Ohio-born Republican 29th President of the United States from 1920 until his death in office in 1923.

Harris, Colleen—1907-19xx—fictitious twin sister of Eddie Harris and daughter of "Harry Harris." Close friend of Helen Webber.

Harris, Eddie—1907-19xx—fictitious Anaheim High baseball teammate.

Harris, E.N. "Harry"—1882-1940—fictitious Klabee of Anaheim Klavern and father of the Harris twins, Eddie and Colleen.

Hollingsworth, Margaret—18xx-19xx—fictitious Los Angeles socialite married to Julian Petroleum executive.

Hornsby, Rogers "The Rajah"—1896-1963—Hall of Fame baseball player, who played for the Chicago Cubs and Saint Louis Cardinals who holds the Major League record for a single season batting average after hitting .424 for the 1924 Cardinals.

Hudnall, Forrest—18xx-19xx—Owner of two soda fountains in Anaheim.

Jackson, Joseph Jefferson "Shoeless Joe"—1897-1951—Baseball player remembered for his performance on the field and his alleged association with the Black Sox Scandal in which members of the Chicago White Sox conspired to fix the 1919

World Series. Despite exceptional play in the 1919 series, setting a record with 12 base hits, Jackson was banned from baseball for conspiring to cover up his teammates scandal.

Johnson, Walter—1887-1946—Fullerton High School Graduate and Hall of Fame baseball pitcher for Washington Senators.

Julian, Courtney Chauncey (C.C.)—18xx-1934—Founder of Los Angeles-based Julian Petroleum Corporation (Julian Pete) convicted for ponzi scheme to sell oil stocks and inflate the stock price. Convicted of bribery in 1929 and sentenced to 14 years in prison, he was pardoned after 19 months and then rearrested in Oklahoma for conspiracy to commit fraud. He jumped bail. Fled to Shanghai, and committed suicide in 1934.

LeSueur, Lucille Fay—1904-1977—Early film star who found fame under her stage name of Joan Crawford.

Lyon, J. T.—18xx-19xx—Anaheim real estate executive whose billboards graced the countryside of Orange County in the Roaring Twenties.

Martin, Alma—1907-1997—Fictitious Catholic Anaheim High School student.

McAdoo, William Gibbs—1863-1941—Democratic presidential candidate in 1924 election heavily backed by the Ku Klux Klan. His loss of the Democratic nomination to John W. Davis of West Virginia triggered the Klanbake demonstration in New Jersey that gave a black eye to the Democratic Party.

Merritt Coach—1888-1953—fictitious Anaheim High School baseball coach and Klan member.

Metcalfe, Elmer H.—**18xx-19xx**—Mayor of Anaheim 1923-1925, voted out of office in 1925 Ku Klux Klan recall election.

Mix, Thomas Edwin—**1880-1940**—Early Hollywood actor who starred in over 200 Westerns and defined the genre.

Moody, Bert—**18xx-19xx**—Ku Klux Klan member and Anaheim Chief of Police until fired in 1925 after Ku Klux Klan recall election.

Moore, Colleen—**1899-1988**—Hollywood silent film actress who popularized Dutchboy bobbed hair cut in the Roaring Twenties.

Morrison, Marion Mitchell "Duke"—**1907-1979**—Personal friend of Florence Barnes and aspiring USC football player who later found fame in Hollywood Westerns under his stage name of John Wayne.

Mosher, Medford—**18xx-1924**—Inglewood policeman allegedly murdered by a fellow Klansman in a well publicized raid on Fidel Elduayen's garage-based moonshine operation.

Myers, Leon—**18xx-19xx**—Clergyman who founded Anaheim Klavern of the Ku Klux Klan in 192x

Nazimova, Alla Marem-Ides (nee Adelaida Yakovlevna) Leventon—**1879-1945**—Russian-born Hollywood silent movie actress, whose private lesbian lifestyle made her controversial. Coined the word "sewing circle" as code for closeted bisexual and lesbian actresses of the day. Her Sunset Boulevard mansion known as the Garden of Alla was later converted into a hotel with 25 villas known for parties and debauchery during the Roaring Twenties.

Negri, Pola (nee Barbara Apolonia Chalupec)—1897-1987— Polish-born silent film actress known for her numerous Hollywood affairs with actors including Charlie Chaplin and Rudolf Valentino.

Norman, Mabel Ethelreid—1892-1930—Silent film comedienne and director linked to murder of William Desmond Taylor but ruled out by L.A.P.D. as a suspect. Rumored to be a heavy cocaine user.

Oswald, Glen—18xx-19xx—Bandleader of Glen Oswald's Serenaders, a West Coast jazz and ragtime band who recorded several hits in 1924-1925.

Pershing, General John Joseph "Black Jack"—1860-1948— commander of the American Expeditionary Force on the Western Front in World War I,

Pickford, Mary (nee Gladys Louise Smith)—1892-1979— Early movie actress, and cofounder of United Artists studio married to Douglas Fairbanks.

Rappe, Virginia Caroline—1895-1921—Hollywood silent film actress allegedly raped and murdered by Fatty Arbuckle in San Francisco's Saint Francis Hotel in 1921. Arbuckle was never convicted.

Reid, Wallace—1891-1923—Hollywood silent film actor known as "The screen's most perfect lover." Died in 1923 of morphine addiction.

Reynolds, Dean Jr. —1907-1990—High school baseball pitching phenom at Anaheim Union High School and aviation pioneer.

Reynolds, Dean Sr. —1888-1918—Father of Dean Reynolds, Jr..

Reynolds, Esther. —1890-1938—Mother of Dean Reynolds, Jr.

Rickenbacker, Eddie—**1890-1973**—American World War I fighter ace in the 94th Aero Squadron, credited with 26 aerial victories. Later president of Eastern Air Lines.

Slayback, Aaron A.—**18xx-19xx** –Anaheim groceryman and city councilman 1923-1925, voted out of office in 1925 Ku Klux Klan recall election.

Smith, Alfred Emmanuel—**1873-1944**—Catholic Democratic governor of New York reviled by the Ku Klux Klan.

Swanson, Gloria May Josephine—**1899-1983**—Hollywood silent film era actress known for her *haute-couture* high fashion.

Taylor, William Desmond—**1872-1922**—Irish-born Hollywood director whose 1922 murder was never solved.

Valentino, Rudolph (Rodolfo Alfonso Raffaello Pierre Fibilbert Guglielmi di Valentina d'Antonguella)—**1895-1926**—Hollywood silent film star and sex symbol.

Waring, Fredrick Malcolm Sr.—**1900-1984**—Bandleader of Fred Waring's Pennsylvanians and inventer of the Waring blender.

Webber, Helen—1908-2001—Daughter of Herbert Webber whose face appeared on Roaring '20's fruit labels, later briefly a silent film star prior to 1928.

Webber, Herbert, Jr. "Bert"—1904-1923—Brother of Helen Webber.

Webber, Herbert Sr. "Bert"—1888-1927—Father of Helen Webber and Sunkist Executive.

Wilson, Harrison Charles "Skeeter"—1907-1959—Friend and classmate of Dean Reynolds Jr.

Wilson, Thomas Woodrow—1856-1924—Virginia-born Democratic 28th President of the United States from 1912 to 1920. Wilson's enthusiastic support for the Ku Klux Klan and the film *The Birth of a Nation* helped to catapult the defunct Ku Klux Klan back into the national spotlight.

AUTHOR Q&A

1. **What in your life prepared you to be a writer? And when did you begin writing fiction?**

   I began writing fiction over 20 years ago after receiving a death threat from an insurance company. Having found success as a civil engineer after the Northridge Earthquake locating and documenting earthquake damage and presenting the engineering basis for repair claims, I encountered a rogue adjuster who preferred to take the low road. That was the first time I became aware of validation rackets, which was the seed from which *The Anaheim Beauties Valencia Queen* emerged.

   Eventually, California Insurance Commissioner, Charles Quackenbush, was forced to resign for taking payoffs from insurance companies he'd been elected to police. At last, the corruption in California became evident. But friends, under the spell of what psychologists call "authority bias," were hesitant to admit insurance companies were so dishonest. Figuring novels were a sneaky way to tell the truth to people who seemed angry about having their beliefs called into question, I took up writing fiction.

It has taken me decades to become a decent writer, but I made so many writer friends I kept at it for years. Plus I had to find out what was going to happen to my characters.

2. *The Anaheim Beauties Valencia Queen* **is your first novel. How long did it take to research and write?**
It's actually the seventh novel I've written, but the first I'm publishing. An author friend gave me the idea to write a story about Anaheim in the year the Ku Klux Klan controlled the city. I had planned to write a short story, but it grew legs and expanded into a novel that took three years to complete.

3. **Speaking of research, you ground your reader with accuracy. A good number of people, places, and events are real. Do you do all your research on your own? And as a writer, how does research impact your process?**
I do most of my own research. Over my lifetime I've acquired a large collection of old maps, pictures, and esoteric data, plus connections that help put forgotten faces and places at my fingertips. A writer never knows what information can launch a story in new directions. I like my research to surprise me. The J.T. Lyon and the Dr. Louis J. Elwood billboards in this story came from real advertisements (complete with eyes) in an old 1924 Anaheim phone book that evoked Fitzgerald's eyes of T.J. Eckleburg. I needed billboards, so these landed in the novel. I'm also fascinated by vanished California landscapes: Valencia groves that sprawled all the way to the horizon, the forgotten pleasure piers of Venice and Santa

Monica, or the Mount Lowe Scenic Railway in the San
Gabriel Mountains

I strive for authenticity, but sometimes have to take some
liberties. I gave Anaheim Union High School a baseball
team in 1924 even though the high school didn't have
one. This was intentional. My portrayal of Coach Merritt
was unsympathetic, and I didn't want to be libeling the
coach of a particular team at a particular high school who
might, in fact, have never joined the Ku Klux Klan.

4. **The themes in *The Anaheim Beauties Valencia Queen*
   are timeless. Please give us a sense of what you consider the most important theme and what you hope
   your readers take away from reading the book.**
   This is a story about wounds left by absent (or in Helen's
   case cruel) parents and the measures people take to salve
   such wounds. While their backstories differ, Dean and
   Helen's parents fail to offer validation or membership
   within their tribes. As a consequence, both Dean and
   Helen make terrible decisions, which empower selfish
   people to ruin their lives.

5. **As a writer, do you outline? And do you know the
   story arc and the ending of the book when you sit
   down to write, or does it develop as you go?**
   I'm more of an organic seat of the pants writer than an
   outline writer. The one thing I outline is a thorough
   historical timeline to keep my facts straight, and the
   details of my characters. Then I turn them loose and hope
   my characters surprise me. I had an ending in mind for
   Dean, but as the story neared the finish, I had to change

it, since it didn't really satisfy. I finally came up with an ending that surprised me, and felt right, using the factual connection between Mount Lowe and "Pancho" (Florence Lowe) Barnes, the larger-than-life pioneer aviatrix and the granddaughter of the Mount Lowe resort developer Thaddeus Lowe.

6. **What drew you to setting the novel in Post-World-War-I southern California? Why 1924 in particular?**

The short answer is that 1924 was the year the Klan took over Anaheim. A more complete answer involves the observation that history can rhyme. I believe there are resonances between 1924 and today.

7. **You use the term "validation rackets." What do you mean by this and who is vulnerable to them?**

I consider validation rackets to have two features.

1. A group of insiders who withhold validation from outsiders who look up to them

2. A structure enabling those insiders to take unfair advantage of the outsiders, or even use them to attack others even further outside their circle

In 1924, the Ku Klux Klan, despite their family-values smokescreen, enabled a clique of insiders to become extremely wealthy. Using slogans like "Don't be half a man. Join the Klan," Klan leaders offered members validation for a $10 fee (Klectoken) that in today's dollars amounts to $150.00. In the case of Hollywood casting couches, the validation rackets are too familiar and have endured, with insiders victimizing struggling entertainers who will do anything to further their careers.

8. **What makes validation rackets insidious? What are some of the more subtle ones existing today?**

   Validation rackets are insidious by urging victims of authoritarians to redirect their anger toward other victims, while allowing their oppressors to go unpunished. In Anaheim, Klan members pledged obedience and paid exorbitant sums to leaders, in exchange for validation. They were then ordered to turn their wrath against the Catholics, diverting their attention from insiders who were using them. In segments of corporate America, underpaid employees follow orders to hurt customers to enrich and impress the higher-ups. Similar behavior occurs in gangs, cliques, cults, paramilitary groups, hierarchies, and even higher education. Scientific research documenting this leveraging of authority bias include Stanley Milgram's experiments at Yale, Philip Zimbardo's Stanford Prison Experiment, the Stockholm Syndrome, the Third Wave Experiment at Palo Alto High School, and on a grander scale, Abu Ghraib, Nazi Germany, or Soviet Russia.

   At the moment we are witnessing the Milgramming of America in which authority figures shame us until we turn against each other. Validation rackets are thriving on both the right (in which mainstream Americans are maligned as "snowflakes," "libtards" or "losers," and on the left (where many of the same mainstream Americans are maligned as "racists", "rapists,""the white cis-heteropatriarchy," or the "basket of deplorables." This intentional behavior promoted by both ends of the spectrum, enriches and empowers power players on the fringes while impoverishing the rest of us. We need to call it what it is.

It is predatory behavior, not all that different from the validation rackets I found in Anaheim.

There is no problem with a preference for one political party's platform, but when that preference empowers cruelty, America is being "Milgrammed." The only antidote is for some of us to validate each other, the way that Pancho Barnes enabled Dean to fly.

9. **Both baseball and aviation are escapes in the book. Why did you choose these two activities for this purpose?**
I have to write what I know. I love baseball, and I had the opportunity to fly while in the Air Force, allowing me to write about these topics with emotion.

10. **Alma, Helen, Dean, Mr. Webber—how real were your main characters to you? What does an author have to feel to be able to breathe life into their characters?**
As an organic writer I try to get into my characters' minds the same way a method actor tries to become their character. This can be challenging when not all of my characters are nice people. As long as I am clear about what each character wants more than life itself, the story flows and writes itself. When I lose track of what each character wants, writers block happens, and I need to spend some more time with my characters.

11. **As the storyteller, you chose to allow Dean to live. Why?**
I thought about killing him off, but I just couldn't. It didn't feel right, even though some purists will argue

noir requires the death of the protagonist. But this is not always the case. Mildred Pierce, for example, only dies symbolically. And similarly Dean only dies symbolically. Banished from baseball and the city that had raised him since he'd moved there, like a caterpillar, Dean must reemerge into a different mode of life.

12. **Often writers pit good against evil. You do this, but it does not seem black and white. There is a lot of shading. Do you agree with this assessment? Why?**
I agree with this assessment. I strive for honest writing, which means no character is all good or all evil. My goal is to show reality, and allow the reader to ask and answer their own questions. I try very hard to make my readers think without telling them what to think. I hope my novel's gift to readers is to help them see and cope with gray in a world presenting itself as black and white.

13. **You end the novel with Dean as a pilot. Why?**
Sometimes when I'm stuck, I ask my characters what they want, and I can often hear their answer in their own words within the novel. There was a throw-away line early in Act 2 where Dean complains when Alma's angry at him that he needs wings instead of strings. That was my clue to what Dean wanted, so I went with it.

14. **What do you see as the most important role of history? Do you think that we have enough of a sense of it in today's society?**
History is how we learn from our mistakes, and to quote George Santayana, those who cannot remember the past are condemned to repeat it. I am concerned we're not

remembering our past. Further, when our collective past is sliced and diced into one-thousand different narratives, we have no sense of who we are as individuals and are ripe for validation rackets.

15. **You call your genre "Red Car Noir." Where does this name come from? What can a reader expect from a Red Car Noir novel?**

I wanted a name to brand the novels I've written and am writing. I boiled it down to "Southern California-based historical fiction chronicling the dark side of the American Dream," which is a mouthful. I needed something catchier and shorter. The Red Car reference is to that period of Southern California history (1901-1961) where the Pacific Electric Red Car trolleys ran throughout Los Angeles. A few works extend into the early 1970's, since the Kennedy Assassination, Vietnam, and Watergate represent the period's sunset. But the bulk of my work is set within the early 1900's, an era underrepresented in our literature.

As for "noir," the genre has both a broad definition and a narrow one, with film-noir being narrower than roman noir or neo-noir. My focus on realism, on the dark side of the American dream, with *femmes fatales* and protagonists who aren't detectives but are victimized by a system that is more corrupt than they are, fits within the broad but not the narrow definition. My primary departure from the full-blown film-noir genre is my self-destructive protagonists don't usually die or go to prison. Amidst tragedy, they find a sadder-but-wiser resolution with jaded resignation and contentment.

Red Car Noir is more like neo-noir. The movie *Chinatown* comes to mind. Jake Gittes makes it out of Chinatown, but with scars.

16. **Are there other Red Car Noir novels in the works?**
I'm halfway through the second installment of my *Angeltown* trilogy set in the early 1900's, amidst labor wars, the Salton Sea floods, and the Owens Valley Aqueduct. The history of Los Angeles is wrapped up in its water, and being a water engineer, I feel compelled to tell the story. The first installment, *Angeltown*, is ready to go to press and deals with all the dirty tricks that brought Los Angeles their water. The story culminates in the bombing of the Los Angeles Times Building in October 1910 where 22 people were murdered.

It is a story that still resonates today.

Two further volumes, *Edendale*, and *Hollywoodland* are also in the works, taking the saga of Los Angeles into the early 1930's through the Saint Francis Dam disaster and the demise of William Mulholland. I'm 30,000 words into writing *Edendale*, and enjoying it.

QUESTIONS FOR DISCUSSION

1. In the opening stanza of the book, Alma Martin, whom we later learn is a character in the novel, expresses regrets over Woodrow Wilson's vision to "make the world safe for democracy." In what ways was Woodrow Wilson a moral or immoral man? How does this foreshadow the theme?

2. In what ways does the Southern California of 1924 resemble Southern California today? In what ways are the 1924 settings different from today?

3. Why do you think the author chose to set this story in 1924 when there are plenty of extremist groups in existence today to write about?

4. What techniques do you see used to transport the reader to 1924?

5. How does your perception of Anaheim evolve as the story progresses?

6. Generally the Ku Klux Klan is not associated with hostility toward Catholics, but the Anaheim Ku Klux Klan did, in fact, attempt to burn down Saint Boniface Church in 1924. Did this surprise you? Why or why not?

7. A famous study of obedience in psychology was carried out at Yale by psychologist Stanley Milgram. In the Milgram experiments, subjects repeatedly chose obedience to authority over personal conscience. What do you think you would do if forced to choose between obeying your conscience versus obeying authority?

8. The author writes of validation rackets, where people in power leverage their ability to give or withhold praise to extract obedience from people seeking validation. In what ways do you think the Anaheim Ku Klux Klan might have been a validation racket?

9. Do you feel the 1920's Hollywood culture might have also been a validation racket?

10. What similarities and what differences do you see between the Anaheim Ku Klux Klan, and the 1920's Hollywood power structure?

11. In what ways do you see Dean being validated by others in Anaheim? In what ways does Anaheim fail to validate him as a member of the community?

12. In what ways do you see Helen being validated? In what ways do others fail to validate her?

13. Discuss the symbolism of elevation (up versus down) as it is used throughout the novel.

14. Discuss the symbolism of strings versus wings used throughout the novel.

15. What is the significance of the Shoeless Joe Jackson baseball glove? Do you think Shoeless Joe Jackson deserved to be banned from baseball for covering up the activities of his teammates who threw the 1919 "Black Sox" World Series? To what extent do you think Dean was guilty or innocent of withholding information about activities of the Ku Klux Klan?

16. How did you feel when the identity of the Exalted Cyclops was revealed. In what ways did the author hide the Ku Klux Klan in plain sight.

17. How did you feel about the resolution of Helen and Dean's relationship?

18. When did you realize what Mr. Webber had done to Helen? Were you satisfied with his suicide? Why, or why not?

19. Is Dean's mother a minor or major character in the book? In what ways does she impact Dean's life?

20. What does the author's handling of Dean's relationship with his father say about the role of fathers in children's lives?

21. The author introduces three characters, Lucille LaSeuer, Florence Lowe Barnes, and Duke Morrison, who later became famous under other names. Was this too obvious or not obvious enough? How is your perception of someone affected by their name?

22. Do you think Dean redeems himself? To what extent do you think bringing in Crazy Florence at the end of the novel was a *deus ex machina* plot device? Did it work, and why or why not?

23. Why does the author end the novel with Dean as a pilot?

24. Discuss some of the validation rackets in existence today. Are they all bad? Do they ever have redeeming qualities?

25. The author calls his book a Red Car Noir novel. Now that you have read and discussed the book, what do you think this means?

ACKNOWLEDGMENTS

If I thanked everyone who in some manner contributed to this book, the names would not fill a dozen pages. I am truly very fortunate. But there are seven individuals I wish to thank profusely for their patience, wisdom, guidance, and contributions to this book. You are my "Magnificent Seven." A huge shout-out and an Elmer Bernstein overture to each of you:

1. To Dennis Coplen, author, who helped me crystallize the idea for the story.

2. To Louella Nelson, author, teacher, and writing mentor, who has been mentoring my writing since the Clinton Administration.

3. To Janet Simcic, author and critique group leader, who kept telling me to publish it.

4. To Maddie Margarita, author, and the foremost cheerleader for authors in Orange County, California, who convinced me that my writing didn't suck.

5. To Antoinette Kuritz, publicist and La Jolla Writers Conference founder, who helped to get the word out on this book.

6. To Jared Kuritz" publishing consultant, who helps me navigate the mysteries of the Internet.

7. To my wife, Sharon, who has patiently allowed me to pursue my writing passion for decades.

ABOUT THE AUTHOR

D. J. Phinney is an Air Force veteran and a licensed civil and mechanical engineer who has been responsible for design and construction of more than $100 million in water and wastewater infrastructure in California and Arizona.

A Southern California native with a passion for history and construction, Mr. Phinney turned to writing fiction, following the Northridge Earthquake, when a death threat from an insurance company helped him see fiction as a sneaky way to write about the truth. While he has published short stories, *The Anaheim Beauties Valencia Queen* is his first novel. When not writing, Mr. Phinney spends time with his wife of 40 years, their grown son, their grandchildren and their golden retriever. Or he can be found exploring local history in anticipation of completing his next Red Car Noir adventure.

CPSIA information can be obtained
at www.ICGtesting.com
Printed in the USA
FSHW012228100919
61860FS